BLOOD & MILK

N.R. WALKER

COPYRIGHT

Cover Artist: Sara York
Editor: Labyrinth Bound Edits
Blood & Milk © 2016 N.R. Walker
Publisher: BlueHeart Press

All Rights Reserved:

This literary work may not be reproduced or transmitted in any form or by any means, including electronic or photographic reproduction, in whole or in part, without express written permission, except in the case of brief quotations embodied in critical articles and reviews.
This is a work of fiction, and any resemblance to persons, living or dead, or business establishments, events or locales is coincidental.
The Licensed Art Material is being used for illustrative purposes only.

Warning:

Intended for an 18+ audience only. This book contains material that maybe offensive to some and is intended for a mature, adult audience. It contains graphic language, explicit sexual content, and adult situations.

The author uses Australian English spelling and grammar.

Trigger Warnings:

Homophobic violence. Reader discretion advised.

Trademarks:

All trademarks are the property of their respective owners.

PRONUNCIATION GUIDE:

Alé: Ah-leh
    Damu: Dah-mu
    Nkorisa: En-kor-issa
    Kijani: Key-yar-nee
    Kasisi: Kah-see-see
    Mposi: Em-poss-ee

Glossary: Common terms used throughout:

Manyatta/Kraal: Maasai village, surrounded by an acacia thorn fence.
    Shuka: Traditional red shawl worn by the Maasai
    Rungu: Wooden club, used/thrown as weapon
    Diviner: Tribal witchdoctor
    Uji: Thin, milk-like consistency drink made from water and maize.
    Ugali: Water and maize mix with the consistency of mashed potatoes.

AUTHOR'S NOTE:

At the date of publication, June 2016, the International Lesbian, Gay, Bisexual, Trans and Intersex Association, or ILGA, lists 73 countries with criminal laws against sexual activity by lesbian, gay, bisexual, transgender or intersex people, punishable by imprisonment, torture, or death. 33 of these countries are in Africa, Tanzania being one of them.

To my African friends who read my books, I am truly honoured, and incredibly humbled. Your strength encourages me, and to know my words give you hope and happiness is a gift that will stay with me forever.

Nawatakiya amani na upendo

The African Human Rights Coalition does some amazing work for LGBTIQ people, and donations are always welcome.

DEDICATION

To Santa Aziz,

For helping me with true Maasai ways, diet, language and culture, and for giving me the courage to publish this story. But especially for reminding me why words are important. This book is for you.

A Very Special Mention:

To the many pre-readers, sensitivity readers, and beta-readers who helped and guided, suggested, and corrected. You made this book better, and I thank you.

BLOOD
&
MILK

N.R. Walker

PROLOGUE

IT WAS TWELVE MONTHS ON. A full year had passed, yet my world had stopped completely. The men who stole my life were charged and would serve time for their crime. No one called it a hate crime, but that's what it was. If I was expecting some sort of finality to come with the court findings, I didn't get it.

I was still hollow. I was still numb to the world, and I was still alone.

I was also awarded damages, civilian victim and medical.

A nice healthy sum that meant I could pay off my debts after not working for twelve months, and more. Though no amount of money would make this right. No amount of money would bring him back.

My mother came along for the final hearing, though I could only guess why. I had barely spoken two words to her in the last year. Maybe she came so she could vie for the sympathy card with her friends. Or maybe she thought she could have one last twist of the knife...

"Now it's all over," she said, nodding her head like her

words were wise and final. "You can put all this homosexual nonsense behind you."

I looked at my mother and smiled. I fucking smiled. I raged inside with a fury to burn the world, and maybe she saw something in my eyes—maybe it was a ferocity she'd never seen before, maybe it was madness—and my words were whisper quiet.

"You are a despicable, bitter human being, and you are a disgrace to mothers everywhere. So, when you go to your church group, instead of praying for my soul, you should be praying for yours. You have only hate and judgement in your heart, and you are doomed to an eternity in hell." I leaned in close and sneered at her. "And I hope you fucking burn." I stood up and stared down at her. She was pale and shocked, and I did not care. "If you think my words are cold and cruel," I added, "I want you to know I learned them from you."

I walked away, for the final time. I knew I'd never see her again, and I had made my peace with that.

I didn't care for the money. I didn't care for anything. I longed for sleep, because in my dreams, I saw him. And that night, almost one year to the day since he was gone, in our too-big bed, in our too-quiet flat, in my too-alone life, I dreamed of Jarrod.

He sat on our bed and grinned. I longed to hear his voice, just once. It'd been a year and I craved the sound of his voice, his touch. But when I reached out for him, even in my dream, as in my waking nightmares, he was gone. I sat up in our bed, reaching out for nothing but air. He was gone, really gone.

But in this dream, on the bed where he'd sat, was a plane ticket. Mr Heath Crowley, it said. One way ticket to Tanzania.

CHAPTER ONE

THE FLIGHT FROM SYDNEY, Australia, to Dar es Salaam, Tanzania, was long, though I didn't remember much of it. Much like the last twelve months of my life, zoning out and staring into space for undetermined lengths of time made my days bearable. My connecting flight to Arusha, with a fly-by view of Mount Kilimanjaro, was much less pleasant.

The Australian couple I had the misfortune of sitting next to were off on some great safari, glamour camping trip, according to their never ending attempt at conversation.

"You have odd coloured eyes," the woman said bluntly, like I might not have known. She stared into each of my eyes like she was looking to see if she could find a way to fix them. "One's brown, one's a greeny-hazel colour."

"Ah, yes. I know. Heterochromia. Don't worry, it's not contagious."

She snorted rudely. "My sister had a dog with odd eyes."

I repressed a sigh. Funnily enough, most people made a similar comment when they first met me. You'd think someone having different coloured eyes was the most absurd thing they'd ever seen, but, to me, it was as obtuse as me telling her she had blonde hair like it was some kind of disease. She clearly didn't pick up on my want for silence.

"Are you travelling alone?"

"Yes."

"In an organised tour?"

"No."

"Are you meeting someone there?"

"Yeah."

She visibly relaxed. "Oh, that's good. I hear it can be very dangerous if you're not in a group tour."

I didn't explain that I'd made one phone call and, for a nominal fee and something akin to a breath of hope, would be meeting a man whose name I couldn't remember, and he would be taking me to a remote tribe of Maasai who had no clue I was coming.

Why? Because I'd dreamed of this.

Not dreamed of, as in a bucket-list aspiration kind of dream. But literally dreamed it. I'd had many instances, where my dreams foretold events that would inevitably shape my life. Not like normal dreams. These premonition-type dreams were the ones that woke me with a piercing weight on my breastbone. I would wake up in a cold sweat with vivid images screaming through my mind. Then, in the near future—a day, a week, a month—the dream would happen in my waking life. I couldn't explain it, and only a few people ever knew about my *talent*.

Or curse.

I had a dream that told me I must go to Tanzania and that I would live with the Maasai. So, with absolutely nothing left to keep me tethered to my life in Sydney, I made a phone call, booked a ticket, and boarded a plane.

The woman beside me was still prattling on, her ignorance and naivety keeping company with her good intentions. "You read the travel warnings, yes? I've heard all the horror stories of people who come to these far-off countries by themselves. You must be so careful, or you might find yourself not coming back at all."

"It wouldn't much matter if I didn't," I mumbled. "Waking up in a bathtub of ice with one less kidney isn't so bad. I've lived through worse."

She blinked back her surprise and stopped talking to me after that. I smiled internally, put on the headphones, and closed my eyes, grateful for the peace and solitude.

When we'd landed, and even as we made it through the concourse and were herded out to the blistering heat of East Africa, I still kept to myself. The majority of other people were ushered onto tourist buses to the right. I went to the left, armed with no more than the backpack I brought with me. The sun was blinding, so I kept my head down and almost missed the guy waiting for me.

"Are you Mister Cowley?"

I looked up to find a man, a few inches taller than my five ten. He had short hair, nubbed at his scalp, dark brown skin, and a smile that showed every single one of his teeth.

"Crowley," I corrected, not that it probably mattered. No one else knew I was coming, except the one person I'd given my name and flight details to, the man who would drive me to the Maasai. "And you are?" I was expecting an Eric, I thankfully remembered, but I wasn't naïve enough to give a stranger the name of the person I was waiting for.

"I am Eric. I wait here for you." His English was broken, but he nodded enthusiastically. "You want to go to the Isikirari people. I take you."

I offered him my hand, which he shook with just as much enthusiasm as he smiled. "Heath Crowley."

"You come with me," he said. His smile never faltered, and without one iota of concern for my safety, I followed him. He stopped at a car—if it could be described as that—and I couldn't believe what I was seeing.

The car itself was an early 60s model Morris Minor, held together by rust and goodwill. But inside the car, piled into the backseat, were two other men... and three goats.

"Um." I wasn't sure what the hell to do.

"You get in front," Eric said. His grin was somewhat reassuring.

I did as he asked and climbed in. The smell inside the car was an unholy mix of sweat and piss—human or goat, I couldn't tell. And for the next hour, Eric drove west. The scenery was beautiful, just like I'd imagined it to be. Arusha was green with Mount Meru as a backdrop to the north, and the countryside as we drove was mostly farmland.

I had no idea where he was taking me, and it occurred to me that I didn't really care. We went through a few smaller towns, and I tried to take in as much as I could. I felt so removed from the fact that I was actually heading toward the Serengeti. Well, I hoped I was. Eric asked me a few questions and pointed out a few landmarks, and the two men who both eyed me warily in the back with the bleating, stinking goats, never said a word.

Eventually we came to the large gateway to the World Heritage's Ngorongoro Conservation Area. It was a name I remembered from the maps I'd studied, so I knew Eric had at least taken me in the right direction. There were a few mudbrick buildings and a flow of safari buses that surprised me but then we passed a huge, westernised looking tourist safari hotel and I understood why.

This really was the gateway to the Serengeti.

Then, at a turn off in what looked like the middle of flat grassland, Eric brought the car to a stop. I was almost hoping we'd lose the two silent guys and their goats but that wasn't what happened at all. Eric stopped in the middle of the road and the two guys got out from the backseat taking their goats with them. Then Eric held out his hand. "Pay now."

Right. I paid him the eighty-thousand Tanzanian shillings I'd agreed to, which equated to about fifty Australian dollars. I folded up the rest of my money and slid some into my backpack, some into my sock, and some into my shirt pocket. I'd travelled enough to know to separate my money. "Where to now?" I asked.

"You go with them," Eric said, pointing in the direction the two men had gone. They were already a hundred yards ahead and were, by all accounts, walking into the middle of nowhere. "They take you."

"The two men with the goats?"

"Yes, yes," he said, still with the grin. "Hurry, hurry."

Shit. I grabbed my backpack and scrambled out of the car. I waved my thanks as I ran after the two men. There was no turning back now. Eric was already driving away and I had to run to catch up to my guides.

"I'm coming with you, yes?" I asked them.

One man, the shorter of the two, turned his head in acknowledgment, though he never spoke. Actually, they never even looked directly at me, but they never stopped or said no, they never hunted me away, so I assumed it was okay to follow them. I stayed a few metres behind, and we walked. And walked, and then we walked some more.

I had no clue where we were going, or how long we would be walking for. From the direction of the setting sun,

I deduced we were heading west. The sun was hotter and brighter than I thought possible, probably because we were walking directly into it. Though I was surprised by how green everything was; the grasses were long and danced in the breeze. I'd always imagined Africa to be arid, much like central Australia, but this was very fertile land.

Still walking, I sipped at my bottled water sparingly. I resisted the urge to complain or even speak. The two men remained silent, but from what I could ascertain, they were happy in their camaraderie, and as we continued to walk, I wondered if they were indeed brothers. They looked alike: both tall and lean, thin even, with dark skin and short, nubbed hair. But it wasn't even their looks. They walked the same: long, confident strides, moving purposefully, yet there was a stillness about them.

And we walked.

I took in the scenery and kept reminding myself that I was walking the Serengeti. The landscape was beautiful. Remote and so removed from anything I'd seen in regional Australia. This was a foreign vastness, a different kind of isolation, than anything I'd experienced back home. The trees that spotted the scenery were no longer eucalypt, as they were back home, but were flat-top African acacias, which were so typical in photos of Africa. A herd of some kind of bison were off in the distance, and I tried hard not to wonder if there were lions anywhere close by.

The two men strode easily over the rocks and tussock grasses. And for the hours I walked behind them, I studied them as well. Their sandals were made from old tyres. Crude and elementary, but functional. Their clothes were threadbare and dirty: not a judgement, merely an observation. They had beaded loops instead of earlobes and I could see necklaces hidden by their shirts.

Were they Maasai or just villagers taking me to the Maasai? I had no idea.

I merely walked behind them, thankful the setting sun had taken the baking heat with it. But the cool change brought with it another element I'd not expected. Darkness.

The men in front of me were obviously familiar with their environment, and as evening became night, their silence as they walked became eerie. Thankfully the noisy goats kept me on track and just when I couldn't see my own hand in front of my face, and just when I was about to ask the men how much further, a faint orange light came into view.

When I'd booked my ticket to come here, I had done some research. Well, all that Google and travel forums would allow. I knew the village itself was called a *manyatta* or *kraal*, with a wall built of thorns to surround and protect the people and livestock within.

In an otherwise all-surrounding blackness, the flickering of orange I didn't realise until we were right up on it, was the fire I was seeing near the thorn walls of the kraal. The two men ahead of me stopped and faced me. "Stop," one of them said.

The other man disappeared through the narrow gateway with the goats, and I stood there under the watchful eye of the other guy. Just a short moment later, I heard voices, then a long line of people filed out of the manyatta. They formed a half-circle around me; my back to the wall. And within half a minute, I was surrounded by dozens of people. Maasai people, tall, imposing, and intimidating. I could barely make them out—the night was too dark—but there was an air of concern and danger to them.

I didn't need to speak Maa to know they were alarmed at my presence. Outraged even. A tall man, well over six foot, confronted me, draped in red cloth and wielding a long spear, he spoke in my face. His eyes and teeth looked yellow in the lack of light; his disposition was formidable. "What you do here?"

Quickly recognising he was a respected tribal man, I kept my head down, knowing my place here was well beneath his. "I mean no harm," I said, surprised by the strength of my own voice. "I have come to live with your people. If you would have me. I want to learn your ways."

Conversation swept through the village, murmurs and rumbles of unease. The man before me raised his hand and a silence hushed over the people. He gripped my chin and forced my face upwards so he could see my face.

His eyes went wide, and he yelled something I couldn't comprehend. Was it a name? Was he calling for someone else?

I should have been afraid. I should have run away. But instead I stood there, without any thought of self-preservation, under the scrutiny of a man who might possibly kill me.

Then another man, much older and smaller, wearing a headdress of some sort—I couldn't quite make it out in the darkness—draped in red, with beaded necklaces, appeared in front of me. The crowd moved for him, a clear mark of respect. He came to stand in front of me, and when he saw my different coloured eyes, he let out a long gasp.

He spoke words in Maa I could not begin to understand—a quiet timbre to his voice, but with strength as well. From his reaction, I could see he was excited and even amazed. Waves of disbelief and murmurs spread through the people encircled around us. Whatever he called me, the words I didn't understand, must have meant something to them.

The small village elder smiled at me by the firelight. Then he spoke in broken English. "Broken man. Incomplete, but he brave. No fear." I wasn't sure what to make of that. But then he said, "He dreams."

Well, I understood that. "Yes. My dreams told me to come here."

The first man, the angry warrior guy, didn't like that at all. He spoke harshly to the elder, stomping his spear to the ground. I made no sense of his words, only his demeanour. He didn't like me or want me here.

The elder stopped him with just his raised hand. A silence so profound settled over the kraal, and the elder looked at me. "He stay. He be ghost of Kafir." He nodded sagely. "He stay with Damu."

CHAPTER TWO
————————

THE PEOPLE in the kraal buzzed in conversations and excitement. Someone at the back started to sing, and I wondered briefly if I was being welcomed or if I was about to be speared.

The tall, angry warrior eyed me, not even trying to hide his disdain. He was only a few feet from me, thumping his spear into the dirt as he spoke to other men. Some women stood back, further into the darkness, and some smiled and giggled behind their hands. Some sneered.

While my fate was being decided, I took a moment to look around. The night was dark, given the moon was no more than a sliver of light in the sky, but my eyes had adjusted somewhat. I could see the people surrounding me were all wearing *shukas*, the traditional red shawl the Maasai were famous for. Some were blue, some a mix of both, but there was mostly red. They wore beaded earrings, beaded necklaces, and most of them were barefoot. Some wore the same tyre sandals the other men had worn.

I noticed the smells then. The fire, of course, but the

unmistakable odour of cattle and cow shit was the most prominent, plus the faint smell of food cooked hours before.

"Damu!" the angry warrior yelled, short and clipped.

The crowd of gatherers whispered in surprise and amusement as a man weaved his way through from the very back. He was tall, had a shaved head, and stared at the ground. The warrior spoke down to him, angry words that, once again, I could not understand. It was very clear, even to me, this man was not held in any regard by his peers. I briefly wondered what he'd done so wrong, what terrible crime he had committed, to be spoken to in such a manner.

Then Damu, still with his head down, turned to me. He glanced up for just a second. He beckoned me with his hand, and the angry warrior pointed in the direction Damu wished for me to go. "You go. Go with him."

I bowed my head, in what I'd hoped was a sign of respect, and quickly followed the man named Damu. Only once we'd got through the gateway and were away from the fire, I couldn't see a damn thing. I was following him blindly, in every sense of the word.

I stopped walking. "Uh," I said, loud enough for Damu to hear me and hopefully quiet enough that the others didn't. "I can't see."

Then, silently, a hand touched my arm. "This way."

He kept his hand on my arm and led me a short distance, where he stopped. My eyes had adjusted a little, and I could see we were in front of a small hut. Damu bent low to get through the doorway, and putting my complete faith in a man I'd not even been introduced to, I followed.

If I thought the African night sky was dark, then inside the hut was a blackness I'd never imagined before. I literally couldn't see my own hand in front of my face. It was warm inside the hut, and it stank. I couldn't stand up; the ceiling was far too low. I crouched down and slung my backpack off to the floor, which I now realised was dirt. I had the sense of being enclosed in a room far too small to contain me, let alone two men.

"Sleep here," Damu said. His voice was soft and kind. There was an edge to his tone, like he was uncertain but didn't want to offend me.

"It's very dark."

"Yes. It is night."

I smiled, grateful he couldn't see me... *hoping* he couldn't see me. I didn't want to offend him either. "You speak English." Very broken, very literal English. It was a shame my profound use of sarcasm would never be used here.

"Some."

"I am grateful. Thank you for allowing me to stay."

"It not my decision."

Oh. "I am grateful nonetheless." I had so many questions. Like what were the names the elder man had called me, who was Kafir, and why was I his ghost?

"Lay. Sleep."

Okay then. My questions could obviously wait. Figuring if there was a bed for me, I'd have been shown to it, so I assumed I was to sleep on the floor. I sat down, edging my back to the wall. I pulled my backpack under my head and curled into a ball. I closed my eyes, not aware of how tired I was, though my mind was still pedaling a thousand miles an hour.

What the hell was I doing? Did I really just fly to East Africa, and walk for the better part of a day across the Serengeti? Did I ask the Maasai warrior wielding a spear if I could stay? Was I really lying in the dirt, on the cold hard ground, in a hut with a man I didn't know?

I resisted the urge to laugh out loud, then I blinked back tears.

Sleep crawled over me, like a slow mist with spindly fingers, wrapping around me and taking me under.

I WOKE to a large hand on my shoulder, shaking me, and a whispered, urgent voice saying words I couldn't understand.

I sat up, my mind in a fog, my heart hammering. The vivid dream of Jarrod's smiling face swirled through my conscience, evaporating like smoke until it was gone. I tried to keep it close, I tried to tell him to stay, but it was too late. Damu was in my face, his hands on my shoulders, and from the concern on his face, I realised I must have been having a nightmare. It was still dark in the hut, though early morning light shone through the door opening. If African summer mornings were anything like Australian summer mornings, I'd guess it was about five a.m.

"You dream," Damu said.

"Sorry," I said, my voice croaking. "Did I wake you?"

He shook his head and moved back away from me as far as the space in the hut allowed. I could see inside the hut now, though only barely. There were no windows and certainly no electrical lighting, so it was still dark. The hut was no more than six feet by four—I'm sure I could touch the walls with my arms outstretched. The ceiling was about five feet off the ground, made from what looked like sticks with mud. The walls were the same, though from my very brief online research I knew the Maasai made their huts from sticks and cow shit. Which would probably explain the smell.

Inside, the hut was divided into two areas: a bedroom

and a kitchen, if they could be called that. There was a bed of sorts, which looked like an old inch-thin mattress on the dirt floor along one wall. On the opposite wall there was what I assumed was a kitchen. Well, there was a bowl on the floor and an old dirty bucket, and there appeared to be a mudbrick fire pit in the corner, where I imagined some food was cooked.

If there was an image used to describe basic, almost ancient living, this could be it.

Yet, I was here to learn, to observe with an open mind, not to judge.

I scrubbed my hand through my hair, suddenly feeling the ache in my back and neck from sleeping on the ground. "Thank you for waking me," I said to Damu. He looked at me warily, and I could only assume my dreaming—or nightmares, as they tended to be—had scared him.

Damu nodded toward the door. "No be late."

"Okay," I said, kind of crawling to the door. I had no idea what I wasn't to be late for or where I was to go, but I had no option but to put my trust in Damu. Only when I was outside could I stand up to my full height. Every vertebra in my back cracked with satisfaction when I stretched, but then I took notice of where I was.

Morning was breaking over the manyatta. The sky was light blues and pinks, the air was cool and fresh, and I still could hardly believe I was in Tanzania with the Maasai. There must have been twelve or fifteen other huts all close together up on end of the enclosed village, yet the hut I'd slept in, Damu's hut, was removed from the other huts. I wondered what that meant but dared not ask. There were animal pens within the walls of the manyatta, filled with cows and goats, and some Maasai, wearing their traditional red shukas, were tending to them.

I couldn't help but smile. I was smiling, truly happy for the first time in so long. It felt strange on my face.

"We go," Damu said. I turned to find him pointing in the opposite direction, toward the huts. "Come."

It was then I noticed Damu. I'd only seen him in the darkness. He'd guided me in the darkness by kindly taking my arm, and I'd slept in his hut, but I hadn't yet really seen his face. Until now.

Damu was, at a guess, six foot three inches. His skin was a deep, dark brown and perfectly smooth, his head shaved to the scalp. He had eyes the colour of onyx, and when he caught me staring, he smiled. He wore the traditional red shuka, though it was open through the chest, and I could see he was thin and muscular, without one ounce of fat on his body. His earlobes bore white and red beads. He wore a string of necklaces made from wooden and black beads, and bracelets which, unlike his necklaces, were of bright colours, and he had a wooden club holstered in his belt. He really was a very striking man.

I felt a strange calmness around him. Which was absurd, because I'd never noticed any such thing before. Some people always gave off angry vibes or nervousness, but I'd always assumed that was from how they were behaving.

But Damu was different.

I felt calm beside him, a gentleness, which surprised me.

As we went around the back of the first hut, we came across a small child. I had no clue whether it was a boy or a girl—it truly didn't matter—who wore westernised clothes. Well, a long shirt, five sizes too big, that had holes and stains, and little sneakers. As soon as the child saw us, they stopped, looked at me with something akin to horror, then let out a scream.

Damu put his hand out, speaking rapid fire words I couldn't begin to understand, but the child's mother quickly appeared, along with several other women, and snatched up the child.

There was now a line of six women staring at me, all wary but curious. They wore dresses of red and blue with dozens of brightly coloured necklaces. They had shaved heads and long drooping earlobes filled with beads like Damu's. Other children hid behind their mothers, peeking at me, then quickly hiding again. I had no clue what they were saying, but I knew a scared kid when I saw one.

I wasn't sure what the cultural etiquette was in this scenario, but I wanted to reassure them. So I bowed my head and smiled, aiming for friendly. "Hello."

The women turned and scurried away, ushering their children before them. *Jesus.* I looked up at Damu. "Did I do something wrong?"

Damu stood at my side like a poor kid designated to show the new kid around at school. "No white man."

I blanched. "They've never seen a white man before?"

Damu shook his head and he smiled. "Women, yes. Children, no."

Oh dear God. No wonder they were scared. I must have looked like an alien or something.

Damu took my arm and pulled me along. "Come. We not be late."

There was a meeting, of sorts, around the fire that had burned last night. The entire Maasai tribe was there. They were split in two groups: the men, and the women and children. Some of the men had shaved heads, some with long hair in tight braids that were held in ponytails by metal clasps. They sat on the ground with their spears and long sticks, with military discipline. They all wore the traditional red shukas and were—there were no other words for it—a formidable sight. The women sat on the ground too, the babies strapped to their backs and the small children jumping and clapping happily around them.

It was like I'd woken up on a movie set.

A group of men, who I could only assume were the tribal elders, sat at the front, and the angry warrior from last night was the first to see me. He stood and thumped his spear into the dirt, yelling fierce words in my direction.

Now the entire tribe stared at me. The children cried out and ran to their mothers.

But it was the small elder, the oldest of all the tribal leaders, who stood up and called for calm. He was the same man who called me the *ghost of Kafir*, the same man who said I could stay. He motioned for me to come forward, which I did obediently. He wore a headdress of beads and feathers and held what I first thought was a stick with a tuft of hair sticking out the end, but I realised, a little belatedly, it was an animal's tail wrapped with twine of some sort. I couldn't tell if it was a zebra tail or a warthog's or a lion's. God, I had no idea. What I did know was that from the headdress and utmost respect from his tribe, this little old man must be what the Maasai called their 'diviner.' Before I knew differently, I probably would have called him a witchdoctor.

It was then I noticed Damu had come forward with me. He stood by my side, facing the elders with his head bowed. I took his cue and did the same.

The diviner pointed his tail-stick thing to the tribesmen who sat to my left, and gave them what appeared to be an order. Without a murmur, they stood and filed out. Then he did the same to the women, and they left, taking the children with them.

"Damu," the elder said. He spoke to him in Maa, then he shooed him away with his hand. Damu hesitated in leaving me, but the diviner repeated his order, and Damu backed away. I didn't see where he went. I didn't dare look.

The diviner smiled, revealing a few missing teeth, and he seemed friendly. He had a kind face, and I liked him. "Sit. Sit," he said.

I sat right where I had been standing, and the diviner sat with his back to the wall of a hut with the other elders. The angry warrior stood for a moment longer, no doubt to remind me of his status, and subsequently, reminding me of mine.

They talked a little amongst themselves, and I realised this was a trial of sorts. My stay here was still being decided. Maybe even my life. I just sat there, staring at the dirt, and waited.

It was only when they spoke in English that I looked up. "White man," one of them said. It wasn't a racist comment, it was merely an observation. I nodded my acknowledgment and looked at each of them in turn, hoping it would show my respect. Of course it allowed them all to see my different coloured eyes, and they started talking amongst themselves again.

"Kafir! Kafir!" one of the men cried. "Eyes of Kafir."

"He dreams," the diviner told them.

They talked amongst themselves some more. All the while the angry warrior never took his eyes off me. "Where you come?"

"I'm from Australia. A city called Sydney, in Australia," I answered.

"You have wife?"

"No."

"You no wife, no children, no cattle?"

"No."

"You come here for wife?"

"No." Even if I wasn't gay, finding a partner was the last, last, *last* thing I wanted.

He stared at me, like my life and intentions were unfathomable.

So I said, "I want to help you. I want to live here and help, be a part of your people."

"How you help our people?" the diviner asked.

I reached into my shirt pocket and pulled out a wad of notes. It was probably fifty thousand Tanzanian shillings or about thirty Australian dollars. I had more money stashed and figured buying my way in for thirty bucks was money well spent. I held out the money. "For your people."

Apparently this was a good thing. They were pleased, even the angry warrior seemed mollified after he'd snatched the money from my hand. So, while I was in their good graces, I needed to know some names. Diviner and angry warrior were apt and all, but hardly polite. Not that they'd made any attempt in asking me my name—I guessed they didn't care.

I kept my head bowed. "May I ask your names? I would like to know what to call you."

After another brief meeting amongst themselves, the diviner nodded. "Kasisi."

Angry warrior's name was Kijani. And the other elders were Makumu and Mposi and Lomunyak.

I put my hand to my chest. "My name is Heath Crowley."

"No," Kasisi said. "You are Alé."

The other men laughed, but they nodded. "Alé. Alé."

Right then. So apparently my name was Alé. It sounded like Ah-leh, and I had no clue what it meant. Probably

Stupid White Man, but as it meant they'd accepted me even as an outsider, I just smiled and nodded.

Then Kijani pointed his spear to the left. "Damu. Go to Damu."

They found something funny about that, repeating "Damu and Alé" as they laughed. I didn't care. I took my leave with a bow of my head.

And under the warm African sky, I shed my name of Heath Crowley, along with my old life, and for the briefest moment, it was the lightest I'd felt in over twelve months. From that day on, I wasn't Heath anymore. There was no dark cloud hanging over me, there was no all-consuming heartache, there was no devastating loss. I was Alé.

And I went in search of Damu.

CHAPTER THREE

DAMU WAS COMING out of his hut with his bucket in hand. "Damu," I called. "Kijani said I was to find you."

Damu gave me a hard nod. "Yes."

His English wasn't great, but I was grateful he spoke any at all. I knew English was common in Tanzania, but I hadn't realised just how difficult it might have been if they spoke none at all. I had to make an effort to learn more Maa words. I doubted I'd ever be fluent—it seemed so fast and very foreign, but I was determined to at least try. I motioned to his bucket. "Where are we going?"

His voice was quiet, his whole demeanour was placid. "Water."

"Oh, of course." I looked around, seeing nothing but thorn fencing, mud huts, and dirt. "Where do we go?"

He nodded over the thorn fence and started to walk. Of course I followed, and as we went through the small gate, we headed in the direction he had nodded. Outside the kraal was something else. When I'd arrived the night before, I couldn't see any of my surroundings. Now it was a perfect summer day: the sun was still hovering over the horizon and the sky, well, I'd never seen a sky so big. The landscape was flat, undulating to low rolling hills on the horizon. The grass was knee-high and browning off, a sign of the blistering heat. There was a line of greener trees to the west, and in an otherwise dry environment, I assumed the thriving vegetation meant water.

I must have assumed right, because we headed in that direction. There were some women walking a few hundred metres ahead, their laughter carried when the wind blew towards us. Damu and I walked without speaking, and yet, I didn't mind it. It was a peaceful silence.

I was still wearing the clothes from yesterday, and I hadn't eaten since... I couldn't remember. The plane flight from Sydney?

"So, what do you eat for breakfast?" My voice sounded loud in the silence. Damu looked at me, confused, so I broke it down and put my hand to my mouth. "Food?"

"Yes, yes," was all he said.

Okay, then. So maybe there would be breakfast after we got water? I had no clue. Now that I'd thought of food, my stomach growled in protest. If Damu had heard it, and I assumed he had, he said nothing.

We walked the rest of the way in silence. It must have been a kilometre away, and as we neared the small river, the women who had been ahead of us were walking back. They carried plastic containers of water, and their chatter and smiles died away when they saw me. They spoke in passing to Damu, pleasantly enough, but it got me thinking...

All the other males had gone, herding their cattle. I'd seen them off in the distance—not only the cows and goats, but the striking tall dark figures draped in red were pretty hard not to notice.

As was the man beside me. So why wasn't Damu with them?

"Were you told to look after me?" I asked, not knowing if he'd understand. "Did Kijani make you mind me?"

Damu eyed me cautiously but stayed quiet as he approached the edge of the river. Just when I thought he hadn't understood me, he said, "Kijani make you responsibility for me. I do what Kijani tell me."

Despite his broken English, I understood him just fine, and I was right. Damu was my babysitter. I couldn't even be offended. I'd much rather spend my days with Damu than Kijani, the spear-wielding warrior with anger management issues.

But it can't have been good for him. My presence had taken him from his daily work with the other men. "I'm sorry."

Damu's gaze shot to mine. Was he shocked at my apology? "Why you be sorry?"

"Looking after me is not what you want. I trouble you?"

"No, no," he said, then stepped down the muddy bank and waded into the water. He filled the bucket and left it on the bank, then went back into the water downstream. He washed his face and cupped his hands in the water and drank.

I sat down and pulled off my sneakers and socks, pulled up the legs of my pants and followed him out. The water was cool and a little muddy, and I paused, wondering if I should drink unboiled water, but considering I hadn't had anything to drink since my flight here, I drank it anyway. And it was good. I hadn't even realised how thirsty I was.

After standing in the cool water for a minute or so, I guessed now was as good a time as any to start with the dialect. "What is your word for water?"

Damu smiled. "Water. *Enk-áre*."

"Enk-áre," I repeated. The ending sounded a little similar to the name Kijani and Kasisi had called me. "What does Alé mean? The elders called me that. The leaders, that's what they called me."

Damu almost smiled. "Milk."

Oh. "Because I'm white?"

Damu gave an unapologetic nod and walked out of the water.

Fair enough, I thought. The Maasai people lived the way they had for thousands of years, almost untouched by time and what we called "progress." Being politically correct to a strange white man was not on their cultural radar. Nor should it be. I understood there would be very few similarities between their world and mine long before I'd set foot in Tanzania. It was half the reason I came here. I wanted no reminders of the world I'd left behind.

Damu was waiting for me on the river bank, so I quickly got out and pulled on my socks and shoes. He waited patiently, and I made a mental note to be more aware of those around me, their ways and practices.

I stood, my wet feet now uncomfortable in dry socks and shoes, and I wasn't really looking forward to the walk back. "Why is the village so far from the river?" I asked. Then I corrected my phrasing. "The manyatta, why is it so far from the enk-árê?"

And just as I'd finished speaking, I swatted a mosquito on my arm, making Damu laugh. It was a contagious sound, but then I had to swish another mozzie from buzzing near my face. "I see why."

"Yes. Yellow... Yellow?" He looked unsure of his wording.

Yellow. Yellow... Oh shit. "Yellow fever?"

"Yes!" Damu said with a bright smile.

Well hell, I certainly didn't want malaria or any other mosquito-borne disease. Even though I'd just gulped mouthfuls of river water. Shit. I'd had a dozen different shots before I came here, but still. "Water make me sick? Enk-áre make me," I pretended to dry retch.

Damu only laughed, which wasn't too comforting.

"Should I boil water?" I asked. Then something else occurred to me. Damu had his water, what the hell was I going to drink. I pointed to the bucket he was now holding. "Ah, your water. Where is my water? I didn't bring a container or a canister."

Damu looked at his bucket. "My water, your water. Responsibility is you to me."

"Then allow me to carry it," I offered, holding out my hand.

"No. Responsibility is you to me."

Okay then. I was his responsibility for all things.

He turned and headed back the way we'd come, and I had to jog to catch up. His long legs strode much quicker than mine. I wondered how much I'd slowed him down already.

"Any mals," Damu said. "Also why we build great far from river."

"Any mals? Oh. *Animals*? What kind of animals?" Because truly, Australia had some scary critters, but we sure as hell didn't have lions and hippos and rhinos.

Damu laughed at my expression. "Animals need water like we need water."

"Are there lions here?" I asked, given he'd not freely given up what kind of friendly wildlife we could encounter.

"Some." He pointed one hand further to the west. "Serengeti. Some here."

Holy shit.

"Mostly beasts."

"Wildebeests?"

Damu nodded. "Yes. Wildebeests come. Many wildebeests."

Oh good. Because if the odd lion here and there wasn't scary enough, stampeding wildebeests kind of was. I shook my head, dumbfounded that I was in a real life game of Jumanji. "Do you see elephants?"

His brow furrowed, so I made a trunk from my arm and made some lame elephant noise. It just made Damu laugh. "*Il-tomíá.*"

"Elephant."

Damu repeated the English word and seemed happy with this exchange, so I kept asking questions. "Giraffe?" I pretended to elongate my neck. "Long neck. Giraffe."

He grinned, his white teeth a stark contrast to his skin. "*E-mára.*"

And as we walked back to the manyatta, we swapped the names of relevant things: all the animals I could think of, trees, birds, day, night. I didn't expect to remember them all but the conversation was good.

"You speak good English," I told him as we neared the familiar thorn fence of the manyatta or kraal. "Did you go to school?"

"No," he replied. "No school. I learn by others."

Wow. He was self-taught. "Do you go to the towns?"

Damu shook his head. "No. I not leave."

"Ever?"

He didn't answer with words, but his silence told me all I needed to know. Jesus. He'd never left the manyatta in which he was born.

"How old are you?" I asked.

Damu didn't answer and the look that crossed his face was one of confusion. Did he not understand my English? I tried rewording my question. "How many years are you?"

He shook his head. "No."

I didn't know if he didn't know what the answer was in English, or if he didn't know what a year was. I had to think more laterally. I had to forget what my culture had taught me and look at it from Damu's perspective. "What are your seasons here?" I asked instead. "Where I'm from, we have summer." I waved my hand at my face like a fan to imply it was hot. Then I pretended to shiver and rub my arms like I was cold. "And winter. And we have spring, when the baby animals are born, and autumn when the leaves fall."

This he seemed to understand. He practised the names of the seasons with me and it was very clear he liked to learn new things. "We have *nkokua*, means the long rains," he said. "*Oloirurujuruj* is the drizzling season, and *oltumuret* for the short rains."

They really did live their entire lives around the land. "Three seasons," I said, holding up three fingers. Damu nodded. "We have four."

He smiled happily, and I couldn't help but like him. Well, the very little I knew of him. "What is your wooden club?" I asked, nodding toward the weapon tied off in his belt.

"*Rungu*." He pulled the wooden club out and held the handle end. It looked like a short, golf driving club or even a wooden human thigh bone. It was smooth and about forty centimetres long. He pulled it back and motioned to throw it, almost like a boomerang.

"You throw it?" I asked. "At animals?"

He grinned and stopped walking. He put the bucket

down and pointed to a tree about thirty metres away, then motioned to the low branch.

"The low branch?" I asked. It stuck out at about ninety degrees, lower than the other branches. "Wait," I said, putting my hand up in a stop signal. I ran over to the tree and pointed up above my head to the branch in question, but also to a discoloured knot in the branch. I wanted to see how good he really was.

He grinned and waited for me to come back to him before he aimed. He walked back about ten metres, simply felt the weight of the rungu in his hand a few times, pulled it back over his shoulder, and taking a few long strides in, he launched it at the tree.

And he hit it, right at the part I'd pointed to. Perfect aim.

I stared, speechless. "Oh my God!" I cried. "You got it!"

He let out a laugh but hurriedly went to retrieve it. He checked it for damage and seeing none, he slipped it back in his belt.

I was still staring, not quite believing what I'd just seen. "Remind me to never make you angry."

"No, no," he said, waving his hands.

I laughed, hoping he meant he wouldn't ever throw his rungu at me, and so we talked the whole way back to the kraal. I wanted to learn as much as I could, and Damu was very patient with me. "You have many questions," he said as we neared the thorned acacia fence that surrounded his village.

"Do I annoy you?" I asked. "Like mosquito?"

Damu laughed and as we walked back in through the gateway, we were met by Kijani. Damu's laughter cut off abruptly. He stopped walking, and he put his head down.

Kijani barked some order at him, and from what I could tell, Damu was in trouble for being late.

"I slowed him down," I said, then realised all too late that it was not my place to speak.

Kijani glared at me with fire and ice in one look. He didn't speak to me, but rather he murmured something low and threatening to Damu instead. If Damu was responsible for me, any anger I caused the warrior leader would fall back on Damu. I wouldn't make the mistake of speaking out of turn again.

Kijani snapped another order at Damu and Damu grabbed my arm and quickly led me back to his hut. Only when we were inside, in the absolute darkness of his home, did I find my voice again. "I'm sorry if I caused you trouble. I won't speak out of turn again."

My eyes burned as they adjusted to the dark, and I strained to see. I was on my knees because of the low ceiling while Damu crouched easily. He carefully put the bucket of water in the corner opposite his bed, then mixed a white powder with water in a small bowl and handed it to me. It looked like glue paste. "Eat."

This was probably the most hideously disgusting looking meal I'd ever eaten, but I was starving hungry and very, very grateful Damu had given me food. "Thank you."

He grabbed my hand. "No. This hand. Never that hand."

"Oh." I bowed my head. "Sorry." Jesus. I had so much to learn, but I was grateful I'd not offended any of the leaders or, God forbid, Kijani. I had read somewhere it was taboo to eat with your left hand—it was, after all, the hand used for wiping one's arse. Apparently. But I'd simply forgotten. As I ate the ground oatmeal goo with the fingers on my right hand, I briefly wondered what would happen if I'd been left-handed...

I wolfed down half of the porridge and held out the bowl with the remainder. "For you?"

My eyes had adjusted, and I could see the smile on Damu's face. He nodded at me. "Eat."

I didn't want him to go hungry, but wasn't going to argue because I had no idea when I would eat again. He was obviously waiting for me to finish using his one and only bowl, yet even in the darkness of his hut I could see the confusion on his face. "You offer me the food?" he asked.

"Of course." I mean, seriously, he'd offered it to me first. I was just being polite. He'd given me shelter, water, food, and conversation.

"Alé has kindness."

Oh. He'd used the name I was given, which was now, I assumed, my Maasai name. "Damu has kindness."

His grin was instantaneous, his teeth gleaming in the darkness. I held out the empty bowl. "Do I clean?"

He ignored that, whether he didn't understand or if he was just in a hurry, I wasn't sure. He simply added more ground meal and water to the bowl and ate his breakfast.

I figured it was a good time to freshen up the best I could, so I rummaged through my backpack for a clean shirt. I rolled on some underarm deodorant and, peeling off my shirt, pulled the new one on. When Damu was done eating, I followed him outside and he pointed to one of the houses. "You this way."

I went blindly, wherever he was telling me I had to go. We walked to one of the far off huts where there were ten or twelve women sitting on the ground in a bit of circle. Each of them was busy, either stringing beads or weaving threads, and their conversation stopped as we approached.

Damu spoke to them, words I couldn't understand—though I think I heard the name Kijani—before he turned to me. "You be here."

Okay then. So Kijani had said that I was to sit with the women. I nodded, indicating I understood, and without another word, he walked away. I stood there with twelve women staring up at me, their faces neutral. They didn't seem to hate me, but they weren't exactly welcoming either. I knew it had to be me who bridged the gap. I found a place in the dirt, shaded by the hut. "May I sit here?" I asked, patting the ground. Some spoke in Maa, but others nodded and I knew without doubt, if it weren't for Kijani's instruction, I wouldn't have been welcome.

I must have been truly bizarre to these women, even a little frightening. So I gave them a smile and put my hand to my chest. "I am Alé."

Of course this made them laugh. I'd just called myself milk. But their smiles were contagious, and it seemed to break the tension because they went back to their conversation like I wasn't even there. Except for one woman who nodded at me. She had a shaved head, beaded earlobes, and from the number of necklaces she wore, I gathered she held some kind of rank and respect amongst the women. She wore a red tartan dress, had bare feet, and sat on an animal hide. She was smiling at me now. "Kafir. Eyes of Kafir."

I put my hand to my eyes. "I have two different coloured eyes," I said, using two fingers on the number and pointing in turn to each eye. I didn't know if they all spoke English, so I hoped they understood what I was saying. "Who is Kafir?"

The woman spoke in very broken English, but I was very grateful she was even speaking to me. "Kafir roam our land. No kill him; he protect us."

Oh, some guy protected them so they didn't kill him. That was nice. The women started talking again as they continued with their handiwork, breaking out in laughter and song as they made bracelets and clothes, and it truly was a privilege to watch. They were such a happy people. They literally lived with the barest of things, such primitive means, but to this outsider, they seemed content.

I tried to imagine the women I'd known in Australia, and even the men, living like this, and the idea was comical. Most of the people I knew thought they wouldn't survive without Wi-Fi, the latest model phones, and their morning hit of over-priced, over-rated "organic" soy latte.

The woman beside me finished a strand of white beads. I nodded toward it. "Very beautiful."

They all laughed again, and I didn't even mind that they were laughing at me. One of the women across from me picked up a single strand of string. "Alé make beads."

I grinned at her. "Can I?"

She threw the string to me and all of them laughed and clapped, but I still didn't mind. I watched how the others started, how they tied off the thin leather strand, and I threaded the beads.

And I have to admit. I rather enjoyed it.

As the morning wore on into the afternoon, the children came a little closer to me, but only for a second. I think they were seeing which of them was the bravest. I helped with the beading, I helped grinding grains on a flat rock with a worn stone, and I did everything the women did. They rarely spoke to me, yet I was comforted by their seeming acceptance of me.

I watched out for Damu, catching sight of him every now and then. He was never far away, always by himself, never with the other Maasai men. While they were off tending cattle and goats, Damu did the work the women did, not the work of the men, and I couldn't help wonder why.

He'd been given the demoralising duty of babysitting the stupid white man, and Kijani spoke down to him. They treated him like an outcast. I assumed there was some cultural reason for this but didn't dare ask.

When the sun was low in the sky and my stomach was torturing me with pangs of hunger, Damu found me. "Come," he said, nodding toward his hut.

If I'd been excited by the prospect of dinner, I shouldn't have been. Damu soon mixed together some of the porridge we'd had at breakfast, and handed me the bowl. But I was so hungry, I was appreciative for anything. "Thank you, Damu. I am very grateful."

I sat on the dirt floor where I'd slept the night before and ate my meal. Damu sat patiently and silent, waiting for me to finish. I handed him the empty bowl, graciously feeling the weight of food in my belly. As he prepared his own meal, I could see the small bowl container from which he scooped the white powdered grains was almost empty. "What do you call the food?" I asked him.

He added water and stirred, then looked at the white goop in his bowl. "*Ugali*. Ugali is thick. *Uji* is thin." He showed me the different consistencies. Uji was just a runnier, milk-like consistency, so he added more flour to make it into ugali. Ugali looked like thick porridge or mashed potatoes. "Ugali eat at dinner. Uji drink at morning."

"Ugali, uji" I repeated, pronouncing it as he had. "Where do you get the grain from?"

"Share. Everyone share."

Fair enough. The entire tribe rationed out equally. But something bothered me, though. "Am I eating your share?"

Damu just continued to eat. "Responsibility to me."

Oh Jesus. I was costing him half his food. I smiled at him, hopeful the horrible way I felt didn't show on my face. I was determined to search out more food tomorrow. I sat back, leaning against the wall, and watched the last slivers of colour fade from the sky. The food in my stomach and possibly jet lag insisted I lay down for a second. I pulled my backpack under my head and closed my eyes, willing the dreams to come as much as I wished they never would.

The hardest thing about saying goodbye to someone was seeing them every night in my dreams.

It was my most favourite, and equally dreaded, part of my day.

CHAPTER FOUR

THE NEXT DAY started the same. We walked for water, which I determined was a job for female tribe members. The men and young boys herded their cattle and goats down into the valley, watching over them carefully. So why were Damu and myself allocated to duties with the women and girls, I didn't have a clue. Not that I minded. Hearing the laughter and songs of the woman ahead of us, and the walk itself, were beautiful. And the river water was the closest thing to a bath or shower as I would get, so once Damu had collected his bucket full of water, I went downstream a little way, stripped off to my underwear and went in. I figured drinking the water yesterday hadn't ill-affected me in anyway, so it had to be okay. I was sure to be quick though, not wanting to anger Kijani if we were late again.

I didn't think I'd broken any Maasai rules about stripping down and swimming in their river. Damu never insisted I stop. In fact, he laughed at me when I shook my hair like a dog. I didn't need to speak Maa to understand a few universal things: smiles and laughter were good; glaring, yelling and pointing a spear at my head was bad.

I was aiming for a day when Kijani didn't want to kill me.

I waded out of the water, pulled on my shorts and shirt, then sat down to once again struggle with putting dry socks on wet feet.

I pointed to Damu's tyre sandals. "Your shoes are much better than mine." I held up my $180 sneakers. Back home, these were the newest and best sneakers on the market. Here, they were more of a pain in the arse. I had to wriggle my foot and use both hands to pull the stupid shoe on.

Damu laughed again. "I think no."

"You prefer these?" I said, tying the laces. "Yours are much easier." I jumped to my feet. "Come, we don't want to be late."

Damu smiled as we walked back to the manyatta. His long, graceful strides weren't easy to keep up with, even with him carrying a bucket of water, but I was determined to walk at his pace. I certainly didn't want him in any trouble on my account.

"It's very beautiful here," I said to him as we walked in the warm Tanzanian morning. I'd seen the Lion King as a kid and didn't really think much of the landscape, until now. The animators got the details right, the vastness and the colours.

"*Enkai* is good," Damu said.

"What is *Enkai*?" I asked, wondering if it were another word for the weather.

He held the bucket in one hand and with his free hand, he drew an arc across the hills and sky. "The word..." He seemed to struggle with his English. "God," he added quickly, as though he'd just remembered it. "Maasai God."

Oh. I gave him a smile and said, "Enkai is very good."

"Good for land, good for people," he said. "Many rains, good for cattle."

It was clear he was very proud of his life here. "It will be cold soon?"

Damu nodded. "In one moon, days be small."

Ah. In one moon, so one full lunar cycle meaning one month, the days will be shorter. "Same for my country."

"You be many places," Damu said.

"Some, yes. I worked for a travel agent, I helped people organise holidays and tours, and it was expected that I travel a lot."

"How many country?"

"Nine or ten," I answered. "A few countries in Europe, America, Canada, Japan, and now Tanzania."

He seemed a little reflective after that, as though he felt bad because I was more worldly than he was. Which was true. I *had* travelled more—a lot more, considering he'd never left his village—but he was Maasai. He had more history and culture in his little finger than I could possibly imagine. "But Damu," I added with a smile. "There's nothing in all the world like what you have here. It's very special."

He seemed to like that, but his smile faded into a frown. "Council law don't agree."

Council law? "The Government?"

"Yes," he said, as though that was the word he was looking for. "Try move us. Want our land for money."

I had seen similar comments and articles that said Maasai were being driven off their land. Their nomadic nature, to live where the land takes them, made them easy targets for money-hungry governments. The Maasai would move their village when the seasons demanded it, only to come back to find it "owned" by someone else. They had no legal recourse, no money, and didn't live by government laws.

It saddened me to hear Damu confirm this.

When we arrived back at the manyatta, we drank our breakfast of uji, and afterwards, Damu went about his chores and I went back to the ever-changing circle of women doing their crafts, beadwork, and sewing of tartans and leathers.

Some of the women from yesterday were now working on their homes, replastering the outside walls with a mix of dung and mud, singing and laughing as they did.

The ladies I sat with also sang and this time, made no fuss at my presence. I quickly took my place beside them, collecting up beads and string and set about doing my work. I'd only threaded a few beads when a small child of maybe five or six, wearing a cotton t-shirt as a dress, edged closer to me. I had no idea of this child's gender—it didn't matter to me. I smiled at them and they turned and ran, only to return a short while later, getting a little closer. This time I smiled at them and they didn't run, so I said, "Hello."

They squealed and ran away, making the women laugh, and I could hear other children laughing as well. I was pleased the children were working up the courage to come up to me.

Next time the child got closer, I put my hand to my chest and introduced myself. "I am Alé."

They didn't run. "*Mzungu.*"

I looked to the older woman from yesterday. "Mzungu?"

"White man," she replied.

I smiled at the child. "Yes. Mzungu." I held out my arm, and the child very bravely reached out to touch the skin on my forearm. Obviously they'd never seen a white person before. As soon as they touched me, they pulled back their hand. Their face lit up with wonder and broke into a huge smile. I found myself grinning as well. "I am Alé," I repeated.

The older woman said, "He is Komboa."

"His name is Komboa?" I asked, still not quite catching all her words. I'd rather question than get it wrong and offend someone. She nodded, so I looked at the little boy and gave him a smile and a wave. "Hello Komboa."

He laughed and ran away, and I went back to beading, happy with the interaction. And then the older woman said, "Amali." And the women around the circle each told me their names. "Nashuru." "Yantai." "Naasha." "Leela."

I bowed my head. "Alé. Thank you. Very honoured," I said. I fought a smile for the rest of the day.

AND SO THE DAYS WENT, each day's routine the same. The chores always varied, but I spent my days with Amali, Nashuru, and Yantai mostly, doing whatever they were doing. Damu was never far away, and I likened his role in the tribe to a maintenance man: he did whatever was asked of him. He never went with the men, and he didn't truly interact with the women either, but he was always around, always busy, always smiling.

Damu and I would talk, usually me asking a bunch of questions about their culture. I was learning some words in Maa, and he was learning new English words. I liked him. He was peaceful and content. He was proud but humble, he had next to no possessions, but he was happy with what he had.

And before I knew it, I'd been there a week.

I drank uji for breakfast and ate ugali as my only two

small meals a day, and in one week, I knew I'd lost some weight. My shorts were too big, but I found I could roll the waistband over a few times to help keep them up. I also still slept on the ground in Damu's hut, but I didn't mind. I usually fell into sleep too tired to care.

And every night I dreamed the same dream.

It was of Jarrod, but that didn't surprise me. My dreams were always of him. I dreamed he was here with me, walking through the long brown grass of the Serengeti, toward the river where Damu and I walked every morning. Jarrod looked beautiful, ethereal, as he moved in slow motion through the field. His hand skimmed the top of the grass, feeling it dance at his touch, and he gave me the most amazing smile. He never spoke, but I understood what he was telling me just fine. He was telling me I was where I should be, and in my dream I called his name but he couldn't hear me. I longed to hear him speak, to smell his skin, and I ached to feel his arms around me. And when I tried to run to him, he was gone.

The dream never changed. I yearned for the ending to be different. I wanted to reach him, to touch him, to hear his voice. I longed to see his face, to hear his voice. But in my dream, as in real life, he was gone. Every morning I woke in a sweat, trying to get my bearings in the darkness of the hut.

Damu was often sitting upright on his mattress, watching me. I knew I'd woken him with my dreams, but he never questioned me. He never pushed me.

Instead, our early morning walks to the river would clear my head, and our conversations were the highlights of my day.

During my day, while Damu was doing his chores, I used a flat rock and rounded stone to grind the ugali to the fine powder for our porridge. It was a primitive mortar and pestle but just as effective. Amali gave me a gourd to store it in, and I went in search of Damu with my score.

"Look!" I said, holding out the makeshift container. He was carting firewood and threw down the load in his arms, the branches clattering to the ground. "I made this for us."

Damu peered inside the gourd, much like a parent would look at art their kids made at school. "You make?"

I was grinning like an idiot, I was sure of it. "Yes!" It was hard to explain how it made me feel to contribute. I was giving something, on equal footing. As meagre as a small amount of ground porridge was, but I no longer was a burden to Damu's rations. "Tomorrow we eat my ugali."

"No."

Oh. I felt like he'd slapped me. I couldn't hide how deflated I was. "Oh."

"No, no," he shook his head, still smiling. "Tomorrow new moon. We drink milk. Tonight we eat ugali, tomorrow milk."

"Oh," I said again, this time with a laugh. "Milk?"

He held up three fingers. "Three days."

"Is that some kind of ritual?" I asked. "Ceremony?"

"Milk three days of new moon, then meat."

Meat. Dear God, I never thought I'd miss meat, but after seven days of polenta-like porridge, even the word meat made my mouth water. Hell, even three days of milk sounded great.

Damu put his hand on the gourd. "Keep. Store."

His fingers brushed mine and the thrill of human touch made my heart flutter. It wasn't a sexual touch. It wasn't intimate in any way, but it had been so long since I'd felt the touch of another person... I hadn't realised how much I'd missed that either.

AT DUSK, Damu didn't come for me as he normally did. I went to his hut anyway and set about making the both of us some porridge. Just before dark, he slid in through the doorway. "I wondered where you were," I admitted.

He held up a small bowl. It was the bottom of a gourd that had been smoothed off. "For you."

I couldn't believe it. He'd made me my very own bowl. "You did this for me?"

Even as the darkness filled in around us, I could see his smile. "Yes. For you."

I was so incredibly touched. It was probably the most incredible gift I'd ever received. It wasn't the value of it or lack thereof, in this case, it was the acceptance. It was the gift of his time and skill, that he hand-crafted this bowl for me, and that something in this village now belonged to me. Because of Damu.

"Thank you," I whispered. "En-ashê, en-ashê," I said. *Gratitude. Gratitude.*

He took the bowl and scooped out porridge for me, then he took his own bowl and did the same. We ate in silence, both of us smiling between mouthfuls.

And as we sat there in the darkened hut, I thought back to what I'd learned in my first week of living with the Maasai.

That it was strictly a patriarchal society. The men made the decisions that ruled over the tribe as a whole, and elders and leading warriors were at the spearhead of that. The men's primary role was to look after and manage their herds and provide safety for the women and children. The men were divided into groups or age-sets of warriors—moran, who were the young warriors, and elders. They were proud and dignified and took their roles very seriously.

Women were regarded in much the same way as their cattle were. It was hard to get my head around, and I had to remind myself that I was here as a guest and it was not my place to judge. Women did most of the manual labour around the manyatta and were responsible for the upkeep of their homes, preparing meals, and looking after the children.

And despite their social standing within this community, the women were some of the happiest people I'd ever met. They sang and danced, they adored and respected their husbands. Many of the women shared husbands, as they were either the first, second, third wife, and each of the wives were like sisters to their fellow wives.

Needless to say, it couldn't have been any further removed from my Catholic upbringing.

It was fascinating and remarkable.

Throughout the manyatta, at any given time of the day, someone would be singing or dancing, and there was always laughter. There was so much joy in the simplest of things.

The children were a highlight for me. Free of any responsibility, it was their duty to learn through play and stories of their ancestors: the young Maasai in the manyatta were like one large kindergarten. They laughed and squealed with delight, they were rarely still, always running and jumping, and role-playing. It was their true belief children of the same age-set, these kids from about four to eight years old, would share everything: food, homes, friendships, brotherhood, and sisterhood. They would remain in that same age-set with their fellow "brothers" and "sisters" until the day they died.

It was a society that remained unchanged for hundreds, if not thousands, of years.

Damu broke my train of thought. "I see Jaali sit with you today."

"Yes!" I laughed. "He sat on me," I said, patting my knee. "When I was sitting with Amali."

"You happy."

Of course it made me happy. The kids were all petrified of me when I first arrived, and now, just a week later, they were climbing all over me and patting me on the head in some Maasai kind of game reminiscent of Duck, Duck, Goose. "Yes, it makes me happy."

"You have children?" Damu asked me.

"No," I answered softly.

"No wife, no child, no goats," Damu said. "Like me."

I nodded slowly. "Tell me, is that why they put us together." I motioned between us. "Did Kijani and Kasisi insist I stay with you because we have no wife, no goats?"

Damu was quiet for a moment, and I wondered whether he would answer me at all. Then he said, "I have no... worth."

"You mean wealth?"

Again, silence, until he replied. "No. No worth."

"Yes you do," I said quickly. "You are very kind and very helpful."

"Not a man."

"You are just as much a man as Kijani," I whispered. "Just because you don't have a spear doesn't make you less of a man."

"He is brave warrior," Damu said, sounding almost offended that I'd said such a thing.

"Why do you not have long hair like him? Why are you not a warrior?" I asked. "You are in the same age-set."

"I do woman's work, not a man."

An irrational anger welled up inside me. I had no right to be mad at his cultural differences, but saying he was not a man when he clearly was, really fucking irked me. "You are a man," I said, with more heat in my tone than I intended. I scrambled over and grabbed the bucket of water then snatched up the empty dirty bowls and went outside.

Being told you're not a man because of someone else's opinion on what they believe makes a man was such a sore point for me. I'd spent years being told I was never a man, would never be a man until I decided to be straight instead of gay. And it raised my hackles every fucking time.

I poured some water into the bowls and angrily scrubbed them clean until the fight in me was gone. My shoulders fell, suddenly weighted down by the fact I'd taken my anger out on Damu—the very person who least deserved it.

It also made me realise that I had been placed with Damu and spent my days with the women—whom I respected immensely and enjoyed their friendship and camaraderie. But in the eyes of the Maasai men, that made me a non-man too.

Somehow it didn't bother me so much that they thought little of me, but they thought the same of Damu, and that upset me. With a defeated sigh, I took our bowls and bucket of water back inside the pitch-black hut and felt my way back to my dirt bed.

Damu was quiet, though I could hear him breathe, and I knew what I must do. "I apologise for my anger," I said softly, hoping he would hear the sincerity. "I apologise if I upset you. I am sorry."

He never said a word.

After a minute or so of silence, I said, "Thank you for my bowl."

I heard him roll over, onto his side or back; I couldn't tell in the darkness. "You leave your country because you are not a man?" he asked. "Who is Jarrod? The one your dreams speak of?"

Hearing his name spoken reopened the wounds I'd tried twelve months to close. I closed my eyes slowly, instant tears pooling in my eyes. "He is... He..." I couldn't answer. I couldn't. I rolled over on my bed of dirt and faced the wall.

I knew my dreams that night would be unforgiving.

I wasn't disappointed.

CHAPTER FIVE

JARROD WALKS amongst the Serengeti grasses, smiling. The sun shines brightly on him, and the breeze gently messes his brown hair. But then he turns, looking sharply over his shoulder, his face quickly overcome with fear.

In the distance on the African plain, lions appear. A pride of them, separating us and herding Jarrod. Hunting him. He sprints, he yells at me, though no sound leaves his mouth, telling me to run. And just as the lions set upon him, I realise they aren't lions at all. They're men in a darkened alley, a Sydney side-street, kicking and punching under the cover of night...

I scream for help and try to fight them, until the darkness takes me too.

I WOKE up in complete blackness, and for a split second, I thought I was reliving my dream: helpless and fading in and out consciousness, unable to move but trying to fight just the same. But then I understood the strong arms around me weren't restraints, but Damu. He pulled me onto his mattress with him and hushed me like a child. It was then I realised I was crying. The dream was so real, the memories too raw. I buried my face into his chest and sobbed.

When sleep finally slithered in around me, it was, for the first time in far too long, thankfully dreamless.

SO APPARENTLY NOT HAVING UJI FOR breakfast or ugali for dinner meant drinking milk for breakfast *and* dinner. Not just any milk, but goat's milk and cow's milk, and it also meant drinking it warm, and while I was respectful and grateful for the gift of food, it was far from my favourite.

I'd already begun to re-evaluate the way I thought of food. Back home, food was something you might take for granted. We demanded a variety of ingredients, insisted it be fresh and prepared in sanitary environments. We also went out for meals that cost ridiculous amounts of money—which seemed absurd to me now. We ate when we were bored. We ate because it was simply there.

Here, in the world of the Maasai, people ate exactly enough food for the nutritional content to get them through their daily activities until their next meal. Of course there were ceremonial meals and feasts. I'd yet to see one. I'd only drank water and uji and eaten some nuts and berries and ugali since I'd been here. It was bland, like a semolina porridge. But it filled my tummy. I didn't miss anything else. Sure, steak or chicken would probably be divine, but I knew my body was getting enough sustenance to survive. And strangely enough, that was all I needed.

But there was much excitement around the manyatta this day. The new moon brought with it a buzz and everyone was looking forward to the festivities. As Damu and I walked to the river, I didn't want him to bring up my nightmare—or how I woke up still cradled in his arms—so I asked non-stop questions about what the new moon signified and what it meant for our diet. Why did we only drink milk? Why for three days? What did the new season mean for the Maasai, and what did it mean for the Serengeti? How cold did the winters get here?

Damu, as always, showed nothing but patience and answered every question, even if he'd explained it before. I was certain he saw through my thinly veiled attempt at distraction, though he had the decency to pretend he didn't.

He simply walked beside me back to the kraal, tall and proud in his red shuka, his smile ever present. When I'd run out of questions, he told me stories of his people and, in particular, how the animals played a part in their history.

"Will you take me to see them?" I asked. "Not today, but one day. I want to see giraffes and elephants."

Damu laughed and pointed to the west. "That way."

"Do they come here?" I pointed to the ground.

"Some. Not always. Down river. No here because of the people."

Ah, right. I nodded in understanding. "Why do the Maasai not hunt antelope or wildebeest?"

"Our law says no."

"Tanzanian law?"

He shook his head. "Maasai law. No harm to animal. Be at one with the animal and the land."

"I understand that. I agree with it," I added. "But some people might wonder why the Maasai struggle for food when it roams so freely in your land."

Damu just smiled. "Why people worry what we do?"

And there it was. *Why* do *people worry about how other*

cultures and people live their lives? Because some people weren't happy unless they were sticking their noses into other people's business, trying to convert their beliefs and way of life. "You speak the truth."

He grinned at the compliment, and he was excited to get back too, walking quicker than normal. "So tell me, you like drinking the milk?"

He nodded quickly. "Very much."

I quickened my pace. "Then come on. Hurry."

He laughed freely and matched my strides without even trying.

THOUGH NOTHING quite prepared me for the taste of the milk. I took my ration, the white liquid sloshing in my bowl, under the watchful eye of Kijani. He'd as good as left me alone for the last few days and not so much as even looked in my direction, and I was kinda glad. He was intimidating and fierce, and his hatred of me was not something he had to hide.

But I took my bowl back to Damu and sat with him, sipping at the milk. Two weeks ago, back in Sydney, if I'd been offered warm goat's milk I would have laughed and refused point blank. But now, after eating the same porridge every meal for a week, the milk wasn't so bad. Well, the first taste was warm and wasn't too bad, but I wasn't sure how much of it I could stomach. I had doubts three days of it would be pleasant.

Damu savoured every sip, smiling to himself as he drank it. The Maasai consumed enough starch and protein to survive, and this ceremonious milk was a crucial part of their diet.

"Good?" he asked, clearly proud and happy.

I would never insult him or his people, and I only had to tell a half-truth. "Yes."

He laughed like he could tell I was lying, earning a pointed stare from Kijani. Maybe he didn't like to see Damu happy. Maybe he'd never heard him laugh before. I didn't know, but I didn't make eye contact and I kept my smile hidden behind my bowl.

The children laughed, the women sang and danced. The plate-like beads around their neck bobbed and swayed in a show of hierarchy and grace. Amali wore the most necklaces, which in turn made her dancing more alluring, and this cemented her position as first wife of Kasisi, the tribal elder chief. She was the grandmother figure to the women here, the most respected for sure.

On the third day, when I thought I couldn't stomach any more tepid goat's milk, and when I thought it couldn't possibly get any worse, it got a whole lot worse. The third day signified the end of the ceremonial days, and to celebrate, the Maasai would drink a mixture of goat's milk and blood.

"*O-saróí*," the people sang, which led them to point and laugh at me and Damu. "O-saróí. O-saróí. Damu, Alé."

"Why are they laughing at us?" I quietly asked Damu. We had taken our bowls of the pink, sloshing liquid, and as usual, gone to drink away from the others.

He smiled as he sipped his meal, slowly closing his eyes and savouring the taste. "Blood and milk."

Realisation sank in. Alé meant milk... "What does your name mean?"

Damu's eyes flinched, his happy façade slipped for the briefest moment. "It is Swahili word. It means blood."

Without any explanation, he nodded to my untouched bowl. "Drink."

I looked at the mixture of blood and milk, and my empty stomach rolled at the thought of actually drinking it. This was their most revered meal. The Maasai were world famous for drinking this mixture of goat's blood and curdled milk. It sustained them when they ate no other food for days or weeks at a time. They'd been known to walk for days, surviving—no, not just surviving, but thriving—on this ghastly mixture.

I noticed then that others were watching me, waiting for me to drink it, Kijani included. I couldn't, *wouldn't*, offend them. But more so, if Damu was responsible for me and I disgraced his people, the punishment of only God knows what would be inflicted on him, not me. And that was something I couldn't bear the thought of. So I put the bowl to my lips and tried not to think of words like *coagulation* and *congealed*, and I drank it. Even though I was starving hungry, the taste was putrid.

Sour and metallic, warm and thick, I willed myself to swallow it down. Not for me, not to sustain or nourish my body, but for Damu.

Instead of thinking about what I was drinking, I concentrated on what questions I would ask him as I drained my bowl.

Damu, grinning widely, clapped my shoulder. "Good. Good."

The others, who had been watching, both men and women, seemed pleased with me, and even Kijani gave me a nod like I'd passed some test. I couldn't let on that the liquid sat like a brick in my stomach and threatened to be expelled at any second.

Instead, I wiped my mouth with the back of my hand

and asked Damu, "How many more of these?" I nodded pointedly to my bowl.

He grinned at me. "Not today. We eat meat this night."

"Oh, thank God."

Damu laughed, and I really did like that sound. "You did good."

Pleased by the compliment and relieved at not vomiting, I gave him a smile. "Thank you. Your approval means a lot to me."

Damu's gaze shot to mine, an intense look—one of shock and gratitude—before he looked away. He had obviously never been given praise before. Was it so bizarre that his opinion be held in high regard of others? Something had definitely happened with Damu. There had to be a reason why he was so excluded from his people.

"Your name means blood?" I asked.

His smile slowly faded away. "Yes. My mother die in birth to me. There was much blood. I was born in blood."

Oh man. "I'm very sorry," I whispered. It was a natural reaction to put my hand on his arm before I'd given thought to whether it was an acceptable gesture between men.

Again, his almost-black eyes met mine, though now he didn't speak. He just stared at me, into me, and I couldn't look away. He didn't seem to mind my touching him, and no one seemed to notice us or even look in our direction, so I didn't pull my hand away.

"Can I ask you something?"

"You ask many questions."

I smiled at that. It was true, but these questions were personal. "Why are you not a warrior? Are you not in the same age-set as Kijani."

He pulled his arm away from me, and my hand burned at the loss. I expected him to get up and walk away, but he didn't. He stayed seated with me, though he looked out across the kraal, at the huts and people. "I not deserve warrior. I kill my mother. Kijani's mother."

Wait, what? "You and Kijani are brothers?" I whispered, not able to hide my surprise.

He nodded. "Chief Kasisi, our father. Mother was first wife, most favoured."

Oh Jesus. "It was *not* your fault. You were just a baby."

He sighed and still wouldn't look at me. "No matter. Amali raise me and Kijani like mother."

"Amali is a very good woman," I said. "I like her."

Damu almost smiled. "Kijani good leader. Good warrior."

"Yes, he is," I agreed. I couldn't deny it. Kijani was a good warrior and protector of his people. Didn't mean he was likeable, though. "You are a good man too."

Damu shook his head immediately. "Not same."

I pursed my lips together so I wouldn't argue. Maasai lore was that all boys, or moran, go through warriorhood. They are circumcised, have long braided hair, and carry spears. Then when the new age-set of boys are ready, they enter warriorhood and the older warriors step down, shave their heads, and hold long white sticks instead of spears. They get married to their first wife and have children and more wives.

That was how things happened here.

But not for Damu.

He had no long hair, he held no spear. His people had basically told him he would forever be in no man's land. Literally.

"I not warrior. So no cattle. So cannot take wife. I not bear children," he said quietly. "Not man."

The last time we had this discussion, it hadn't ended

well. I needed to curb my temper. It wasn't even the whole man-qualifying thing that annoyed me, but the use of cows and goats as currency to buy wives was, to put it bluntly, an insulting mindfuck. *Don't get angry. Don't judge their culture,* I repeated this in my head over and over until I could think of a more objective thing to say.

"Whose decision was it that you not enter warriorhood?"

"Kasisi, he see, he dream of future. He see Kijani be great warrior. They make decision for our people."

His own father and brother basically sentenced him to a life of nothing. I bit back my anger and frustration on his behalf.

"Kasisi say I have hearts," Damu said quietly, holding up two fingers. "One heart for this people, one heart not here."

I blinked, trying to guess the significance. "What does that mean?"

"He see I not belong here with whole heart. So I not be warrior."

I took a steadying breath to tamp down my temper. "What do you think?"

"I belong here. I not know how to belong in other place when I am only here."

Damu's logic was sound. How could he belong somewhere else, when he'd never *been* anywhere else? He'd never set foot outside this valley or away from his people. Of course it would be absurd to consider belonging somewhere he'd never been.

"I don't belong in my home either," I told him. "Not any more than I belong here."

Damu turned to face me. "Is that why you come here?"

If I stripped away the complexities, the horrors I'd lived

through, and if I stripped away the emotions, the answer was quite simple. "Yes."

"Are you man in your country?"

"Yes." *Though some would argue*, I thought humourlessly to myself. Those men in the alley certainly would.

"You have not wife or children?" He'd asked me this before, so it clearly confused him that I was a certain age and not married and had no children.

"No. In my country, it's very different." I couldn't even begin to quantify how different *very different* was. Jesus Christ. "We don't need wife or husband to be a man or woman. In my country, your age and how you treat people makes you a man." It was more complex than I could explain, but I gave him the shortest version I could think of. "If I am older than eighteen years and treat people with respect, if I contribute to my people and city by working and paying taxes, then I am an adult. And that makes me a man, and it makes a female a woman. There are many variables," I added. "Someone doesn't have to over eighteen years. They might be sixteen and looking after brothers and sisters and working full-time to feed them. I would call them an adult and therefore a man or a woman. Or they might not work or have a family, but they are still an adult, therefore a man or a woman."

He seemed to ponder this foreign concept for a long hard moment. "Why so complicated?"

I laughed because the Maasai way, although completely foreign and bizarre to me, was so much easier. "It is complicated, I agree."

We set about our chores, though this time I helped Damu. I wasn't given any directive to stay with the women, so I took it as an opportunity to spend the day with him. As the milk drinking ceremony had suggested, the change of season meant winter was coming, and so we collected the firewood for the manyatta.

One aspect of the Maasai people which I truly admired, was that everything was shared. All food, all water, and all tools. The entire kraal worked together in that respect, to see the betterment of the whole, not the individual. It was a principle many world leaders could learn from.

Damu and I took swathes of cloth, much like old blankets, and headed toward the river and the trees which lined it. We worked in a happy silence, collecting sticks and small dried branches into piles on our blankets.

At one point, Damu picked up two sticks and held them to his head like antlers. He stomped the ground with his foot like he was going to charge at me, so I wielded one long stick like a sword. Damu roared and ran at me. His height and expression made him terrifying. I threw the stick, squealed like a child, and hid behind a tree. I stuck my head out to find him laughing, like *really* laughing at me. He was doubled over, holding his sides.

I stomped over, much like a petulant child, and shoved his shoulder as I walked past. "Not funny."

"Much funny," he said, wiping his eyes. "Much funny."

I stole sticks from his pile to make mine bigger. "Now it's funny."

He sobered, looking at my now-bigger-than-his pile. "Not funny."

I grinned at him. "Much funny."

He relented with his usual grin, and as he brushed past me, he slid his hand up my arm. It was a gentle touch, a lingering touch, and one that caught my breath. I hadn't been expecting it, and despite my damaged heart, I welcomed it. If Damu noticed my reaction, he didn't let on.

We wrapped up the kindling and secured them in

bundles on our back. When Damu had helped me with mine, I put my hand on his shoulder. "Thank you."

He gently touched my face and smiled warmly at me. "Welcome."

It was an intimate thing to do. Well, it was to me, though I had no way of knowing what it meant to him. Not without outing myself and possibly getting thrown out of the kraal or even killed.

But so began the smallest touches between us. I had put my hand on his arm first, I remembered, as a gesture of friendship and comfort. Maybe that's all his were to me as well, I reasoned. Maybe I was reading way more into it than I should. Maybe I was so starved of human touch, I was seeing things where things simply were not.

I made it my mission to watch the others and see how the Maasai treated the act of touch. I'd been there over a week but hadn't paid any attention to if and how they acted intimately. But hopefully, I could interpret what Damu's touches meant and what they didn't mean, without landing either one of us in trouble.

When we walked back to the manyatta, Damu walked a little closer than he did before. Or maybe I imagined that as well. Maybe drinking blood and milk made people hallucinate or delusional, or maybe the hit of protein made my brain work cognitively and I could now see what had always been there.

We got back to the kraal around midday, and there was much excitement. Some of the warriors and young moran were taking a goat to be slaughtered for dinner. I noticed two younger warriors holding hands as they ran with the unlucky goat.

"They must take it away from kraal," Damu explained. "No kill it here." I was thankful, because as good as eating meat sounded, I certainly didn't want to watch them slay it.

"Why is everyone leaving the kraal?" I asked, as all the people left the safety of the acacia fence.

"No eat meat in manyatta," Damu explained.

I was pretty much resigned to not being surprised by any new developments in what I learned about the Maasai. All new cultural findings were just taken in stride, and again, I didn't want to judge. Maybe the Maasai would think it completely absurd that we'd use a telephone to order food in plastic containers, then pay extra to have them deliver it to our front door.

The women prepared a fire, all while laughing and singing, and the children sang and clapped, play-acting and jumping. I'd never known such truly happy people. Always smiling, always laughing.

And, as I'd started to notice, always touching.

The women touched the women, and the men touched the men, while men and women didn't touch in public, even those who were married. Which, in such a homophobic society, struck me as odd. Especially with guys I'd noticed holding hands. And this was a homophobic society, as was much of East Africa. I'd known that before I came here, but I never considered it a problem because I wasn't travelling with a male partner and certainly had no intention of finding one.

Damu was tending to the roof of his hut, and while we were afforded privacy, I decided I would ask. "Can I ask you a question?"

"Always with you questions," he said, smiling as he continued his work.

I looked around, just to make sure we were out of earshot. "I've noticed people touching. The women touch other women, fixing beads or wiping faces," I said, then took a deep breath. "And the men touch men and hold hands. But the men don't touch the women."

Damu's hands stilled. He blinked and licked his lips. "No touching. Not allowed."

"But the men were holding hands?"

"Warrior brothers will do this," Damu explained, patting down some mud on the roof. "It is... acceptable we touch in this way."

"But not married people?"

Damu shook his head, which I took as no.

I don't know why I needed to ask this—I knew what the answer was going to be—but the masochist in me needed to hear him say it. "And in your country, men can't be married to men?"

Damu's gaze shot to mine, and there was something in his eyes. A flicker of fear? Of knowing? I couldn't tell. "No." He shook his head. "No. Marriage is for purpose of children."

I nodded slowly. I understood. In the eyes of the Maasai, wealth was determined by how many wives, children, and cattle a man had. It was bizarre to me, archaic even, yet I forced myself not to pass judgement. "In my country," I said softly, "marriage is for love. Man or woman, it doesn't matter."

Okay, so that was boiling a complex societal institution into one very short sentence. But I needed to simplify it so he understood. No, Australia didn't have marriage equality, but marriage back home was a wedding ceremony and a legal document between two people, with permissions by a church. Here, in Maasai culture, it was simply an agreement within or between tribes. There were no marriage certificates, no prenups or other legalities, apart from the promise and exchange of dowry. So, by Maasai law, any two people who declared themselves to married, simply were. Sure, the tribal priest performed ceremonies to qualify the act of marriage, but the bindings were that of word and honour.

So, to simplify it, in Damu's eyes, a marriage was two people who were bound together by a promise. And I had to admit, I liked that.

It meant that what Jarrod and I had would have been considered a marriage, and that both warmed me and devastated me, in equal measure.

I didn't wait for Damu's response. He seemed stuck for words anyway and I needed to take a breath. Usually whenever I thought of Jarrod, be it while awake or asleep, it wrecked me.

Though this time, I had no time to drown in my own thoughts and misery.

CHAPTER SIX

MOMBOA RACED up to me and grabbed my hand. He pulled me along, speaking so fast I couldn't understand, but his excitement was universal. "Alé, Alé," he sang my name, dragging me with him. "*Adumu, adumu.*"

Adumu was the Maa word for what basically meant to stand in a circle and jump. And all the young boys, no older than eight or ten, were standing in a circle pretending to be warriors. They had shirts and strips of cloth tied around their heads, pretending to have long warrior hair. They were singing and jumping like the Maasai were famous for.

The basic rule was whoever jumped the highest won.

Momboa pointed at me. "Alé!"

So I jumped too, and all the boys laughed and clapped. I noticed the women were watching and laughing as well, even Damu had stopped fixing his roof and was watching. I waved him over. "Damu!" He shook his head, but I wasn't giving in. Kijani wasn't here, and he was the only one who seemed to care. "Damu, adumu."

Momboa ran over and grabbed Damu's hand, pulling

him into the circle. The little boy jumped, his eyes as wide as his smile, and eventually Damu gave in. And he jumped.

He was a striking figure, tall, lean, and graceful. He stood completely still, then launched upwards, jumping at least a foot from the ground. He landed silently, then jumped again, only three times in total, and stopped still. All the boys laughed and cheered, and I clapped, unable to hide my shock.

Shock that he was so profound, so striking, and completely humble. And shock that I liked what I saw.

Damu simply bowed his head, a gesture of grace and nobility. The boys all ran off, singing as they went, which left me with Damu. "You win at jumping," I said. "I'm very impressed."

He tried not to smile, and I'm sure he blushed. It was hard to tell, the way he ducked his head. But the sound of the returning butcher party singing and chanting broke the moment between us, and Damu quickly went back to being hidden as Kijani came in carrying the carcass of the goat.

The excitement was hard to ignore. The feast had brought with it much anticipation, and not only did it distract me from thinking about Jarrod, but I saw the dynamics of the tribe in its full hierarchical glory. The men, being the elders, warriors and moran, ate first. They ate the best cuts of meat and they ate as a group, away from the others. Only when they were done did the women and children eat. And not only did they eat what meat was left, but all chargrilled innards and even the skin, fur attached.

Damu and I were, of course, included with the women. My enthusiasm for meat lagged a little when I saw what was left, and in accordance with my customs, I waited for the women to eat first.

Damu eyed me warily as he ate, and he nodded toward the scraps of meat and offal. "Eat."

Amali handed me a chunk of charred meat without a word, a silent insistence that I eat.

I didn't know whether it was meat or grilled innards, and as I put it to my mouth, I realised I didn't want to know. I was grateful to be included, and I was grateful for the food. "Thank you."

The children chewed on rib bones and the women sang as we ate, and I stopped overthinking and just enjoyed it for what it was.

After all, I was eating a ceremonial season feast with the Maasai in the heart of the Serengeti, Tanzania.

And with that in mind, I had a second helping.

When the meat was gone, the children sat around with the women and their matriarchal leader, Amali, retold the story of the hyena and the hare. I understood parts, but Damu translated, explaining how two creatures who were once close friends became eternal enemies after each deceived the other for his own gain. I had no doubt the children had heard these stories before, but they listened intently.

I sat with my legs crossed, like a school kid at story time, and Momboa climbed into my lap. And when they finished singing songs, Momboa asked me to sing a song. "Alé sing."

I had no clue what I was supposed to sing, and I looked to Damu for help. He just laughed. "Sing song," he said, grinning as though he knew how much I didn't want to. God, there was no getting out of it. So, with Momboa in my lap, I took his hands in mine and clapped his hands together. And I don't know why, but I sang the alphabet song.

And when I'd done A through to Z, the kids all clapped and bounced, then demanded I sing it again.

By the third time I'd sung it, they were singing along with me and even some of the women, Yantai and Damisi, were singing along too.

Just when I was sure I was going to be singing it all night long, the warriors all stood in an adumu, a circle for jumping. The women stood near them and began a chanting beat, completely a cappella and completely hypnotic. The warriors took turns to jump, leaping tall in the air. As the sun set on the horizon, the sky changed from blues to oranges and purples. The Maasai, as a whole, the Serengeti, mesmerised me. I nudged Damu to join the adumu, but he shook his head no. "Not my place," he whispered to me. He watched the warriors, not with jealousy or longing like one might expect, but with admiration and respect.

And that was why I liked him. He had an inner strength I admired, and I wished the others would see him like I did.

That night, I expected my dreams to taunt me. Not only had I thought of Jarrod and had those emotions of loss and longing pummel through me, but I'd also admitted to myself that, even for the briefest second, I looked at another man like I swore I never would again.

But I didn't dream that night. And I woke up with a new sense of purpose. I knew what I had to do.

Damu was already awake, standing outside the hut. He was watching the sun rise. I squeezed out the small door and stretched my back, feeling every kink pop as I did. "You sleep without dream," Damu said.

I looked up at him. "I did."

I wondered if he missed my nightmares and the excuse to pull me onto his mattress. I hated to admit that, while I didn't miss the vivid, haunting dreams, I did miss the safety of his arms.

But I wouldn't allow myself to think like that. That wasn't why I was here.

"Where is Kijani?" I asked.

"Why?"

"I need to ask a favour of him."

Damu looked at me like I'd lost my mind.

I smiled at him. "I want to teach the children English. I want to teach them how to read and write."

KIJANI WAS TALKING with Kasisi and Mposi when I approached them. I figured it would work in my favour to have Kasisi there, as he'd always been favourable toward me. Kijani, not so much.

"May I interrupt?" I asked, my head bowed with respect.

Kijani looked at me with his usual contempt, and when his gaze shot over my shoulder, I turned to see Damu was behind me.

"Ah," Kasisi, the small elder addressed me with a smile. "Eyes of Kafir. *Ol-óíborr.*"

Nice. My knowledge of Maa wasn't great, but I knew enough to know he'd basically just called me "white man with weird eyes," and this was from the one that liked me.

I nodded. "I have come to ask a favour," I said, still with my head bowed, but not low enough to miss Kijani tightening his grip on his spear. They waited for me to speak. "If the elders approve, I would like to teach the children. Like a school, to read and write English."

Kijani's immediate reaction was to stomp his spear. "No."

Without taking his eyes off me, Kasisi raised his hand to silence the angry warrior. "Why you do this?" he asked me.

I looked up then, into their eyes, so they would see the sincerity in mine. "Because I am able to. I can teach them, basic words, so they don't have to leave to go to school."

Maybe that was a low blow on my behalf. I knew from what little research I'd done before I came here, that not only was displacement a threat to their culture, but so was the fact the younger Maasai needed to leave their lands to get schooling.

The three elders spoke then, too fast and all at once, so I couldn't understand. Kijani looked at Damu, and I couldn't believe they were brothers. Sure, they looked alike, but their demeanours were polar opposites of each other. Kijani was stress and anger, and Damu was calm and peace.

Kijani barked something at Damu, and I didn't have to understand the words to know what he was implying. I put my hand up. "No. This was my idea. Damu is not to blame."

Damu dropped his head like this was the worst thing I could have said. I didn't know what was customary and what was forbidden. But I wanted to do this, and it would be on my head, not Damu's. "Damu." I waited for him to look at me. "If it was wrong of me to ask, then I am sorry. I just want to help."

Apparently this was not to Kijani's liking. "You seek his forgive?"

"Yes," I answered, looking Kijani right in the eye. "Damu is my guide. He has shown me my way here. He has shown me kindness."

Kijani leaned toward me, never breaking eye contact,

and I briefly wondered if people had died for speaking to him in such a way.

Again Kasisi raised his hand, silently quelling all talk. He spoke again in rapid Maa and he, Mposi, and Kijani quickly fell into conversation like I wasn't there. They turned and started to walk away, their conversation never stopped.

Damu put his hand on my arm. "They will discuss."

I turned to him. "I am sorry. If I caused you problems, that was not my intention."

He replied with a small smile and a nod. "Come. We must get water."

And just like that, he collected his bucket and we made the trek to the river.

"Do you think they'll allow me to do it?" I asked. "To teach the children?"

"Do not know."

"But it'd be good, right?"

Damu just smiled as he walked but didn't answer.

"Then they wouldn't have to leave," I added. "They could stay with their own people. They could learn here, and they could teach me more words in Maa." The more I spoke about it, the more I was convinced it was the right thing to do.

We approached the river, and given the women and children were long gone, Damu sat on the bank and took off his shoes. Then he proceeded to unwrap his shuka and let the red cloth fall on the rocks. He stood, wearing only a small wrap that was more a codpiece than underwear.

I tried not to ogle, but I couldn't look away. He was tall, lean, his movements fluid and graceful. I'd used the word "striking" to describe him before, but he was more than that. He was stunning.

Then he dropped the codpiece and stepped into the water.

I looked away to give him some privacy, but not before I saw him completely naked. He was, well, to put it politely, he was in proportion. His flaccid cock hung, long and thin. Just like the rest of him, tall, dark, and beautiful.

He immersed himself in the water, finally surfacing with a deep breath and a smile. He began to bathe himself.

I wondered if I could do the same, because the water sure looked inviting... I stripped down too, completely naked and not caring for modesty, and dived into the water. It was cool and fresh and felt heavenly against my skin. I didn't realise how gritty I'd become. Sure, I'd dived into the water a few times in my time here but never fully naked.

It was sublime.

Underwater, I raked my hands through my hair letting the water sluice through the strands to remove any grit and sand. Daily face washes, shaving, and teeth brushing served its purpose, but a proper bath was unbeatable.

I'd forgotten what a shower felt like. And as amazing as the water felt, I didn't miss running water. I didn't miss electricity. I didn't miss anything.

Except Jarrod.

I broke the surface, gasping for air. As usual, the memory of Jarrod squeezed my heart and crippled my lungs.

Damu laughed at me, oblivious to my struggle to breathe. And strangely enough, his laughter, his smiling face, calmed me. I exhaled with a rush and laid back, allowing myself to float, feeling my lungs expand and contract with every inhale, exhale, inhale, exhale, until my panic attack passed.

Damu floated beside me and without a word between

us, with a peace that soothed me, we floated naked in the water under the Tanzanian sky.

WHEN WE CLIMBED out of the water, still naked, I almost slipped on the rocks. Damu caught me before I fell, holding me close, and for a moment neither one of us moved. He kept his hands on the tops of my arms, our fronts almost touching. He was half a foot taller than me, and when I finally looked from his bare chest up to his face, I found he was looking down at me. His lips were parted, his eyes alight with fire, and I thought for a second he was going to kiss me.

I didn't know how I would react. I didn't know what that meant for me, to be held and touched by another man—I was sure my heart wasn't ready. But what I *did* know was that no matter how unsure I was of moving forward, I knew I couldn't go backwards. I might not have wanted him to kiss me, but I didn't want him to *not* kiss me either.

I was so conflicted.

Then I felt his cock brush against my stomach. I instinctively looked down. He was hard, his reaction to me was undeniable. He turned quickly and grabbed his clothes, dressing quickly, scrambling to hide himself. He was not only embarrassed, but he was ashamed, and that saddened me. It also worried me.

I dressed hurriedly, and before Damu could walk away, I grabbed his arm. "Damu."

He wouldn't look at me. His eyes were fixed on the ground to the side of us.

I wanted to touch his face so he would look at me, but I

didn't dare scaring him off even more. "Don't be embarrassed. You don't have to be ashamed of your body around me."

He shook his head and pulled his arm from my grasp, but he didn't step away. He seemed stuck for words but eventually settled on, "No. No."

Was he worried he'd offended me? Or was he worried that I would tell someone else? "I don't mind, and no one else needs to know." I motioned between us. "Just us. Just us."

His gaze shot to mine then, his eyes filled with fear and uncertainty. "Forgive."

"There's nothing to forgive. You did nothing wrong." He squinted his eyes closed, like I'd just told him the sky wasn't blue. I said it again, this time with more conviction. "You did nothing wrong."

He took a step back, and I knew this conversation was over, for now at least. He turned and walked away. I pulled on my sneakers, which wasn't easy, given my feet were still wet. I needed to change the subject, to let him know things were still good between us.

"Hey, Damu," I called out. He stopped walking and begrudgingly turned to look at me. I pointed to the line of trees further up. "Should we grab some sticks and branches for firewood?"

He looked at me for a long moment, then relented with a nod and a small smile.

I picked up a branch and then another, and soon Damu was beside me. "Figured it'd save us a trip back here," I said as we collected wood together. "And if anyone wonders why we were so long."

I dropped my sticks to the ground and pulled my shirt over my head, laying it flat on the ground. I piled the wood across my shirt and after we'd collected a decent amount, I wrapped my shirt around the firewood and tied it off. It made it so much easier to carry. It also made me shirtless.

Looking down at myself, I could see my shorts were now far too big for me. Even with the waistband doubled over, they still hung low on my hips. My abs were noticeable, which was funny because I never realised I even had abs.

"You *aronkenu*," Damu said, holding up one finger. "No fat."

"Skinny," I said with a laugh. "Or are you saying I was fat when I got here?" I was hardly overweight when I arrived here—hell, my weight loss in the last twelve months had been a concern for my doctor. He'd almost certainly keel over if he saw me now. Ideals of body shape were vastly different between my country and Damu's. I grinned at him and tapped his visible ribs. "Not as skinny as you."

He jumped. "Ah!"

"You're ticklish?" I laughed. "Good to know!"

Ignoring his shy smile, I picked up the stack of wood and slung it over my shoulder so it rested on my back.

"You wish me to carry?"

"No. It's fine. Come on, we better not be too late."

We'd walked about a quarter mile when I nodded toward the ridge line. "Will you take me there one day?"

"Into Serengeti?"

"Yes." I mean it wasn't far, and the Serengeti itself was huge. Technically this land was part of the Serengeti, but I meant into the valley. "Where the animals are."

"If you wish."

"Do we need permission from Kasisi or Kijani?" I asked. I wasn't sure on what the actual protocol was for leaving the kraal for anything other than chores.

"No permission. I tell them I take you, but ask when it be good time. It must not interfere with everyone."

Okay, fair enough, I thought. Everything everyone in the kraal did was always in fair consideration of everyone else. It was how the Maasai lived. As a whole entity. United.

"I would like that. I would like to see elephants and giraffes."

Damu smiled. "I ask for you. The moran will leave soon for *Eunoto.*"

"What is Eunoto?"

"Warrior ceremony."

"Really?" I couldn't hide my surprise. Or my curiosity. "What happens at the Eunoto? Who will go? Will Komboa go?" I doubted he would, he was no older than six... but I had no idea.

Damu chuckled and shook his head. "Always with questions."

"Always."

"Komboa is wrong age-set. Nampasso's age-set will go."

"All of them?"

"Yes."

"For how long?"

He held up four fingers. "Moons."

"Four months?"

Damu laughed again. "They will go with other warriors and learn their ways."

"Where do they go?"

"Away from kraal. Many days walk."

"Will Kijani take them?"

Damu smiled again, knowing very well why I asked. Four months without Kijani sounded pretty good to me.

Damu nodded. "Kijani will go for some, not all of this. One or two moons only."

I couldn't help but smile. Hell, even one month without Kijani sounded good. But then something dawned on me. "Who will protect the kraal if he and the other warriors are not here?"

"Not all go. Kasisi will see who stays."

It had to hurt knowing his father and brother were tribal leaders and he was completely disregarded. He acted like he didn't mind, but I had to wonder just how well he hid it. "Did you go to Eunoto?"

Damu shook his head. "Not for me."

We walked in silence for a while, and I couldn't help but think of something I'd read... But it wasn't like I could just come out ask something like that.

"You have questions," Damu said, smiling at me.

"I do, but it is very personal."

Damu looked at me warily, his smile lifted one corner of his mouth. "You will ask it anyway."

My smile was slow spreading. "You know me so well!" *What the hell?* "If you didn't go through a warrior ceremony, why are you circumcised?"

Damu surprised me by bursting out laughing. He play-fully pushed my shoulder, causing me to lose my step. He covered his mouth with his hand. "You pay attention?"

"It was hard not to notice," I told him, grinning widely. "You have a very... um, what is the Maa word for elephant penis?"

Damu stopped walking and his mouth fell open. This time I pushed his shoulder, and we both fell about laughing.

I noticed then that Kijani was watching us from the gate of the kraal, but I didn't care. Damu and I laughed the rest of the way home.

Kijani watched us again that afternoon, when we worked patching the roof of our hut, and he watched me again as I sat with the women, making beads and darning clothes. It probably didn't help that Momboa sat on my lap begging me to sing the alphabet song with him again and again.

When Kijani called Damu over to where he and Kasisi were watching, I stood up too. I wasn't sure what I could do or say to defend him, but if they had an issue with my asking permission to teach the kids, then they could speak to me about it.

"*Awúên, awúên,*" Amali said. *Sit down. Sit down.*

Kijani and Kasisi led Damu away, where no one could hear them speak. The longer he was gone, the more I worried.

"He be fine," Amali said.

I tried to smile for her, but my concern was too great. "I don't want to cause him trouble."

She waved me off with a smile and went about her chores. Soon they were singing again, but I remained silent and kept looking for Damu to return. The sun was getting lower and lower and the light was almost gone when Damu returned. He found me waiting outside our hut, and I was so relieved to see him.

"Are you okay?"

He took my hand—a Maasai gesture of friends, I reminded myself—and led me inside. It was, as always, dark inside, but when we sat facing each other, I could see his face. "I am fine. They have decision on school."

Oh. "Really? Well, what did they say?"

"They say, yes."

My relief and grin was instantaneous. "Really?"

Damu laughed. "Yes. Condition, they have condition."

I wouldn't expect anything else. "Of course. That's fine. When can I start?"

"Tomorrow. We start tomorrow."

I couldn't help myself. I was so excited and happy, I acted without thinking. I leaned up on my knees and hugged him. "Thank you!" I pulled back. "Sorry." I put some distance between us, as much as the small hut allowed anyway. "Here, let me cook the ugali," I said, scooting over to start the porridge. I busied myself with dinner, but when I risked a glance back at Damu, I found him looking at me with a smile that might have been half shy, half smitten.

I handed him his bowl. "Let's eat."

CHAPTER SEVEN

JARROD SMILES as he picks up branches. He looks different under the Tanzanian sunlight, brighter somehow, like a light shone from within. The women help me build an open shelter, the children too, and there is singing and humming as a constant background noise.

Jarrod lifts one branch, laying it flat on the roof, while Amali and Yantai weigh the leaves down with mud. I can't stop staring at him, much like I always did. Feeling my eyes upon him, he stares right back at me. He gives a pointed nod to Damu and chuckles like he knows something I don't.

"What's so funny?" I ask.

Jarrod's smile slowly fades, his gaze never leaves mine, as though he's speaking to me with his mind. He's so close, I reach out to touch him, but my hand feels nothing but air. "Say something," I plead. "If I can just hear your voice."

The corner of Jarrod's lip curls upwards and looks fondly at Damu. And with a wistful smile, he disappears like he was never there. The man I loved, the man I lived for, is gone.

Again.

"ALÉ." Damu's voice was low, his breath warm on my neck. He shook me gently. "Shhh."

I realised I was asleep in his arms again, on his tiny mattress. My heart was hammering, and I knew immediately my dreaming had woken him. My eyes burned with tears and my throat was thick. I breathed in a ragged sob, feeling Jarrod leave me all over again bore with it a physical ache.

It was still dark outside, I could see through the doorway, and I reckoned it was about three in the morning. I should have scrambled over to my bed of dirt in the corner, but I couldn't bring myself to move.

Instead, I pulled Damu's arm tighter around me, snuggled right back against him, feeling the safety of his hold, and closed my eyes.

I WOKE BEFORE DAMU. His arm was still wrapped tight around my waist, his soft breaths at the nape of my neck, and his red shuka draped over us like a blanket. I could also feel his cock pressed against the crack of my arse.

It felt so good. Hot and hard and right there. It was something I hadn't felt in over a year, physical intimacy, sexual attraction.

Not since Jarrod. Not since that awful day... we'd woken up, like any other normal day. Sex before work wasn't that unusual. It was usually just a quick fuck or mutual blowjobs or handjobs in the shower. We saved our lengthy lovemaking sessions for night time when we could, and quite often did, spend hours in bed.

He'd woken me that day by pressing his lubed up fingers inside me, nipping teeth at my shoulder, pleading with me to "wake up, baby" before he slipped his cock into me. Afterwards, he made me coffee and toast, told me he loved me, stole a bite of my peanut butter, kissed me, and went to work. Just like any normal day. Work was normal, and we went to the pub for dinner after work, just like normal.

Everything was normal.

Until it wasn't.

Nothing was normal again after that day. Not one thing. Not me, not my life, not the stars or the moon. Not the air I breathed, not how people looked at me.

Nothing.

And when the memories brought with them their leaden weight of loss and grief, they brought with it something new.

Guilt.

Guilt for breathing, for surviving. Guilt for living when he does not. Guilt for lying in the arms of another man.

I didn't dare move.

I wanted to grind back harder. I wanted to grip his hips behind me and pull him closer still. I wanted to feel him slide between my arsecheeks. I wanted him inside me.

I wanted to feel... something.

Anything

Alive, mostly. I wanted to feel alive.

But I didn't move. Well, not the way I wanted to. I peeled Damu's arm off me and crawled out of the hut. The sun was rising, shedding strands of brilliant golds over the horizon. The air was crisp, the birds were singing their praises, and the kraal was waking.

It wasn't long until Damu stood beside me and stretched the kinks out of his back. "Excited for this day?" he asked.

"What?"

He eyed me cautiously. "Start school for you."

"Oh," I said. There was no point in pretending I hadn't forgotten. "I had other things on my mind."

Damu nodded slowly. "He speak to you," he said, looking over the kraal. "In your dreams. The one you left behind."

I swallowed down my heart and breathed hard against the cage that squeezed my lungs. "He doesn't speak. In my dreams, he doesn't speak. I would kill to hear his voice. Just one more time. I would give anything—" my voice cracked "—I would give *anything*, just to hear his voice, but he never speaks. And I didn't leave him behind. He left me."

I was on the verge of tears and tried blinking them back but had to scrub them away with my hands. Damu put his hand on my shoulder. "We get water."

I nodded, and ducked back into the hut to grab the bucket, and it was then I noticed Kijani had come out of his home. Damu was clearly making sure Kijani didn't see me upset. I doubted the brave warrior would take my tears as anything short of weakness.

Not that I cared what Kijani thought of me. I cared about what Damu thought of me. "Sorry about this morning," I said to him as we walked to the river.

He shrugged it off. His ever-silent way of saying 'no problem.' He held up the empty bucket. "Need more water to make school."

My gaze shot to his. "We're *making* a school?"

Damu laughed. He put his hand up, flat, then upright. "Roof. Side. Block sun and wind."

I put my hand on his shoulder and bounced with excitement. "We're making a school!"

Damu laughed, and it turned out to be the best thing ever. Distraction, purpose, and a real sense of belonging.

For the next week, myself and Damu, along with the women of the manyatta and even the children helped us build a basic shelter. It was exactly as Damu had said. Roof and sides, and not much more.

But it was ours. We built it. We did it together. We sang and hummed as we trussed a frame, then just as my dream had shown, we fixed dried branches and leaves and weighed them down with mud and cow shit. The only thing missing from my dream was Jarrod. But somehow he was here with me. I couldn't explain it, but I felt closer to him now than I had in twelve months.

And every night, I didn't bother lying down on my dirt bed. Damu lay down on his thin mattress and I melded to him, my back to his front. I used his arm as a pillow and wrapped his other arm around me. He pulled his shuka over us, and we slept.

We never spoke about it. We never questioned it. I couldn't afford to: he was my only comfort, and it would seem I was his only comfort too. In a world that turned without me, Damu was my fixed point. He was the only shining light I'd had in twelve months of empty darkness.

Even when I'd wake with my face buried in his neck or resting on his chest, his arms were always around me. He couldn't hide his body's reaction to the contact, and neither could I.

At first I thought my body betrayed me. The physical reaction I could justify—my body craved touch, it was as simple as that—but my emotional reaction to him was one I simply wasn't prepared for.

I wasn't ready for that.

I was certain I never would be.

And I didn't know what was worse. Having dreams of Jarrod that were so vivid, so real I swear I could almost touch him.

Or not dreaming of him at all.

Whether it was sleeping next to Damu, in the comfort of his embrace, or whether it was the exhaustion from working from sun up till sun down, I didn't know. But my sleep was absent of dreams. I didn't know if that was me letting go of Jarrod, or if it was Jarrod letting go of me... I'm not sure which one hurt the most.

"WHAT ARE YOU DOING?" Damu asked.

I had emptied out my backpack and found the notepad and pen I had in there. It was the size of a journal, and I had intended to keep notes or an itinerary of my travels but never had. I had now been in Tanzania, living with Damu and his people for three weeks. It felt like both a lifetime and the blink of an eye and yet, I hadn't written a word about my being here. My stay in the kraal, no matter how long it ended up being, would be something I'd need time to process before I started to document. I'd need time to decompress, to appreciate and evaluate everything I'd experienced. So knowing I wouldn't be using the notepad made the decision pretty easy.

"I'm going to use this," I said, holding up the notepad, "to help teach." It was ridiculous how basic my resources were, but that made me even more keen to do it. "We need more things," I admitted. "A chalkboard, paper, pencils."

Damu looked at me like I'd told him we needed free wifi.

Good Lord, the Internet seemed a century ahead of time. I guessed, out in the Serengeti plains, it was.

Or was it…?

"How far away is the closest market?"

Damu blinked back his surprise. "One day walk."

"When I came here, I walked with Joseph and Mbaya and some goats. Had they been to market?" Joseph and Mbaya, as it turned out, quite often went to market and did the bidding set out by the senior elders. It was quite often a two-day venture, apparently. "Can you and I go to the markets?"

"No, no, I not go," he said quickly.

"Why not?"

He rocked back on his heels, shook his head, and wiped his hands on his clothes. Even the thought of going to the closest town was daunting for him. "I cannot."

"Will you not be given permission?"

He opened his mouth, then closed it again. "I have not ever."

"Would you like to?" I asked. "Go to the city?"

He laughed incredulously, like I'd asked him if he'd like to go to the moon.

I held up two fingers. "Two days. Just two days."

Damu bit his lip. He was clearly torn. "You will go even if I not go?"

He didn't want me to go on my own, either for fear of my safety, or because he didn't want to not be with me. I liked that, more than I should. "I would not want to go without you," I told him, my voice soft.

He fought a smile and a slight blush tinted his cheeks, and I could see I almost had him won over. "Will we cross the Serengeti?" I asked.

He nodded. "The way you came. Did you not see it when you walked through it?"

"It was dark, and I was following two strange men with goats. I wasn't exactly paying much attention," I reasoned. "I want to see it with you."

Damu's gaze met mine and his eyes swam with unspoken words. Eventually he nodded. "I will ask."

I grinned at him. I was ridiculously excited about the prospect. The two days of walking not so much, but I wanted Damu to experience life outside his tribe, even for just two days. I wanted to be with him when he stepped out of his comfort zone, to show him there was a whole world on the other side of that acacia thorn fence. I wanted to be with him when I saw African wildlife roaming free on the Serengeti.

I clutched my notepad. "I will tell the children," I said, before leaving him with the arduous task of asking his brother and father when we could go.

I had six kids in the lean-to, under the watchful eyes of their mothers, of course. "We will have a chalkboard," I told them, waving my hand at the wall. "Where we can write and draw. And we can have paper and pencils for writing," I held out my notepad and pretended to draw with my pen, and the excited smiles on their little faces matched my own.

Until I saw Damu talking to Kijani. It was pretty clear what the outcome would be by Kijani's tone. I didn't need to know what Kijani had said to him, because the look on Damu's face as he walked back to the classroom said it all.

No.

My words trailed away and the kids followed my line of sight. When Damu realised we were watching him, he tried to smile, but it didn't quite work. He gave me a small shake of his head.

"Momboa," I called the young boy to where I stood. "Can you sing the alphabet song for the class?" I asked. I started him off, singing ABC, then once he was in full swing—and probably getting the letters mixed up—I walked over to where Kijani was standing.

God, didn't he have some fucking goats to herd or something?

I tried to keep my tone neutral, but it was strained at best. "I wish to request items for our school," I said to him. I half expected him to push me over or spear me through the throat, I wasn't sure. But I held his steely gaze. "If it pleases the elders, I want to buy school items. I have money to buy such things. I will pay for it. If Damu and I can't go, then I will give the money to Joseph and Mbaya and they can get them. I can make a list." He hadn't killed me yet, so I kept on going. "This is not for me. It is not for Damu. It is for the children."

Kijani stared at me, amused. In the same way a lion might be humoured by the bravado of a field mouse.

I bowed my head. "I would be most grateful." And with that, I turned and walked back to the classroom. The children were singing, blissfully unaware, but Damu looked worried and cautious. Amali, Nashuru, and Yantai watched on curiously, warily.

No one said a word to me, though. So I sat on the sandy ground next to Momboa and continued to sing the alphabet song.

I really had no clue how to teach a class of basic English to a bunch of kindergarten kids. I was a travel consultant at a flight and holiday destination office, for God's sake. But I could remember the basics from when I was a kid, surely. So I took my notepad and wrote, in big writing, the letter A, then the letter B on the next page, and C the one after that and so forth, right through to Z. I pointed to each letter in turn as I sang the alphabet song again. Then, because we didn't have any paper to spare, I got the kids to draw the shape of the letters in the air, then on the dirt floor.

It was rudimentary, and I had no clue if what I was doing was right, but when we were done, the children all clapped and sang as they followed their mothers home.

I sat in the lean-to classroom and watched as they walked away. It was primitive by any education standards I was used to, and I'd literally spent a few hours or more singing the goddamn alphabet song and clapping along with six kids, yet I'd never felt like I'd accomplished so much before in my entire life.

When Damu found me, I was still sitting in my empty classroom with my notepad in my lap, smiling. "You be happy," he said.

"I am. I accomplished much today." Then I amended, "Actually, this week, you and I have accomplished a great deal. I couldn't have done this without you."

He bowed his head in acknowledgement. "My father and brother have agreed. Joseph and Mbaya will go to market with money."

My smile was immediate. "Really?"

He looked around, I assumed, to see if anyone could hear us. "We can talk away?"

"Yes of course. Let's go home." Whatever he wanted to say, clearly needed saying in private, and that was fine with me. It was getting dark anyway, and it wasn't like anyone would miss us. We ducked through the small doorway and, as usual, sat cross-legged on the dirt floor facing each other. "What is it?"

He hesitated for a second. "I believe Kijani will use money for other things."

"Like what?"

"Sugar and rice." Damu made a face. "I should not say. My loyalties are for my people and for my brother and father. But I have loyalty to you too."

His words warmed my chest. I reached out and took his hand. "And I have loyalty to you too."

He smiled in the darkening room, and his fingers threaded with mine.

"But Damu, if they buy what I need for the school, then I will happily buy them sugar and rice. And a goat too, if they want."

"You would do that?"

I squeezed his fingers and rubbed my thumbs over his knuckles. His hands were huge, his fingers long, his touch was warm and smooth. It felt... nice. "I would do that," I said. While there was still a little light left in the day and with my notepad in my lap, I peeled out a piece of paper. I folded it as Damu watched on. Before he could ask, I explained, "A few years ago, I spent two weeks in Japan." I kept folding the paper, losing daylight quickly, going by feel. Damu watched intently as I produced a small paper crane. "I learned how to make these. The gift, or message, isn't the crane but the paper it's made from. And this paper I brought with me from Australia." I held it out for him. "For you."

He was stunned. "For me?"

"Yes, of course."

He took it cautiously, as though it were the most precious thing in the world. "I give many thanks," he whispered.

I took his free hand and gave it a squeeze. "You're very welcome."

He grinned. "Let me make dinner." He let go of my

hand and shuffled over to his makeshift kitchen. I didn't see what he did with the paper crane. He mixed the ugali and divvied my portion into my bowl before handing it to me. "Today was good day," he said with his trademark smile.

I found myself smiling right back at him. "Yes. Today was a very good day."

AFTER WE'D EATEN and when night had settled over the manyatta, Damu and I sat on his mattress, leaning against the wall with our legs stretched out in front of us. It was pitch black, I couldn't see my own hand in front of my face, but I could feel Damu's side against mine. From our shoulders to our thighs, and it was a reassuring comfort, the simplest of human touches felt so good.

I had taken out one of my hidden stashes of folded shillings and given them to Damu. He would find Kijani in the morning, and hopefully in a few days' time, we'd have our blackboard and supplies.

"You have money in Australia?" Damu asked. I understood he was asking if I had personal wealth, not if we actually had currency in my country.

"Some," I answered with a nod. It was hard to fathom the money in my bank accounts when I was sitting on a dirt floor in a hut made of mud and cow shit, with no water or lights.

"We not have money here. Need it but not have it. The Maasai were a people who lived by the land. Everything we need came from land and cattle. But not anymore. This country, this... government... make us live like white man, but we are not that way."

"How does that make you feel?"

He was quiet a moment. "I cannot change it, so I give it no mind."

"But you don't like it."

"I am not like Kijani. I not believe everything should have price."

I smiled at the darkness. "You're a good man, Damu."

He stilled and was silent a while, then he said, "We sleep now."

We shuffled down until we were comfortable on the mattress. Like every night, I was the little spoon and his arm was my pillow. Damu pulled his shuka over the both of us so his bare chest pressed against my back, and he settled his arm around me. I could have sworn I heard him sigh, and soon after, the tension left his body and he slept.

I revelled in the feel of him, the hard planes of his body, his strength. His safety, his comfort...

I closed my eyes, and this time when sleep crept in to take me, I went willingly.

CHAPTER EIGHT

"TELL JARROD I SAID HI," Becky says with a sweet smile and wave as she picks up her handbag.

"Will do," I reply.

"Usual Friday night then?"

"Yes, we're boring." I roll my eyes. "Dinner, drinks, home in bed before ten."

"You're the oldest twenty-five year olds I know." She winks. "Have fun, and I'll see you on Monday."

"Yes, you will." The door closes behind her. The office is quiet just after six, so I make one more note for the Janson's family holiday trip to New Zealand and shut my computer off.

"You're here late," my boss says as she closes up the office around me. I've worked here for four years and quite often work late... "Thought you had plans tonight?"

"I do. Meeting Jarrod at the pub. It'll be quicker if I leave from here instead of going home first."

She waits for me at the door. I collect my jacket from the back of my chair, pat down my pockets, looking for keys, wallet, and phone, and walk out into the still-warm Sydney evening.

"Have a good weekend," I say to her as she locks the front door.

"You too, Heath. Take care."

I walk the two blocks to the pub, finding Jarrod sitting at a table, waiting for me. He's wearing his work suit, his tie pulled down to expose his first button, undone, and his whole face lights up when he sees me.

I want to take his face in my hands and kiss my hello, but it's something we aren't comfortable in doing in public. We're both out, but public displays of affection, especially in pubs we aren't too familiar with; it's not an option.

"Hey," I say quietly, sitting across from him at the table.

He sips his beer with smiling lips and never says a word.

I just want to hear him speak.

I would give anything to hear his voice.

Then we're leaving, a few beers happy, and step into the street. The night is dark and my heart is hammering, dread and fear spiking my blood, because I know what's coming.

"Hey faggots! Where you going? Party's this way."

I turn to get a look at the man who spoke, but there isn't one. There are three... and they come at us in the dark, their intentions as obvious as the bats they're holding.

Jarrod looks at me, his face etched with fear and panic. He opens his mouth to scream at me to run, run, run, just like he did that night.

But before he makes a sound, everything snaps back.

The alley is gone and we're on the Tanzanian plain, in the sunlight and fresh air. Jarrod takes my hand and we run, and I laugh, freer than I've felt in forever. And when I look at the hand I'm holding, the man I'm running with isn't Jarrod at all.

It's Damu.

"YOU ARE OKAY, ALÉ?" Damu whispered in my ear, his arm was around my chest.

I relaxed straight away, and although my heart was racing, I could tell it wasn't a full-blown episode.

From the colour of the sky outside the door, I knew we'd be getting up soon. But I sunk back against Damu's chest and held his arm where it was wrapped around me until my breathing was back to normal.

When he made no effort to move, or put distance between us, I sighed with relief. "Thank you," I said quietly. I didn't know what exactly I was thanking him for. For comforting me, for not pushing me away, for being my only ray of sunshine in an otherwise dark and lonely world. For everything.

WHEN WE'D COLLECTED water and drank our uji, I went about my morning chores and Damu went in search of Kijani. He gave him the money and a list I'd made with the few things I was after. I had to hope the people at the market could read, because no one at the village could. I'd written in English and the best translations Damu and I could come up with.

I'd also explained, with the help of Damu being my translator, to Joseph and Mbaya what I was after. It would be a miracle if they came back with anything close. I was just grateful that they were trying.

Kijani's initial "no" to my request was because he assumed I expected the village to pay for the school items. They certainly didn't have money to spare on such things, so I couldn't blame him for his kneejerk reaction. I still don't think he liked me, but he tolerated me and I considered that a win.

Though as the morning went on, I noticed things were different. First off, most of the women were gone. The older women remained, tending to the children, and the middle age-set of boys, ages from around ten to eighteen, were wearing black instead of red.

"What's going on?" I asked Damu. "Why is Nampasso wearing black?"

"This begins the *eunoto*."

"When they will be circumcised?" Then I thought about it. "Ouch."

Damu laughed. "Yes. Very painful."

"What happens at eunoto?"

"Their mothers will build a *inkajijik*, a house, for them to stay in. They will have circumcision, but no sound. Not make noise."

I'm pretty sure my mouth fell open. "At all?"

"No sound or dishonour."

I squinted at him. "At all?"

He chuckled. "No."

Jesus. That hurt just thinking about it. "Wow. Did you make a noise?"

He shook his head proudly. "No."

"Good Lord. I'm pretty sure I would scream like a stuck pig."

Damu laughed again. "You have it done, yes?"

"Well, yes. When I was about two weeks old. And I'm pretty sure I would have screamed like a stuck pig."

Damu chuckled. "Then they will stay there and learn the warrior ways. When this is done, there will be ceremony. New warriors return, old warriors return as elders."

"Will Kijani not be a warrior anymore?"

Damu tried not to smile. "You not like him?"

"He scares me. He's intimidating and angry."

"Yes. Because he is warrior. His job very serious. As he should. He's important job." Damu spoke of such reverence for a man that treated him like shit. It boggled my mind. "He will remain warrior. Then he be chief when Kasisi is not. He will take wife after this eunoto."

I mulled this over for a while. Then I asked, "What about you?"

"What of me?"

"What does that mean to you? Will you become an elder? You're in the same age-set as Kijani, yes?"

He took a long while to answer, and he gave me a tight smile. "I not warrior. I have no age-set."

Oh, that's right. Because his mother died during child-birth. The favoured wife of Kasisi, revered mother to Kijani. And for some reason they blamed Damu.

"Does that make you angry?" I asked.

He shook his head. "No. I cannot change it. One is not show anger at the sun for setting. I am not angry that the water runs or that the lion hunts."

"Well, it pisses me off," I told him. "Makes me very angry that they would treat you this way."

His lips twitched as he fought a smile. "It is no matter."

"Well, it matters to me. I wish they'd see you like I do."

He scoffed, like the whole notion of a compliment was absurd. Then an idea came to me. "Who will tend to the cattle when the boys are gone?"

"Komboa," Damu answered.

"But he's just a baby! He can't be more than five."

"Maasai learn very young. It is the way we live for many lives."

I sighed. Centuries-old traditions be damned. "Could you and I look after the cattle?"

"We will, yes."

"We will? For real? Do we get to see the Serengeti?"

Damu grinned at my excitement. "Yes. Everyone does this when warriors are gone."

Everyone chipped in when the tribe was halved in number. Awesome! Herding cattle and goats and teaching the kids in our spare time. I clapped my hands together. "This is good news. Good news."

Damu laughed.

So that's what we did for the next month. We grazed cattle in the mornings, then I sat with the children in our little school until the sun called it a day. Joseph and Mbaya did come back with a blackboard. It was old chipboard that had been painted over with blackboard paint, and it had also been well used. I didn't ask if they'd stolen it from a school somewhere, because I truthfully didn't want to know, and I didn't particularly care. Because we had ourselves a blackboard for our school! It was cause for major celebrations with the children, who were fascinated by chalk and the ability to draw then wipe it away and to draw it again.

Finding such joy in the simplest of things was a truly grounding and humbling experience. I was so far removed from the life I'd once known... and it was the happiest I could remember being in a long, long time.

But as good as it was to see the children so excited and to watch their faces as they learned to draw letters on the chalkboard, my most favourite thing was to herd the goats.

After water collection and breakfast, at Kasisi's instruction, Damu and I would take goats into the plains to graze. We would head northwest to the rockier outcrops while the younger boys, like Momboa and Jaali, would take the cattle south. Goats were peskier, more stubborn, so the much easier cattle were shepherded by the kids.

They were probably better at it than I was, but that was a thought I kept to myself.

Kasisi had given Damu and me long sticks. Not the long white sticks of the elders and certainly not a spear like the warriors had. It was merely a tool for herding, not a status of rank, though Damu was still very proud to have received it. I followed Damu's cues by bowing my head and thanking Kasisi, as though we'd been bestowed with a great honour.

Some customs I could understand, some I could appreciate, and some I could respect. But some were a test to my resolve of not judging. Some I didn't think I would ever understand.

"What you be thinking?" Damu asked, breaking me from my train of thought.

I looked out across the Serengeti. "That if I ever questioned why the Maasai chose to live so removed from the rest of the world, then this is my answer." I waved my hand across the panoramic view. The grasses were brown now, the colder weather had put an end to the afternoon storms, and the days of rain were few and far between. But there were a few spots of animals in the distance. Antelopes and possibly some buffalo. I hadn't seen many animals roaming free—mostly oryx, gazelles, and some wildebeest. They were truly magnificent to watch, even from this distance. The scenery was so beautiful, so remote, and so perfectly disconnected. I loved it. "This is very good."

"You happy here?"

Well, there was a question I hadn't truly asked myself. It made me think. *Am I happy here? Or am I happier than where I was?* I guessed it didn't matter. "I am."

"I can tell. You have quiet dreams now."

"Oh."

He laughed. "Not always but most."

"Sorry." I nodded slowly and kept my eyes on the goats. It was easier not to look at him. "Can I ask you a question?"

"Why you ask if you can ask? You only ask it anyway."

That made me smile. "True. Do my dreams bother you?"

"No. Scare me at first, but not now. I calm you."

"You do," I said, risking a quick glance at him. "You do calm me." I let out a slow and steady breath. "Does it bother you that I sleep on your bed with you?"

He bit his lip and took a while to answer. "No. I calm you."

"You do," I agreed, again. "Tell me, do other men share beds here in your country?" His gaze shot to mine, so I rephrased my question. "What would Kijani do if he saw us?"

Damu stared out across the Serengeti, and after a long silence, he shook his head. "Kijani cannot know." I nodded slowly, as what he said registered. He frowned, his brow furrowed deeply. "Only share bed if married."

"Oh." Jesus. Okay. Well, um, I wasn't sure what to say to that. "And in your country, men cannot be with men?"

He still wouldn't look at me. "No, not allowed."

I swallowed hard. *Here goes nothing. Or everything,* I wasn't sure. "Sometimes in my country it is allowed." I still wasn't about to get into the politics of marriage equality. While gay and lesbian people still couldn't get married in Australia, they certainly weren't executed for it. "Sometimes in my country, there is man and woman. Sometimes it is two men, no wife. Or two women, no husband."

Damu wouldn't look at me. "No. *A-isarkin.*"

I repeated the word, though I was pretty sure I already knew the answer. "What is that in English?"

"Taboo. Great unholy sin. Insult to god and village."

I let out a steadying breath, my heart was in my throat, my stomach in knots. "In my country, it's okay."

Damu shot me a look, half fear, half disbelief. "It is?"

I nodded. "Some people don't like it, but most don't mind at all. It's not illegal." I swallowed hard. "In this country, in your village, what would happen to a man who loved another man?"

Damu looked out over the valley, the goats, and the horizon, but what he saw I could only guess. "In Tanzania, it mean jail. For Maasai, it mean death."

"Fuck." I didn't really mean to say that out loud. My mind was swimming. I knew this fact. I knew homosexuality was regarded as sin here, but all I read were harmless words on a screen from the other side of the world. To hear it spoken by a man, who could very well report my questions to the village elders, in a village that could very well kill me, was something else entirely. It wasn't the fear of being killed that stopped me from back-pedalling, it was that I was unwilling to lie. I had been through too much, I had lost too much to deny the part of me that cost the most.

After a long silence, Damu asked, "Is it that way for you?"

I let out a steadying breath. Here it was. He was asking me if I was homosexual. "Yes."

Damu stared at me. Was he curious? Was he disgusted? I couldn't tell. A dozen emotions crossed his features, and my fear of admitting this truth was only exceeded by my fear in disappointing him. "Is that what your Jarrod was? Your husband, not your brother?"

My brother? It never occurred to me that he would

assume Jarrod was my brother. Jarrod wasn't technically my husband either, but for the sake of Damu's idea of what a marriage was, I guess we were. "Yes. Husband. He was not my brother."

"You lay with him, like you lay with a woman?"

"I've never lain with a woman," I answered, though I was pretty sure that wasn't his point.

His eyes swam with emotions I couldn't name. He put his hand to his chest, his voice cracked, "Like you lay with me?"

I swallowed back my tears. "Yes."

"Is that what you think I do?"

I scrambled to answer. I couldn't bear the thought of him pushing me away. I needed him: a fact I only realised in this second. "I don't know what you do," I told him. "I don't care. It doesn't matter me to me if you lie with woman or man. I need you Damu. You calm me. I can't be here if I don't have you."

He stared at me. His mouth opened like he had so much to say, but in the end, he shrugged. "I not ever lay with man," he whispered. "Or woman."

"Do you like lying with me?" I asked. He recoiled at my blunt and confronting question, so I softened it. "I like lying with you. You make me safe and warm. Do you feel safe and warm when I lie next to you?"

He still didn't answer, and I doubted he ever would. I wanted to tell him it was okay, there was nothing wrong with him, there was nothing broken or evil inside him. He was not a great sin against his village or god, no matter what his customs and religion said. "In my country—" I started to say.

"This is *not* your country!" he said abruptly, fire and anger in his tone. It was the most emotion I'd seen from him, and as he shot to his feet and walked away, I was pretty sure his anger was not directed at me.

It was aimed within.

WE SPENT the rest of the afternoon in silence. I wanted to say so much. I wanted to embrace him and hold him until the band around my lungs eased up a bit. But of course I couldn't.

When nightfall forced us inside, Damu cooked a cabbage soup on the small fire in his kitchen. The colder weather permitted a fire in each house, and with it came hot meals, mostly soups of beans or cabbage. It was a welcome change after weeks of ugali for every evening meal, and it was delicious compared to drinking milk and blood.

"Thank you." I quietly sipped soup from my bowl. "It's very good." Truthfully, it was literally boiled cabbage water, but it was still good.

He nodded, a gesture I barely saw in the darkness. He remained silent, which wasn't too uncommon for Damu, but after our argument earlier, the silence was a heavy one.

I rinsed out our bowls and put them by the fire to dry. Inside was completely dark now, and I didn't know how to move past this void of silence between us. I scooted over to my patch of dirt that had been my bed before I'd started sharing Damu's. It was only a few seconds before he realised. "Alé?"

"Yes?"

I heard him swallow. "Why you... do you not..." His broken sentence ended in a sigh.

The complete darkness allowed me to speak my mind. "Do you want me to sleep next to you?"

I heard him swallow. "Yes. It is confuse to me. I should not want it. But I do."

I shuffled over to him and we lay down together. I was, as always, the little spoon. The fire gave good warmth, but Damu flicked his shuka out and I snuggled back against him. I could feel my anxiety drift away as his arm settled over my waist. His breath at my ear was a soothing sound. He was my calm, my peace.

"You don't need to be confused with me," I murmured. "You are safe with me. No one needs to know. No one has to know what we do." He was quiet and still, letting my whispered words hang loud in the darkness. "For what it's worth, Damu. I'm glad you want this. Because I want it too."

He never said anything, but he nuzzled his nose along the back of my head and he tightened his arm around me.

I relaxed into him, my head on his arm. Sleep came for me, creeping in like a chemical mist, and I fell into the abyss.

HIS STRONG HANDS hold my hips as he slides inside me from behind, impaling me with each thrust. God I love this, being filled and fucked, losing myself in desire. Being his desire. His lips kiss my nape, his teeth scrape my shoulder as his fingers dig into my skin. He drives up into me, giving me every inch, making me moan.

"Alé," he whispers. His voice is thick with want and desperation.

"Mmm," I moan, arching my back and giving him a better angle to thrust into.

"Alé," he whispers, more urgent this time. He's close and so am I.

"ALÉ. WAKE, WAKE." The hand that gripped my hip shook me. "Wake."

I blinked, then blinked again. It was a dream. Just a dream. But it wasn't really. I was breathless, my cock full and aching with need. My back was pressed against Damu, his erection wedged hot against the crack of my arse. Fuck. That would explain the dream...

I tried to move forward but his hand on my hip kept me right where I was. *Oh.* I didn't mind. I didn't mind at all. Then I noticed his breaths were short and sharp, his chest heaving. He gasped softly and whined on the exhale. Then my body reacted before my mind, and I ground my arse against his cock. His fingernails bit into my hip and his teeth scraped my shoulder as he shuddered, flexing rigid as he came. Spurts of come splashed between us, smearing on my back.

Damu shook and let out a strangled cry as his orgasm rolled through him. Then he went completely still, resting his forehead against my shoulder, and very slowly started to push me away.

I remembered then, that he said he'd never laid with a man or a woman before. In all likelihood, this was his first sexual encounter, and coupled with the guilt and shame his people believed went hand in hand with what we'd just done—two men together—I couldn't imagine what was going through his mind.

I rolled over quickly and put my hand to his face. The morning light allowed me to see the outline of his features. His eyes were closed. He was clearly embarrassed and ashamed. "Thank you," I whispered. "Thank you." I pressed my lips to his. His eyes shot open, surprised by my kiss. "We better get to the river early. I'll need to wash my back and my shirt."

I rolled off the mattress, grabbed the bucket, and made my way outside. I was barely a hundred metres from the manyatta by the time he caught up to me. He fell into stride beside me, and we walked to the river.

"What kind of birds are those?" I asked, pointing to some kind of crane flying overhead.

"*N-káítoliá*." He smiled. "Live in lake of crater."

He proceeded to explain the birdlife of the Serengeti, and we talked of other inconsequential things until we reached the river. We never mentioned what happened between us in bed, and he appeared grateful, or happy, at least that things were "normal" between us.

I sat on the river bank and stripped to my underwear. Leaving only my shoes on the rocks, I waded into the water and dunked myself. The water was colder now, fresh and invigorating. I broke the surface. "Phwar, that's cold," I said, shaking myself.

Damu laughed. He was stripped down to his loin cloth, his shuka a red heap on the river bank at his feet. Then, with a hesitant—reluctant?—sigh, he unwrapped the last of his clothes and he stepped into the water. He tried to cover his penis with his hand until he was covered by the river, and it stung that he felt he had to hide any part of himself.

Standing waist-deep in the river, I hand-washed my shirt and socks the best I could. Once white, they were now brown, the Tanzanian dirt well and truly permanently embedded into the fabric. I used my wet shirt to wipe over my body, especially my back where Damu had come on me.

When he realised what I was doing, he quickly looked

away. "Hey," I said. "Don't be embarrassed. Damu." I waited until he looked at me. "It's okay."

"Your dream," he said, looking to the water. He stood, the water rippling low on his hips, his groin hidden underwater. "Dreams not be like that before."

Oh, so my sex-dream got a little interactive. I laughed, which made him look at me. I slung my wet shirt and socks over my shoulder and started to scrub at my shorts. "I'm sorry. I didn't mean for that to happen. But I don't regret it. In fact, I liked it."

He sunk down in the water with a frustrated growl, right down until the water reached his nose. I could tell by his eyes he was smiling, and that, of course, made me smile. He rose slowly so he could speak. "You... *n-gusotó* to me."

"*Ingoosoto?* What does that mean?"

He bought his fingers to his mouth, letting them linger on his lips.

"Kiss?" I asked. I puckered my lips and made a kissing sound. "Kiss?"

He nodded, ever so slightly.

"I did. N-gusotó you." I scrubbed at my shorts and after a moment, I added, "And I would like to do that again. Would that be okay?"

He submerged half his face again to hide his smile, but then he sobered and stood up tall. "No here."

I put my hand up and shook my head. "No. Not here. Never where someone might see." I was glad he was talking about this. I didn't want him to clam up and push me away. I didn't exactly know what I wanted, but I knew what I *didn't* want, and that was to lose Damu. "No one but you and me."

He seemed pleased by this. He nodded slowly, and I wasn't sure what he meant. "Are you nodding"—I nodded my head—"because you understand? Or are you nodding because yes, it's okay for me to kiss you again?"

He sunk back down in the water with a whining noise and rolled his eyes before going completely under. I was still laughing when he came back up for air. "I take it that's a yes," I said, getting out of the water. I clambered up the bank, and wearing nothing but my underwear, I twisted my shirt and shorts, then each sock, trying to get the water out of them before putting them back on again. "Come on, or we'll be late to herd the goats," I said. I held up his clothes. "The women will be here soon."

He must have forgotten that we were earlier than them today, because he hurried to the river bank. His long, lean frame was a rich brown all over. His palms and the soles of his feet were a lighter pink colour. His dark cock hung long, even flaccid from the cool water. He wasn't exactly difficult to look at.

He wrapped the loin cloth around his waist and tucked himself in and tied it off. I was a little disappointed. "You stare at me."

"You're very handsome." I cleared my throat.

He laughed at me, pulled his shuka around himself, and all he could do was shake his head at me as we began the walk back to the manyatta. I was pretty sure no one had ever given him a compliment because every time I did, he was truly baffled.

As we passed the women on their way to the river, I greeted them with, "Enk-are a-iopijú," I said, telling them the water is cold. They nodded and laughed as they kept on walking.

Damu smiled, pleased. "You learn Maa well."

"Like you learn English well."

He mulled that over. "You like to learn our ways."

"I do."

He was quiet a while, his eyes trained on the distance. Then he asked, "You long stay for?"

Oh. My stomach twisted and my heart squeezed. I didn't like the idea of leaving him just yet. "I don't know. How long am I welcome for?"

"Kasisi did not say."

Shit. I hadn't even considered there being a time limit. "If it were up to you, how long could I stay?"

He smiled shyly. "*Intarasi.*"

Always.

CHAPTER NINE

I HAD WONDERED if things would be different between myself and Damu once night fell, but they weren't. Well, not in a bad way. After we'd eaten and were lying on his mattress, I used his arm as a pillow like always, and after he'd covered us in his shuka, he snaked his arm around my waist and pulled me close.

I could feel every part of him against me. His hardening cock fit snug against my arse. I didn't push him, I didn't coerce him. I wanted him to be the one to initiate anything between us. I understood he was completely inexperienced, but I didn't want him to feel pressured.

"Damu," I murmured into the darkness. He froze, so I knew he was awake. "If you have any questions or if you are curious about anything, you can ask me. Okay?"

His only response was to press his lips to my shoulder and give me a gentle squeeze. I relaxed in his arms and fell into a Damu-induced dreamless, peaceful sleep.

The next morning, I woke to his erection pressing against my arsecheek. His breathing told me was awake, though he remained still. "Morning," I said croakily.

"Mmm," he hummed. Then, with his hand on my hip, he pushed me forward a little, but enough to put some room between us.

Okay then. He clearly wasn't ready for more, and that was perfectly fine. "We should get to the river," I said, getting up. The sun was teasing the horizon, slivers of blues and pinks lined the sky. The air was brisk, and I knew my thin T-shirt wouldn't cut the cold for much longer. I rubbed my arms and shivered.

"You need shuka," Damu said, standing beside me. He stretched up and wrapped his shuka around his shoulder like a scarf.

"How do I go about getting myself a shuka?" I asked, as we started to walk to the gate in the acacia-thorn fence.

"I will ask Amali," he said. "It get colder yet."

"And she'll just give me one?"

He nodded with a smile. "She like you."

"I like her too."

He seemed pleased by this, and he smiled as we walked. His peacefulness was back, that aura of calm and quiet confidence, and even walking beside him made me feel at ease.

If he had any uncertainty about what he wanted or who he was, he never let on. Every day and every night for the next two weeks was the same. We herded goats during the day, and I taught the kids in the afternoons. We learned our letters and numbers, words for lions and zebras, we drew pictures, and we sang songs. The mood over the manyatta was happy and serene, everyone did their part, each cog in the machine running with a fine precision.

Each night, Damu and I ate our dinner and lay down on his mattress. He held me tight, sometimes kissing my shoulder, sometimes threading our fingers, his shuka kept us warm, and he kept my dreams at bay. And every morning his arousal pressed hot and hard between us.

But he never acted on it. Sometimes he groaned, sometimes he gripped my hips and shuddered, but he never asked for more. His self-control was extraordinary.

Then one morning when winter was settling in, I woke up as warm as toast in Damu's arms. Though this time, we were on our sides and I was facing him with my face buried in his neck. He had both his arms wrapped around me, our bodies pressed tight together, from our heads to our thighs.

I could feel everything.

His erection pressed against mine, his breathing was sharp and short. He was definitely awake, and he was definitely not pushing me away. I moved my face a little, letting my lips lightly trail up his neck. He gasped in my ear; the sound sent shivers straight to my cock.

I looked into his eyes then, searching for a hint of doubt or fear. There was none. "Damu," I whispered. "Can I kiss you?"

He answered by pressing his lips to mine, hard and urgent, unpractised. I put my hand to his cheek and slowly pulled back, only to kiss him again, softer this time. My lips opened his, and I gently deepened the kiss, tasting his bottom lip with my tongue.

He gasped again when our tongues touched, and I answered by covering his mouth with mine. I pushed him back, never breaking our kiss, and rolled on top of him. He was still for a second and I wondered if I'd gone too far, but then he held me tight and rocked his hips into me, kissing me wildly, passionately. We rutted against each other, and he gripped my hips with desperate fingers, making a strangled sound as he came.

It was enough to push me over the edge, and I followed

suit. I came hard, shooting come into my shorts and shirt, and I collapsed on top of him. My orgasm haze dissipated, leaving behind the cold realisation that I had just had a sexual encounter with a man who was not my boyfriend.

I rolled off Damu and sat up, scrubbing my hands over my face and through my hair. "We should get to the river," I said.

Damu was sitting up behind me now. I glanced back to see him nod, and for the first time in the four months I'd been there, we walked to the river in silence. An uncomfortable, heavy, heart-aching silence.

I cleaned myself up and washed my face. I'd shave later or maybe tomorrow. I guessed it didn't matter too much. Damu did the same, then filled his bucket, and before I could walk away, he grabbed my arm. "Did I do wrong?"

"What?"

"Did I do wrong?" he asked again. He looked stricken: worried, sad, and lost.

"No, no," I said quickly, putting my hand on his arm. "You did nothing wrong. Everything you did was perfect."

"But you not happy?"

I wanted to tell him I was happy, but I couldn't stomach the lie. "I feel like I've betrayed Ja—" I couldn't even bring myself to say his name. "Him. By being with you, I've broken his trust. I've betrayed him, what we had."

Confusion crossed his face. "Your Jarrod, the one you speak of in dreams, he knows you're here?"

"He told me to come here," I answered, without really thinking. "In my dreams, it was him that told me to come here."

"You see him only in dreams?"

Looking at the ground between us, I nodded.

His voice was barely a whisper. "You wish to see him again?"

My eyes filled with tears. "I wish I could hear his voice or feel his touch, just one more time."

"I not understand. You want to be with him but you are here?"

"He told me to come here. In my dreams, it was him that told me come here."

He put his hand to his forehead then scrubbed his face, clearly confused. "I not understand. Why he tell you to come here?"

"I think..." I swallowed back more tears. "I think he told me to come here to find you. He led me to you."

His eyes narrowed at me, flickering with emotions and uncertainty. "What?"

Before I could reply, the sound of the woman talking and laughing interrupted us as they approached.

We smiled as we passed the women, though the silence crept along with us like a shadow, an all-too-real presence I couldn't seem to shake. There were things too difficult to talk about, too painful to revisit, but as we walked, I saw Damu was frowning. His normally always-present smile and peacefulness was gone.

I came here to this country, bearing a weight I could barely carry. I hadn't exactly healed or lessened my burden any; I'd simply given it to someone else to carry.

The realisation that I'd hurt Damu stopped me in the middle of the track. In the Serengeti grass, my feet simply refused to move. He turned back to look at me. "Alé? What is it?"

The words, which I'd struggled to find, came out in a rush. "I'm sorry. I am so busy drowning in my own misery that I didn't realise I'd hurt you too. This is all so new to you. This." I motioned between us. "My being here has jeopardised everything for you, put you at risk of being ostracised by your own people. You have sacrificed all you have for me. Your religious beliefs, your everything. Not to mention how confusing it must be for you—this is your first time... God, Damu, I am so sorry."

He looked at me for a long moment, and eventually his lip curled upwards into a slow smile. "You came here like Kasisi said. You broken. You searching for something to fix you."

"But this is about you too. Not just me. I was selfish to ever think this was just about me."

He shook his head like I was missing the obvious. "You be here, fix me too."

Oh.

He looked torn. "I not ever know why I be different. Why I not want women like men do." Then his face fell and he whispered, "Why I dream of men." He shrugged. "Then you come here and I see I am not the only one."

"You're not. Damu, you're not alone. There's nothing wrong with you. There's nothing wrong with the way you feel, no matter what anyone else says. It took me a long time to learn that, to believe it."

His lips made a twisted smile. "My body likes it."

That made me laugh. "Mine does too."

He grinned properly now. "I try to control it but cannot."

"Don't ignore it. If you are curious, if you have questions, you can ask me."

"Even if you worry what your Jarrod will think?"

My chest ached like it always did when I thought of him, but I tried to smile for Damu. "Even then."

I WAS COUNTING pebbles with the children, using the little rocks as pretend money to buy imaginary things like shirts and melons, when Kasisi called me to see him.

He was sitting outside in the shade of his hut. He quite often liked to watch the children play. Like most of the elders, he took pride and a great deal of joy from the happiness of children. He could see the open classroom from where he sat, and he would watch them often, and Kasisi would smile every time the children sang and clapped.

"Chief," I said, my head bowed. "You wanted to see me."

"You make happy," he said, nodding toward the classroom.

"They make me happy," I replied.

"Not only them," he said. His eyes glanced away, and when I followed his line of sight, I saw he had looked at Damu.

Shit. I worded my answer carefully. "Damu is a good man," I said, diplomatically. "He has been very kind to me."

"He smile."

"He always smiles."

"Hmm," he said, as though he didn't believe me. "You ask Joseph and Mbaya to market."

Oh crap. "I did, yes. I'm sorry I didn't ask if it was okay. I didn't mean any disrespect. I just forgot. I didn't know they were going. When I was herding the goats with Damu the other day, I saw Joseph and Mbaya leaving and I ran to catch them. I gave them money. I would never expect the village to pay for what I request." I'd given them the equivalent of about twenty Australian dollars and a very quick list of what I wanted. "I'm sorry if this was wrong."

He nodded slowly. "You like be here?"

I understood his broken English just fine. "Yes. I like being here. I am grateful. Thank you." Then I wondered how he knew I'd given Joseph and Mbaya money. "Have they returned?"

Kasisi gave one hard nod. "You not buy for you?"

"No," I answered. "I wanted some things for the children."

"You not miss..." He searched for the right word and eventually settled on the Maa equivalent, "...*il-áshumpá* things?"

Did I miss my white man things? I smiled. "No. Being here without any white man things makes me feel free. No burden."

He smiled at that, then turned his head and called for one of his wives to bring him something.

Amali came from inside Kasisi's house, carrying a netted bag, and I could easily see what was inside it. I smiled at her as she handed it to me. "Thank you. Ashê, ashê." Then I looked back at Kasisi and bowed my head. "Ashê. Thank you." I pulled out the notepads of paper. Each page was yellowed with age and a little dusty, but I didn't care. The kids would love them. But then I pulled out the soccer ball and grinned. I glanced back at the kids still in the classroom, then back to Kasisi. "May I show them? Can we play outside the kraal? You can watch over us?"

He gave a nod, and I quickly got to my feet and raced back to the classroom. "Look!" I cried, showing them the ball. "Who wants to play soccer?"

All the kids clapped and cheered, but they were also confused, clearly having no clue what a soccer ball was. I put the ball at my feet and gently tapped it so it rolled toward them, but then I stopped it with my other foot and tapped it in the other direction. "Come," I called, waving my hand toward the gate in the fence. "Come."

I called for Damu to come with us, and the children ran after me. The area on the outside of the fence near the gate was grassless, and the high foot traffic had rendered it clear of any debris. It was roughly square in shape, with about twenty metres each side, and mostly soft dirt. I marked some makeshift goalposts with sticks on two sides and divided us into two teams. Me with three kids, and Damu with three kids.

Trying to explain the basic rules of soccer wasn't easy, given the language barrier. I was getting pretty good at Maa, and they were pretty good at English, but there was a lot lost in translation.

And it was the most I'd laughed in a long, long time.

We ran, mostly in circles, and the kids kicked the ball and chased each other, more a game of tag than soccer. They would stop to jump and sing, showing their Maasai joy the only way they knew how. The women watched from the fence, laughing at the happiness of their children, and even Kasisi and the other elders were smiling.

And as fulfilling as that was, as heart-warming and rewarding as it was, it was Damu's smile that made it perfect for me. He grinned and laughed as he helped the smaller children run and kick the ball. He cheered with them when they made a good kick, and even after the evening put a stop to play, Damu didn't stop smiling.

"You enjoyed soccer," I said. It wasn't a question. It was written all over his face.

"Much." We'd gone into our hut and were having our soup for dinner. It was dark inside but I could still see his face.

"It is great fun."

"We can do soccer every day."

"I hope so."

"Amali give me gift for you."

"She did?"

He reached behind him and handed me a neatly folded square of material. "Is it a shuka? For me?"

"Yes. Amali give."

I lifted it to my face and inhaled. It smelled new and felt scratchy like a picnic blanket. "It's perfect," I said. It was more than just getting a shuka, a blanket even, it was a sign of acceptance and even gratitude for my efforts to school the children. It was a gift from people who had very little to give. "I am very grateful."

"I know this. Amali know this."

I wrapped the shuka around my shoulders. "We will be twice as warm at night."

He chuckled. "Sleep now?"

When we lay down, as always, I had my back to his chest. But before he could flick his shuka out over us, I rolled over and faced him instead. I wasn't even sure why. I just needed to feel human contact. I needed to feel alive.

It was the first time I'd faced him while lying down from the beginning. Sure, I'd woken up in this position, but there was something intimate about starting out like this. I could barely make out the whites of his eyes, though he remained very still. I gently put my hand on his cheek. "Is this okay?"

His breath hitched. "Yes."

"Tell me if you don't want this."

He nodded and swallowed hard. "I want this touch. Very much," he whispered.

I pulled our shukas over us, then ran my thumb across his jaw and kissed him. His lips were full and plump, soft and open. I offered him my tongue, with light and caressing strokes, making him whine with need. He let me kiss him this way, my mouth on his, my hand to his face, until we both needed to come up for air. I slung my leg over his thigh and pulled his hips into mine, feeling every inch of his arousal. He shuddered with pleasure. "Alé," he murmured against my lips.

I slid my hand between us and trailed my hand down past his navel. "Can I touch you?"

His reply was a whispered, gruff, "Yes."

I reached down further and brushed my hand against his erection. He gasped, so this time I slid my palm along his length and slowly, gently, wrapped my fingers around him. He shut his eyes tight and moaned, so to keep him quiet, I covered his mouth with my lips and kissed him.

When I teased his tongue with mine, his cock jerked in my hand. Like the rest of him, his cock was long and thin, and I squeezed him, imagining how incredible he'd feel inside me when he arched into me and let out a strangled cry as he came between us.

It was so powerful and such a turn on, it only took a quick few pulls on my own cock to bring me over the edge.

I thought he'd pull away as the cold realisation of what we'd just done settled over us. But he didn't. He put his hand to my face, his long, gentle fingers tracing the outline of my cheek, my eyebrow, my jaw, and finally my lips. He pulled me closer, wrapping his arm around my waist, and he pressed his lips to mine.

It was a soft kiss, a sleepy kiss, and the emotion behind it took me by surprise. Despite the mess now sticking between us, cooling on our bellies, Damu kissed me again, then tucked me into his neck and sighed. His breathing evened out, his hold on me tightened even as he slept.

I wondered what dreams would haunt me that night as I

fell asleep in the arms of Damu, a man that was, with every Tanzanian sunrise, healing something inside me. I waited for the bony fingers of my nightmares to curl themselves around me, but they didn't.

I slept like a baby and woke with the sun.

THE NEXT TWO weeks played out the same. Damu and I herded the goats, letting them graze further out each day as winter took its toll on the landscape. Then I'd spend time with the kids in the classroom—we were learning shapes, colours, and words in English and their Maa equivalent—and every lesson ended in a game of soccer. Each night ended in Damu's arms, his appetite for exploring his newfound sex life was increasing every night. We didn't always end up in some post orgasmic slumber, but we did, every night without fail, fall asleep in each other's arms.

"I forget that this is all new to you," I said, kissing up his chest. As it turned out, he liked having his nipples tweaked, so I rolled the sensitive nub between my lips just to make him squirm.

It was true though. He'd completely tamped down any sexual urges for his entire life, because to be homosexual in his world meant certain death. So now, with my arrival, he was free to explore every whim he could imagine. We'd yet to have intercourse—we had no condoms or lube—but we'd done just about everything else. When I'd given him his first blowjob, I thought I'd killed him. He lay there, catatonic, his eyes like white saucers in the dark, until a slow smile spread across his face, and then he began to laugh.

Needless to say, it was his new favourite thing.

He rolled me over, manoeuvring me on his thin mattress and skimmed down my stomach and kissed the skin above the waistband of my shorts. He'd never reciprocated before...

"I do for you," he murmured. "What you do for me."

I certainly wasn't going to argue. He freed my erection and started off slowly. He was new to physical intimacy, though he certainly wasn't shy. He was keen to try as much as he could, and he was definitely a quick learner. He did everything to me that I'd done to him. He licked and tasted, enjoying the act and not just the reward.

By no means perfect, but still so, *so* good.

It was hard to be quiet. I used to be so vocal in bed, but being here, where anyone might hear us, warranted absolute silence. When I couldn't hold back my orgasm any longer, I tried to warn him, but he kept his mouth on me and sucked harder...

He gagged, and I couldn't help it, but I laughed. Eventually he fell onto the mattress beside me, and with my mind still swirling in a post-orgasmic haze, I chuckled.

"You drink that of me?" he asked. "It was... not expected taste."

That only made me laugh more. "It's not sweet, if that's what you mean."

"No. Not sweet." He shook his head as I curled into his arms. I was still smiling as I rest my head on his chest, safe and protected. His heart beat in my ear and his voice rumbled through his chest. "But please I do it more?"

I barked out a laugh, trying to muffle the sound. "You can do that any time you like."

He pressed his lips to my temple. "Thank you, Alé."

I kissed his chest. "Thank you, Damu." I closed my eyes,

still smiling, and tumbled slowly into another perfectly dreamless sleep.

———

DAYS ROLLED INTO WEEKS, and without the warriors—well, without Kijani and all the younger warriors—life was very peaceful. I wouldn't say it was better for the village to have them permanently absent, but I'd be lying if I said it wasn't better for Damu and me. We were a little freer, less scrutinised, without the watchful glare of Damu's older brother.

One wintery afternoon, we were playing soccer with the children. They'd become good at it now, and the mothers and elders watched from afar, looking our way with smiles on their faces when one of us laughed or cheered.

But then Makumu, one of the elder guards, started to yell, quick-fired words I'd not heard before. The children stopped running and the women hurried to collect them, leading them back inside the safety of the thorn fence.

I turned to Damu. "What is it?"

"Someone is coming."

Damu's unease put a shiver through me. I scanned the horizon and finally saw what Makumu was looking at. There were two lone figures approaching. Still some distance away but most definitely heading this way. One of them was tall, one shorter, and from the way they walked, I'd guessed one was male, the other female.

"It is Kijani," Makumu said and sighed with relief.

Just then, the taller of the two figures waved. Makumu waved back. "Kijani return," Makumu called out, and a moment later, Kasisi came to stand beside us.

His return was clearly not expected and neither was the

guest he brought with him. *I thought he was at an all-male warrior initiation? What on earth was the woman doing with him…?*

I got a heavy hollow feeling in my belly at the thought of what might have happened to her. I had come to accept many cultural differences here, especially when it came to the social standing of women in this society. I had bitten my tongue so many times, but this I could not leave alone.

"Why is she with him? What has happened to her?" I asked.

I was standing with Damu, Kasisi, and Makumu, watching as Kijani and this woman approached us, but no one answered.

I looked to Damu. "Has she been harmed?"

Damu looked at me then, his brow furrowed. Maybe he didn't like what I was implying, and that was fine with me. Because I didn't like it either.

It was Kasisi who answered. "We wait to hear what Kijani says."

I took a deep breath and let it out slowly. I rationalised that my anger was unfounded, and hearing what Kijani had to say first was a wise choice. If she had been harmed or sold or traded like a fucking goat, *then* I would speak my mind.

Which would probably find me at the pointy end of a spear…

I breathed in deep again and repeated the breathing techniques that my therapist had once taught me. I could only imagine what she would think if she saw me now…

When Kijani was closer, he yelled, "*A-ipót*, Amali."

He was asking for Amali to come. Damu turned and ran through the gate and I heard him call for Amali and a few seconds later, Amali came through the gate with Damu right behind her.

By this time, Kijani and the woman had arrived. She had her head down and her red shuka pulled over her head like a blanket to keep warm against the cold winds on the plains. I could barely see her face, though I noted she was barefoot and without any beads, bracelets, necklaces or anklets.

In Maasai terms, that meant she had no worth.

Then Kijani said, "*Kitalâ.*"

I didn't know what that meant, but Amali went quickly to the woman and took her arm, leading her hurriedly into the kraal.

When the women were gone, Kijani nodded to his father, murmured something I didn't quite catch, and without even so much as a look at me and Damu, he and Kasisi went inside the kraal.

Makumu went back to his guarding duties, while Damu and I just stood there.

"What just happened?" I asked. "What does *kitalâ* mean?"

"Refuge. That woman need refuge."

I turned to look at the gateway into the kraal, to where the woman had gone. Standing there, holding the dusty soccer ball, I felt like a fraud. I had assumed the very worst of these people, people who had offered me a place to live and food to eat when they themselves had very little to offer.

I had assumed wrong of Kijani, and I felt horrible for that.

"Who does she need refuge from?"

Damu shrugged. "Her family."

My shoulders fell. "Oh."

Damu studied me for a long time, then suggested we go inside. The days were shorter, evening was closing in around us, and we'd need to start a fire if we wanted to have soup for dinner. He was unusually quiet while we cooked and ate, as though he was struggling to ask me something.

"What are you thinking about?" I asked, draining my bowl.

"You," he said quietly. He'd hardly had any of his soup, so I knew what he wanted to ask couldn't have been good. "When I said woman need refuge from family, you be scared for her."

I swallowed hard. "Yes. I wonder what horrible things she ran away from."

Damu nodded slowly. "Why you not talk of family?"

The soup in my belly roiled. "My family..." I had to push the air out of my lungs to make my voice work. "I don't have a family."

"At all?"

I shook my head. "They didn't like that I am gay, that I love men and not women."

He looked alarmed. "You said your country is okay with such things."

"My country is. Well, most people are. But not my parents or my sister." I let out a shaky breath. The silence in the hut was deafening. "They wanted me to choose between them and who I really am."

"You choose you."

"I chose truth and honesty. And I chose love not hate."

He slid his hand over mine and was quiet for the longest time. "You are brave. Much brave than me."

I could have laughed at that. The worst my family did was throw me out for being gay. Damu's family, on the other hand, would punish him with the most humiliating, unpleasant death imaginable. "No. Not as brave as you."

"But you are."

A solitary tear ran down my cheek. "But I'm not."

He leaned in and pressed his lips to mine, and whether or not he knew my dreams would be bad that night, I can't be sure. But he pulled me in close, covered me with our shukas, and held me so, so tight.

I was grateful, though it didn't stop the nightmares.

CHAPTER TEN

THE MEN in the alley outside the pub give us a beating. I remember seeing Jarrod's head hit the pavement and taking a kick to the head, before my world goes dark. Someone calls the cops and I wake up in the ambulance. Jarrod doesn't. He hasn't woken up at all.

I'm sitting in the room with him, holding his hand, pleading with every God and deity to save him. I tell him I love him, I tell him I need him to live. Doesn't he understand? I can't do this without him. We are all we have. It's just me and him—it's only ever been me and him—and I can't do life without him.

But I have to, they say. It doesn't look good, they say. His next of kin have been called.

Then his parents turn up, running into the room like they actually care and kicking me out. "He's the reason our boy's in here," Jarrod's mother says with a teary sneer at me.

Detective Don Walmsley escorts me out. "You're not family, son. You can't stay," he whispers. But then he sits with me... He was the one to find us. He hasn't left us yet. He taps my thigh. "It's okay, son. You're not alone."

But I am.

I'm in the hospital corridor alone. My left eye is swollen shut, stitches in the back of my head, my cheek cut, my lip split. I have two broken ribs, cuts and bruises everywhere.

Yet I'm numb to it all.

Jarrod lies in a hospital bed, intubated and bandaged. He has a punctured lung from a broken rib and massive head trauma.

Then my mother turns up. I don't even look at her. I certainly have nothing to say. She sighs when she sees me. Not a relieved sound. More of an inconvenienced, unsaid I-told-you-so. She sits in the chair opposite me, and I stare at her until she looks away.

Then Jarrod's parents come out crying. He's gone, they say. It's my fault, they say.

Detective Don Walmsley stands and defends me, saying the attackers have been caught, and it was in no way my fault.

They don't believe him. My mother doesn't either.

I don't hear what they say after that. My mind is stuck, filled with a roaring white noise.

He is gone.

Jarrod's gone.

I didn't even get to say goodbye.

It's okay, son. You're not alone.

But I am.

I really am.

I WOKE up in complete darkness, feeling like I'd been hit by a truck. My body ached, my bones ached, and my heart... I hadn't even realised the weight in my heart had lessened since I'd arrived here, until it was back in full force.

My dreams had always been vivid. But this one, well it was all too real. I recalled the first morning I woke up after Jarrod died, how I rolled over, waking slowly, and only remembering he was gone when his side of the bed was empty.

My ribs hurt, my face—my eye, my cheek, my jaw—was swollen and sore, the headache was skull-cracking, but nothing prepared me for the pain in my heart.

It was no different now.

It was as if no time had passed at all. It was as if someone had taken the knife of grief and ripped me from sternum to stomach all over again.

I sucked back a breath. My lungs felt like they were filled with concrete. My heart was squeezing, squeezing...

I was alone again.

It's okay, son. You're not alone.

But I was.

"Alé," Damu whispered in my ear. "Alé. Wake, Alé."

I couldn't bring myself to tell him I was already awake and this, me sobbing and unable to breathe, was real. Instead I turned in his arms and buried my face into his neck as I sobbed. "They killed him," I said. "Jarrod died and I didn't. They took him from me."

He held me tighter and kissed the side of my head. "Shhh. I have you," he murmured. "Not alone. You not alone."

I closed my eyes, too exhausted to protest when sleep came for me again.

The next time I woke up, it was sunlight outside. Damu was making me uji, which meant he'd already gone to the river.

I sat up and immediately fell back onto the mattress. My head throbbed and my stomach roiled. "Ugh. What time is it?"

"Sleep," Damu answered.

"I don't feel well."

He looked at me and frowned. "I tell others you sick. They worry. I make you... medicine?"

"Is it not ugali?"

He shook his head and stirred the pot. "You fever. Need this."

I put my hand to my forehead. My skin was clammy and cold, but I felt hot. *Fever*. Great. Just what I need.

Damu scooted over to me and offered me the bowl. A sudden wave of nausea rolled through me and I put my hand up. "No."

Damu nodded. "Yes. You must."

"Sick."

Damu lifted my head off the mattress and put the bowl to my lips, making me drink. It was warm and brewed like a tea, but it tasted of grass and piss. "Ugh. That's awful," I said, gagging as I tried to keep it down.

Damu smiled. "Sleep."

That sounded like a great idea. I closed my eyes, and when I opened them again, the light outside had changed. Damu was there and when he saw me wake up, he forced more medicine down my throat and ordered me to sleep some more. I don't know what the hell he put in that medicine, but I didn't really have a choice. I closed my eyes and only woke again when it was getting dark.

I couldn't tell if my body still ached. My mind was kind of foggy and Damu wiped a wet cloth across my forehead. "Medicine," he said, and poured more of that ghastly tea down my throat.

The next thing I knew it was almost morning. The sky outside was the faintest of purples, which meant it was about five o'clock. Damu was asleep in front of me, on the dirt floor. He was curled into himself, no doubt cold. The fire was barely embers, and his heavier shuka was draped over me while my thinner skuka was all he had. He can't have been comfortable, and he'd obviously spent the day watching over me, tending to me.

"Damu," I roused him gently, quietly. "Come here."

He stirred, barely. "Fever?"

"No. I'm better. Come sleep here."

He sighed and half-asleep, crawled onto the mattress with me. I lifted his shuka and he settled in with me, though this time he was the little spoon. I'd no sooner covered him with the shuka than I felt the tension leave his body. He relaxed into me and I wrapped my arm around his waist. I was about to ask him if he was comfortable, but he was already asleep.

I'D MISSED A WHOLE DAY. Whether it was the illness that brought on my horrible dreams of Jarrod's death or if it were the dreams that brought on the illness, I wasn't sure.

But that medicine, whatever the hell was in it, worked. I was tempted to ask if I could have a dose every night before sleep, to keep my dreams at bay, but was pretty sure Damu wouldn't allow it.

I woke up feeling pretty good, all things considered. But I was keen to get to the river to bathe, to wash away the sweat and stench that being sick left behind. Damu walked with me, as always, but he looked tired.

"Thank you for looking after me yesterday," I said. "It means a lot to me that you would do that."

Damu gave me a solitary nod. "Welcome."

"What was in that medicine?" I asked. "I mean, it tasted unbelievably bad, but it fixed me."

Damu chuckled. "It is tea from bark and roots. I get it for you from far valley."

"You went all that way, just for me?"

It was kind of hard to tell, with the colour of his skin, but I'm sure he blushed. "Yes."

"You should rest today, and I will do your chores."

He smiled then. "No. I'm able."

"I would do them for you. I would do your share, so Kijani won't know."

He chuckled quietly to himself. "Kijani gone back to eunoto."

"Oh. He came back for just one day?" I wasn't exactly sad to have missed seeing him yesterday. "Is everything okay?"

Damu smiled, his usual peaceful demeanour was back. "Yes."

"Kijani stay for one night only. He was offered meat and milk, spent the night talking with Kasisi, and was gone again in the morning." Damu talked proudly of his brother, and I tried to not let that bother me. "He be obligated to go back to eunoto, the boys who would be warriors. He waste no time in getting back there."

"Fair enough," I said. "What of the new woman? Is she okay?"

Damu nodded again. "She stay inside house for one moon."

I had to think about that for a second. Maybe the lack of

food was starting to take its toll. "She won't come out for a whole month?"

"No."

"Why? Is that a custom?" I wasn't judging, I was merely curious. "She came here for safety, is she okay?"

"She is. Amali take care of her."

"Amali is a very good woman."

Damu looked at me and a slow smile spread across his face. "She is very kind." But then he said, "After *e-múráta* a woman stay in house, not come out, for one moon. This way she heal."

"What is e-múráta?"

"Circumcision. On woman."

I felt the blood drain from my face, and I stopped walking. "You what?" I had spent my time here learning their culture and lived by my motto of not judging them, no matter how fucked up things were. But *this*? This crossed a line. That being said, what was deemed barbaric to most of the world was a very significant part of their culture, and I couldn't dismiss that. I shook my head, not knowing what to think. "That is..." I didn't want to use the word wrong, because it was not my moral or ethical place to make such a statement that disrespected an entire race of people. So I went with, "...not good. Not good at all."

Damu had stopped walking, now facing me. He put his hand up, a gesture of peace. "Many Maasai still do e-múráta. Circumcision woman. As it has been done for many years. But no. Our tribe, the Isikirari people not do this. We do different. A ceremony for girls who become woman, but not circumcision. Ceremony the same, but girl gets a cut on her leg instead. Small cut on leg." He lifted his foot off the ground and touched the inside of his thigh. "Here. But some choose old ways. They want circumcision done. Believe it is their right. Some believe not. Kasisi allows this girl choice. If girl from other Maasai tribe choose no circumcision, they be safe here."

I let his words sink in. "You offer them refuge?"

"Kasisi offer them. Kijani bring girl here to be safe. Like Oni and Fajima, they not be born here. They come here, for choice not to be circumcised."

Oni and Fajima were two women in the tribe, wives to Makumu. I let out a deep breath. "Okay then."

Damu laughed. "This please you?"

"Yes. Having the choice is important. If the woman choose it, that's fine. If they choose not to have it, then Kasisi respects that." I couldn't even explain the relief I felt. The Maasai people lived by customs centuries old, yet here was a feminist stronghold in a very patriarchal world. It made me happy.

Damu shook his head. "Not woman choice. Girl choice. She not be woman until ceremony."

Aaaaaaand there it was. Back to the 1800s in one comment. Though, in reminding myself to look at the world through Maasai eyes, I was beginning to understand the dilemmas of the Maasai people. The very roots of their culture were at such odds with the world I came from.

We started walking again as I processed what I had learned, and as we neared the river bank, Damu put his hand out and stopped me. He nodded silently downriver, and when I followed his line of sight, I saw the reason for his smile.

Two giraffes were drinking from the river. Seeing these African creatures roaming wildly, up close and personal, would never not amaze me. Damu wasn't too impressed—much like I'd imagine my reaction to seeing a kangaroo or koala—but I was floored. They were maybe a hundred metres away, with their long legs splayed out so they could drink the water.

"They're beautiful," I whispered. "Why are they here? I mean, why are we only seeing them now?"

"No rains mean river Mara dry up. Smaller water to drink from, easier for predator."

"Makes sense."

The giraffes noticed us, then, and scampered away, all legs and neck. I watched with a smile plastered on my face until they were gone from view and unfortunately missed Damu getting undressed. I only saw a quick glimpse of his arse before it disappeared under the water.

I quickly stripped and joined him. The cold water was heavenly: invigorating and cleansing, washing away the stench of illness. I dunked my head under and scrubbed at my scalp with my fingers. It wasn't anything close to sanitary—it was a muddy river after all—but it was the best it got out here.

From all the creature comforts I'd left behind—toilet paper, hot showers, soap, and shaving cream—it was toothpaste I missed the most. I still had my toothbrush, but it wasn't much use without toothpaste.

When we were out of the river and dressed, we walked a little further downriver to the o'remiti plant. Damu picked a few twigs and handed them to me. It was what the Maasai used to clean their teeth. "You trying to tell me my breath smells?"

He looked horrified. "No."

I burst out laughing and put my hand on his arm. "I was kidding! I'm joking."

He narrowed his eyes at me. "Not the o'remiti, but we will get you some *mswaki*." He looked at my armpits, then sniffed with a scrunched up nose like I was rank.

Mswaki was the plant they used as a deodorant. I barked out a laugh and pushed his shoulder. "I don't smell!" Well, I didn't think I did. I smelled my own armpit. I didn't stink at all. Much.

Damu pushed my shoulder and laughed. "Joking."

I shook my head at him but couldn't help but laugh. "You totally got me!" I shoved the twig in my mouth and chewed, scrubbing it against my teeth. "I really miss toothpaste," I said, the words a jumbled sound around the twig in my mouth. "Your brand of Colgate really sucks."

"Our brand of what? What is brand?"

I waved him off. "Never mind."

Then Damu turned and his smile slid away. He looked to the ground and took a discernible step away from me. There could only be one reason. Given Kijani was away, it had to be Kasisi. And sure enough, there he was. Up the river where we normally bathed, he stood on the riverbank watching us.

I smiled at the chief. I think he liked me. Either that or he thought I was completely insane and therefore good entertainment. Kasisi smiled back at me, just as other elders joined him. As they prepared to bathe, Damu and I took our leave.

"You okay?" I asked as we made our way back to the kraal.

Damu nodded, but he hardly looked convincing.

"He never saw us do anything," I said to reassure him. "We were laughing, that is all." Damu never responded. "If it bothers you, we don't have to... you know, do what we do in bed. It is a risk, I know that. And if you say no more, then it's no more."

Damu shot me a nervous look, and his lips twitched. "You want no more?"

"Oh, I want lots more," I said. He almost smiled. "But I will do whatever you want."

Damu stopped walking. "What we do, Alé..." He struggled for the right words. "What we do, is my only joy."

"Oh." And just like that, his words squeezed my heart.

"It is in all my life that I have something for me. That make sense of my heart. Not toward women, but to men, it make sense now. Because of you."

I reached out to touch him, needing to comfort him, but given our exposed location, I pulled my hand back. I could only hope he saw compassion in my eyes. "Damu."

"So please you not tell me I don't have you."

I shook my head. "You have me. I won't deny you anything. That I have made you happy and made you see that what you desire is not wrong"—I put my hand to my heart—"that heals something inside me."

He looked at me for a long, silent moment and smiled. "You not want to stop?"

I shook my head. "Never."

He started to walk again, his peaceful demeanour back in place. I wasn't sure why I'd said I'd never want to stop. Never was just as much a promise as the word forever. I should have been stunned by my choice of words, but somehow they felt right. I hadn't yet explored what Damu meant to me exactly, I hadn't allowed myself to think anything of it. Was it simply opportunity? A sexual fix after what felt like an eternity of being alone?

I didn't know what to call it or what classification of relationship to name what we had.

At the end of the day, it didn't matter. We just were. Damu had spent his entire life on the outside of his family, of his people, for reasons that were not his fault.

I couldn't help but draw the parallels to my own life.

I understood his pain because I'd lived it. My family wanted nothing to do with me unless I stopped being gay.

It had taken me eighteen years to realise that love shouldn't come with terms and conditions. When I'd finally found the courage to stand on my own two feet, to not deny who I was, then Jarrod walked into my life.

It was similar for Damu. I'd literally walked into his manyatta and been the first person in his entire life to treat him as an equal, to treat him with the respect he deserved.

When I'd struggled with my desires and where my fantasies had taken me, at least I had television and the Internet to help me. I could read and research, I could join forums that were safe places, and we could talk anonymously about our greatest fears and hopes.

But Damu had none of that. He'd admitted he'd had desires for men, and knowing that would be a death sentence, he had no one to turn to. He had no one to talk to, no one to tell him it was okay. He must have spent his entire life in a permanent state of confusion and thinking there was something wrong with him.

Until I got here.

I just hoped it wasn't going to be his downfall.

"We herd in crater today," he said brightly.

"Really?"

"Yes. No grass here until the rains."

"Will we see elephants?"

Damu grinned at me. "Possibly."

I had a bounce in my step the whole way there.

WALKING down into the Serengeti crater was something not to be believed. The sky was an incredible blue, the air was clean and crisp, and the endless grasslands were browns tinged with swirls of green, making the waterways easy to pick out.

Damu and I had to spread out, keeping the small herd of goats between us. Bringing the farm animals into the crater in the small-rains season came with risks. Predators saw them and us as easy targets.

"Lions?" My voice was an octave higher than normal.

Damu laughed. "Yes. Just keep watch for other animals."

"Why?"

"Other animals will see and run away. But you not see lion coming."

I stopped cold. "Oh thanks. That is *not* reassuring."

All he could do was laugh. We herded the goats down the rocky embankment, which the goats navigated easily. Damu did too, each step carefully placed and expertly taken, whereas my old sneakers let me down. The grip was gone—the soles completely smooth—the mesh material on top was torn, and the original colour was no longer recognisable. I slipped and slid down the rocky incline, and when Damu was certain I was okay, he laughed at me some more.

I went to one end of the herd, Damu at the other and we held the long sticks that Kasisi had given us and kept the goats in line. I kept looking around me, checking the longer grasses for movements of a possible lion or cheetah.

Considering the hundred metres between us, Damu had to whistle to get my attention. "Watch the goats," he said, pointing to his eyes then to the herd.

"What if a lion comes?" I yelled back.

"Roar at it," he answered. I think he was joking. I mean, seriously...

I yelled loud enough for him to hear. "People give

Australians a hard time about our wildlife, but at least we don't have lions and cheetahs and rhinos and hippos."

"Not to forget the black mamba snake," Damu said with a grin. I could almost see every tooth in his head. "Make eyes bleed."

Oh, Jesus Christ. I spun around, looking at the ground, and Damu laughed so hard he had to hold his side.

I had to wait until he'd finished before I could reply. "Not funny!"

He just laughed and went back to tending to the goats, and after an hour or so of quiet between us, he whistled again, but this time he pointed his stick to the far horizon. I spun around to see a family of elephants, walking in the distance. Probably a few hundred metres from us, three full-grown female elephants, a juvenile, and a calf were plodding along, no doubt on their way to find water.

I put my hand to my mouth, in shock and awe. *Oh my God.* Real elephants, wild and free, right in front of me.

Then I noticed some zebras a ways off and some gazelle, some water buffalo. It looked like a postcard picture or something out of one of the travel brochures I'd seen a thousand times but never really appreciated. Until now.

I hadn't heard Damu approach me. "You like?"

He was beside me now, so I turned to look up at him. "It's beautiful. It's so perfect, it doesn't even look real." But then I took him in as well. Standing proud in his red shuka and holding his long stick as he surveyed the Serengeti, he looked just as remarkable. "You are beautiful too," I said. My own words surprised me. "This land, the animals, you. Everything."

My heart started to hammer, a nervous flutter. Something I hadn't felt in a long time. It was foreign and strange, and I recognised it for what it was. It was affection. I still couldn't put a name to what Damu meant to me. Not because there wasn't a name that applied, but because I wasn't ready. But I could no longer deny that I had feelings for him...

Does that mean I'm letting go of Jarrod?

I didn't think I ever would. He had been part of my life for a reason, and by the same logic, he'd left my life for a reason too. I had screamed at any god who would listen. *Why, why, why take him? What sense did it make that his life was cut short? What was the purpose of such a senseless death?*

And now I was faced with a possible answer.

Had it been to find Damu? Was it not Jarrod who, in my dreams, led me here? Was he telling me to come here, not to find myself or not to learn to live again, but to find Damu?

My mind reeled, splintered into a dozen different directions, and all the while my heart thundered, my blood pounded in my veins.

And standing in the open plains of the Serengeti, as the African wildlife meandered in the distance, I realised one thing. I was alive. My heart beat, my blood pumped, my lungs squeezed, and nerves fluttered in my belly. I was alive.

It had only taken me over twelve months of non-living to realise. To get on a plane and fly to the other side of the world, to live a life so foreign to my own, to meet one man who would bring me such comfort and warmth when I had none.

Damu, seemingly oblivious to my internal revelations, chuckled and shook his head. "Men cannot be beautiful. Women, yes. The sunrise, the breeze, the rain, yes. Me? No."

I put my hand on his arm and hoped he could see the sincerity in my eyes. "You are the beauty in those things for me. The sunrise every morning, how the breeze moves the tall grass, the rains to nourish the ground. Without you Damu, none of these things would exist for me. You make them beautiful."

He stared at me for the longest moment before a shy smile crept over his face, and he looked away. Only then did he realise some of the goats had wandered from the rest of the herd. He ran after them, and we spent the next few hours at opposite ends of the herd. I would catch him looking at me, though, with a hint of wonder and confusion in his eyes, and he'd quickly look away as he fought a smile.

I was reminded that this was very new to him. Not just our relationship, but friendship in general was new to him. I imagined he looked at me the same way I looked at my first high school crush.

It was sweet.

It made my heart happy, twinged with a little sadness, but mostly happy.

I expected my dreams that night to be brutal. My subconscious had, after all, conceded that my *affections* for Damu were real.

I lay in his arms, cradled and protected, my face in his neck, and I waited for what horrors would come for me.

I slept like a baby.

THE NEW WOMAN that Kijani had returned with, whose name was Razina apparently, never came out of Amali's hut. Damu told me she would stay in the house for a month, and he was right. For the weeks that followed, I never saw her.

The first time I saw her was when Damu and I were

walking to the river. We met the women as they were walking home, and Razina was with them.

"*Éjó áá entedekenyá?*" I asked them. Which, when translated, literally meant 'what does the morning say?' It was the Maa way of saying good morning.

"*Sídái olêŋ!*" they replied. *Very good.*

It was then I noticed Razina. She balked when she saw me, her eyes going wide. "Mzungu," she mumbled. I was used to that now. It meant white man. And truthfully, that's what I was to these people. I didn't have a problem with that.

Then she noticed my eyes and her stare widened even further. "*Enkong'u a-paashari,*" she whispered. I understood enough to decipher that she'd basically just muttered that I had different eyes.

Amali and Yantai pulled her to keep walking, and they all giggled. I could hear them telling her I was a white man with different eyes that lived with them as we went our separate ways.

I forgot about my heterochromia. It had been so long since I'd looked in a mirror. I know the women in the kraal did have a mirror, but I hadn't seen myself in all the time I'd been here.

God, how long had it been? Six months? Had I really been here for six months? "How many months have I been here?" I asked Damu as we got to the river.

"Six moons." He eyed me cautiously. "Why you ask?"

"I couldn't remember, that's all," I answered. "I've lost all sense of time here. There's no TV, no Internet, no phones."

He frowned. "Do you miss those things?"

I unwrapped my shuka and let it fall in a heap on the rocks, then I pulled off my threadbare shirt. *Did I miss those things? My old life?* I thought about how my old life, up until Jarrod died, was a stress of emails, sales quotas, and conference meetings. Not to mention how everyone was glued to their phones and social media updates. *Did I miss that?* "Nope. Not at all."

Did anyone back home miss me? That was the real question. Probably not, I reasoned. Lord knows my family were history, and I'd all but withdrawn from my friends. Those who still called around after Jarrod was killed had eventually stopped trying to get me out of the flat. The visits stopped and eventually the phone calls and tags on Facebook stopped too. I didn't blame them... I just didn't want them trying so damn hard or fumbling over not saying the wrong thing. It was awkward, they knew it as well as I did, and every time they'd look at me with pity, it did nothing but remind me that Jarrod was gone forever.

But here, in the middle of winter, deep in the western Tanzanian wilds, I was free of all of that.

I stripped down to my undies and toed off my shoes. I took hold of Damu's hand, and together, laughing, we dived into the icy cold river.

CHAPTER ELEVEN

THE SWELL of the bellies of the female goats and cows could only mean one thing: spring was coming. The nights were still cold, the mornings brisk, but the days were warming up and a flourish of new growth tinged the Serengeti green. The mood in the kraal was lifted, proof with random outbursts of songs and laughter.

Talk soon filtered through of the return of the warriors at the end of the week, and with it, came much excitement.

The children in our classroom role-played of being warriors, hunting lions and jumping. They taught me new songs, and we continued with our letter and number recognition, in both Maa and English, making both words and sums. Then we played soccer in the evenings before the children were called inside, and Damu and I spent our nights in bed, exploring each other's bodies.

It was both erotic and endearing, watching him learn what his own body liked and how to make my body writhe. We'd done everything else we possibly could without having penetrative sex. Damu's culture had told him all his life that anything to do with the anus was dirty and wrong.

It had been a miracle that he was even open to his own sexuality now, knowing what the ramifications could be if we were caught, but it seemed anal play was a bigger obstacle than I'd first thought.

The reasonable part of my brain knew that some men, when in bed with another man, never partook in anal sex. It wasn't for them, and that was perfectly okay. But I loved to bottom. For me, there was nothing better than being laid on a bed, manhandled even, and being fucked into the mattress. I loved having anal sex, and I wasn't ashamed about it.

Damu, on the other hand, was.

Once when we'd been fooling around in bed and I was jerking him off and fondling his balls, I'd tried teasing him with a gentle touch there, but he froze. I never pushed the issue with him of course, but it didn't stop me from doing it to myself.

I lay back on the mattress, Damu at my side. He had his hand firmly wrapped around my cock and I slipped my hand—my left hand, not my right—down to my balls, tugging and rolling, then I slipped it further down. I massaged my perineum, spread my legs wider and traced circles over my hole. God I'd missed this. My back arched with pleasure and Damu's hand stilled.

"Alé," he whispered.

Still with my left hand, I swiped the precome from the tip of my cock, then applied the sticky wetness to my arsehole. I took my dick with my right hand, pumping and pulling, and with my left hand, I pushed a finger into myself.

"Alé," Damu whispered again. This time he sounded alarmed.

I concentrated on him, but I never stopped working

myself over. "It feels so good," I murmured. I inserted another finger and couldn't help but moan. It had been so long... I pumped my cock harder and pushed deeper inside myself, curling my fingers just enough to touch my gland, over and over, forcing my orgasm free. My back arched one final time, my entire body straining, as come shot onto my stomach. It had been over a year and a half since I'd had an experience so powerful, and it took a few moments for my senses to come back to me.

When the room stopped spinning, Damu had his hand to my cheek. His face was so close to mine, I could see his eyes, even in the darkness. He was staring at me with disbelief. "What is your real name?" he asked, a quiet whisper. "Not Alé."

My name? I had to think... "Heath Crowley."

"Heath Crowley," he repeated like a prayer, before crushing his lips to mine. He deepened the kiss, frantically, then rolled on top of me.

His weight was divine, his kiss deep and thorough. He was owning me, and it was perfect. I opened my legs for him, feeling him in all the right places, and he rutted against me. I drew my knees up, giving him better angles, his long cock was hard and hot against mine. Driving his hips into me, using the friction between us, he brought himself to climax.

I held him tighter, kissed him deeper, as his orgasm ripped through him. He trembled and shook, whining into my mouth as he came, and his come shot between us. He collapsed on top of me, and I wrapped my arms around him. It was so erotic, so hot. I imagined what it would feel like to have him come inside me, and it sent a shiver through me.

Damu stirred, and I tightened my hold on him. "Don't move," I whispered. "I want you right where you are." I pulled our shukas up and over us, covering us the best I could. "That was amazing," I murmured, kissing his ear.

"I have not known such things," he mumbled into my neck. "What you did made me lose my mind. I could not stop."

I chuckled. "You're welcome. And for what it's worth Damu, you can do that to me anytime."

He rolled to the side, taking me with him, so we were on our sides, wrapped in each other's arms. "You like, with your fingers in... there?"

I smiled into his neck. "Yes."

"The way you come in such pleasure..." he whispered, "I can't imagine it. Does it not pain?"

"If it's done right, slow and with a lubricant, it feels amazing. It's strange at first, but then it is very good."

"What is lubricant?"

Oh. "Something to make it slippery and smooth." I tried to think of something he could identify with. "Like fat or grease."

"Make slick."

"Yes."

"And sometimes men put penis there?"

"Sometimes, not always."

He paused for a moment, and his voice was tight. "And you've done this many times?" Was he jealous or curious?

I chuckled. "A few."

Again with a pause. "And this is safe?"

I pulled back and put my right hand to his face. The hut was completely black now and I could just make out the whites of his eyes. I knew HIV and AIDS were a great health concern in Africa, and I could have kicked myself for not addressing this sooner. "Damu, are you worried about your health?"

He just stared at me. His silence was his answer.

I needed to make this clear, so nothing was lost in translation. "I have had many blood tests and each one came back all clear. I have no disease or illness. You are safe with me." Then I asked, "And you have never had sex before?"

"No. Until you."

I knew sex wasn't the only way STIs could spread, but he was a virgin, he'd never left this camp, and he was an absolute picture of health. I didn't have the heart to tell him that it wasn't just anal sex that could spread disease. We'd been giving and receiving blowjobs for a while now... God, I was so stupid. I should have brought this up before the very first time. When he'd told me he was a virgin, I never thought any more on risks, to either of us, because he couldn't have STIs if he was a virgin, right? I was too busy enjoying the feeling of being alive and desired to worry about HIV and AIDS. The fucking irony in that was hideous.

"Damu, please understand. If I thought it was a risk, I wouldn't have done anything with you. I would never harm you, in any way." I pressed my lips to his and traced my fingers over his eyebrow. "You are safe with me."

"You wish me to do the sex to you?"

His nerves were showing in his English. I kissed him softly again. "I would never ask you to do something you didn't want to do."

"But you wish it?"

Here went nothing. "I do. I like it, but it's not essential. I like everything we do. Even just spending time with you and being around you makes me happy."

I could just make out his smile in the darkness. "You make me happy too, Heath Crowley."

I chuckled. "My real name."

"Yes. It is a true name."

"A true name?"

"Heath. Heath is like *Ol-osinkō*."

"It's like what?"

"Centre of home. Heath means home fire, warmth of home."

"Oh." *Heath is like hearth.*

"It is your true name, warmth of my home, Heath Crowley."

I snuggled into his embrace, breathing in his earthy scent and relishing the warmth that surrounded me. He kissed the side of my head, and the strong and steady beat of his heart, lulled me to sleep.

***

EVERY NIGHT THAT WEEK, after we'd spent our days in the cool winds of the Serengeti and our afternoons in the classroom and playing soccer. We spent our nights talking while we ate our soup, and when it was time to go lie down, Damu would end up on top of me, snug between my thighs.

Most nights we frotted, rubbing our cocks together, until release. Some nights we just rocked against each other, our cocks pressed between us, but each night I'd wrap my legs around him or bring my knees up to our sides, each night getting a little closer. Sometimes he rubbed the head of his dick across my hole, like he was testing himself. He was curious, that much was clear, but also uncertain and a little afraid.

On the night before the warriors were to return, I lay on the mattress naked while Damu sat back on his haunches with my thighs across his. His long cock jutted proudly toward me, and he positioned himself at my entrance. I could see the uncertainty on his face, even in the darkened room.

I gripped my own dick with one hand and rubbed a nipple with my other, unable to bite back the moan. He pushed against me, not quite hard enough to penetrate, but he groaned out a cry as he came, shooting come across my arse and balls. I was so turned on, I followed directly after.

When we'd cleaned up a bit and were lying in each other's arms, Damu took a deep breath and let it out as a sigh.

"Are you okay?" I asked.

"Never this better, Heath Crowley. Never this better."

I chuckled and kissed his chest, content to bask in the silence and his happiness.

THE WOMEN STOOD in a line at the gates of the kraal, their gourds filled with fresh milk, and as the new warriors came home, the women splashed them with milk. It probably wasn't the weirdest thing I'd seen in all my time here, but it was an anointing, as such, and that I could respect. They used milk, according to Damu, because it nourished and sustained, it was the sacred lifeblood of the Maasai people.

Kijani followed the new warriors inside, their smiles huge and contagious. The newly appointed elders, or junior elders as they were called, came in last.

When we got back inside the kraal, I couldn't see anyone. "Where is everyone?" I whispered.

"The new warriors go to their mothers," Damu answered. "Be prepared for showing. New shukas, red now, not black. New beads for them too."

"Is that what they've been busy making?" I asked. "When I'm in the classroom with the children, they've been busy stitching and beading."

Damu smiled. "Yes. Very exciting time. Feast tonight. New warriors kill goat. It is tradition."

It was exciting, I couldn't deny it. There was a buzz throughout the whole kraal, and I could hear bursts of laughter coming from inside some of the huts, while the elders stood in closed circles trading stories. All the while, Damu was on the outer. If I hadn't been here with him, he'd have been completely alone. He was never included, he was never part of anything. He simply stood on the outside looking in and seemingly happy to do so. He smiled as they smiled, never an inkling of jealousy or yearning. He was happy because *they* were happy. His own joy, his own place of belonging, never entered into the equation.

It boggled my mind.

As the new warriors came out, dressed in their new red shukas, holding their new warrior spears, they stood in a proud line. Heads held high, chests out, this was their crowning glory, their social status as high as it would get.

The women began to sing, a low bass with perfect rhythm. Amali sang the higher notes, singing words of praise for these new men, of bravery and virility. And they danced, a jerky movement that made their dinner-plate-like necklaces bob and sway.

Then the men began to jump. They'd take turns, leaping high into the air, all while chanting and singing. It was a sight to behold.

It was an incredible thing to witness.

The meat was prepared, the blood kept in gourds, and everyone left the kraal to eat. No meat was ever consumed inside the walls of the kraal, as was customary, and the men never ate with the women and children.

Damu and I stayed with the women, of course. It was just our natural place in the manyatta; they accepted us, included us. I really liked them, especially Amali and Yantai, though I'd be lying if I said it didn't bother me a little bit. Not for me, but for Damu. I had no misconceptions about my status. I was, and would always be, an outsider. But Damu wasn't. He was born here. He was one of them, and he would defend those men with his own life, but he was treated like dirt.

I took comfort in knowing he wasn't bothered by it, and that eased my concerns a great deal. If it upset him, or if it ate away at him, it would have upset me more. But he seemed happy enough, or maybe he was completely resigned to his place in this society.

"What you think of?" he asked, handing me a strip of roasted meat. "It is time for happiness, not frowns."

I took the meat gratefully. "Thank you. Yes, I'm happy... Can I ask you something?"

He laughed. "You always have questions when you be frowning."

I smiled at that. "Would you tell me honestly, does it bother you that you are here when the other men are over there?" I nodded toward the group of warriors and elders.

"You ask this before."

"I did."

"So it bother you?"

"Not for me, but for you. You deserve to be with them."

He chuckled and shook his head. "I am at peace with where I am, Heath Crowley."

I smiled at how he said my name. Not only did he say my full name, but he only ever called me that when we were alone. In front of anyone else, he used my Maasai name, Alé.

"Hey, what's your last name?" I asked. "Do you have a family name?"

"Yes," he said, as he bit into some meat. "We take father's family name."

"And what is yours?"

"Nkorisa."

"Damu Nkorisa?" I asked, just to be certain I had it right.

He nodded slowly and looked to where the children were playing soccer. He smiled wistfully as they laughed.

"Damu Nkorisa," I repeated his full name. "I like how that sounds."

He turned his gaze to me. He never spoke but there was something in his eyes, a depth, an emotion that gave me butterflies.

It wasn't a reaction I was expecting, and I was grateful for the distraction when all the women stood up. I looked over and saw why. Kijani was on his way over. It must have been something special if the warrior leader approached. Amali stepped forward—she was, for all intents and purposes, Kijani's mother. The woman who had taken both Kijani and Damu in as her own—and he bowed his head to her before they had a quiet conversation while everyone watched on.

I had to admit, I admired the way all Maasai men, even in such a patriarchal society, respected their mothers. It was the mother who they came to for advice, it was the mother's approval they sought for many things. Even though Kijani was basically the second in charge of all his people, only after his father, the witchdoctor chief Kasisi, Kijani still sought counsel from his mum.

Kijani and Amali turned and walked away to speak in private, looking back at the men and women in turn.

"What's going on?" I whispered to Damu.

"I not know. I have guess," he answered, a slight smile on his face.

Before he could finish, Kijani and Amali returned to the group of women, and Amali said, "Razina."

Razina, the woman Kijani had bought here seeking refuge, was clearly surprised and nervous, but stepped forward. She was a pretty woman, with high cheekbones and delicate features, though it was hard to tell because she kept her head down, subservient at all times.

"*En-kírínâ*," Amali said.

Why would she be asking for a bracelet?

When Razina dutifully produced a white beaded bracelet from her wrist, about two inches wide, and held it atop her hand, I realised what I witnessing.

A Maasai courting.

Without a word, Kijani took the bracelet and walked away. Okay, so that was weird, and kinda cute. Some of the women giggled, hiding their smiles with their hands and crowding around a blushing Razina, yet Amali didn't seem too amused.

"Why is Amali not happy?" I whispered to Damu.

Damu was obviously amused by what we just saw, his playful smile gave him away. "Maasai man not choose bride. Father choose bride for him. It is the way. Kasisi not want Razina for Kijani's bride."

"Why not?"

"She has no cattle. No wealth."

I took a deep breath and bit my tongue. "But Kijani wants her?"

"It seem so, yes." Damu's smile got wider. "What you

see just now, not usual what happens. Kijani just made stand for bride."

I glanced over at Kasisi and saw that he didn't look terribly impressed. But Kijani looked back at Razina, then ducked his head and was promptly heckled by some guys in his age-set. It was funny to watch.

The ceremony continued until dusk. We took our turns drinking the goat's blood, the metallic liquid had almost congealed by then, and although it nearly made me vomit, I wouldn't disrespect them.

Afterwards we cleaned up, and I saw Damu taking something into his hut. I didn't give it another thought until we'd both gone inside after dark. There was no soup tonight, as we'd eaten our fill of meat and cabbage, but Damu stoked the fire anyway. The nights were still cold, and the small mudbrick stove provided a welcome warmth and light inside the otherwise darkened hut. It was then I noticed the cabbage leaf near our bucket of water. It had something on it.

"What's that for?" I asked, pointing to the mystery leaf.

Damu mumbled something and stoked the fire with vigour instead of answering.

Okay then.

"Damu?"

He wouldn't look at me, but at least he answered. "It is fat from the meat."

Well, that was strange... "Is it for eating?"

He paused for a moment, then shook his head, but didn't say anything else.

I scooted over and picked it up. I was closer to the fire now, and I could see his face more clearly. The fat was more what I would call grease. It was smeared and white. It was clean. Had he got this before the meat was cooked? "Damu?"

He spoke to the fire, still unwilling to look at me. "It is for you. I not know the word. Slick?"

Slick. Slick...? *Oh my God.* I whispered, "Is this for sex?"

He seemed to shrink in on himself, embarrassed. "You said..." He shook his head. "Burn in fire if you not want it. I collect this because you talked of it, and there is no meat now until next moon."

He collected it for me, because I'd told him anal sex was better with some kind of lube, and he didn't want me to wait another month. "Damu, look at me?" I waited for his eyes to meet mine. He was so horribly embarrassed. "Thank you. You are a very kind and generous man, Damu Nkorisa. It means a lot to me that you thought of me, and I am grateful."

He blinked a few times before a shy smile pulled at his lips. "You like it?"

Well, I never thought I'd like to use goat fat as a lube before, that was certain. But, whatever worked. "Yes. But just so you know, you don't have to do anything you don't want to do. Please tell me you understand that?"

He nodded. "Yes." He still looked uncertain though, like he didn't understand my meaning. I tried to think of how to word it so he'd understand, but without using the words *fucking* and *anal sex.*

"Damu, what we've been doing together makes me very happy. I don't need this"—I held up the Maasai-style lube —"to be with you. If you want to use this on me *that way,* I'm happy. If you don't want to, I'm still happy. Okay?"

He smiled, more relaxed now. "Yes."

I put the cabbage leaf back near the bucket. "Are you

tired? I am tired," I told him and scooted back over to the thin mattress.

He loaded up the fire and seemed to hesitate. He glanced quickly at me, then back to the fire.

"Damu?" I asked quietly. "Did you want to try it?"

He shot me a look, and even by the flickering light of the fire, I could see the hesitation in his face. He pretended something about the stove was fascinating. "I uh... I not..."

"Damu," I said, this time with a smile on my face. His awkwardness was rather adorable. "Bring it over."

He quickly grabbed the cabbage leaf and scooted over to the bed, making me laugh. He obviously wanted to try it, very much. I sat up on the mattress and patted the spot beside me, urging him to move closer. Once he was right beside me, I said, "Damu, if you want something, don't ever be embarrassed or ashamed to tell me. If you want it, ask me. We're in this together, okay?" I took the leaf from him and lay it on the ground near our bed, then manoeuvred my legs around him. I pulled him down with me as I lay back, and he came willingly.

We were still fully clothed, but his weight on me was welcome. His scent filling my senses, his hardening erection pressed into my groin, and his lips were barely an inch from mine. I put my hand to his face, and lifting my head a little, I kissed him softly. I knew he was too incredibly shy and inexperienced to tell me exactly what he wanted to do, so I thought I'd help him out.

"Can I tell you what I want?" I asked.

He nodded, then leaned down for another kiss. He was clearly into kissing... When I pulled my mouth away for a breath, I said, "What I want, is for us to be naked. I want to feel you against me—all of you—and I want you between my legs just like you are now. I want you to kiss me, taste me with your tongue."

He shuddered but remained silent.

"I want your hands all over me, but most all Damu, I want you inside me."

He gasped and froze. "I want too. But I not know how."

I cradled his face in my hands. "I will show you."

He nodded again. "I want, but I am also nerves and scared."

I traced my fingers over his eyebrow and down his cheek. "It's okay to be scared, and nervous." I kissed him. "I'll talk you through it, and you can stop any time you want, okay?"

He nodded again, but this time he chuckled. "I'm certain I not stop. Not want to stop."

I kissed him with smiling lips. "I'm certain you won't want to stop either. It will feel really good. Now, Damu?"

"Yes?"

"Undress me. Take my clothes off, and I'll show you how to get my body ready for you."

He'd helped me undress before, though this was different. We both knew what this meant, where this was headed, and my cock filled with anticipation. When we were both naked and Damu had covered us with our shukas, he lay beside me. I took the cabbage leaf and laid it on my chest for easy access. I was oddly reminded of that godawful novelty bacon scented lube and bit back a laugh as I realised just how absurd this Maasai kind of personal lubricant was.

"Okay," I whispered in the dark. "Did you want to touch my arse, or do you want me to do it?"

It took him a second to gather his thoughts and possibly his courage. "I want to do it. To do it for you."

I couldn't help it. I just had to kiss him for saying that.

Then I took his left hand and scooped a generous amount of the lard onto his fingers, and holding his hand in mine, I guided him toward my arse.

"You need to spread it around and inside me." I held his fingers and directed his actions, showing him where I needed it, how much pressure to apply, and how slow to do it. And my God, the slick feeling... "Oh, Damu," I whispered, my voice strained. "That feels really good. Now push inside me. One finger first." I piloted his index finger, slipping the tip into my arsehole up to the knuckle. "Oh yeah, just like that."

Soon we added a second finger, and I was pushing back against him, rolling my hips and imagining what was to come. "Now use the same amount and rub it over you."

He froze and I wasn't sure if what I'd said got mangled in translation.

"Let me do that for you," I said, swiping my finger through the makeshift lube and coating his cock with it.

"Ah, that is good." He bucked his hips forward into my fist. "So good."

"Are you ready?" I asked, letting go of his hard on. "Because I am."

He nodded again and I moved the cabbage leaf to the side. "On top of me, Damu," I said to him. "Get between my legs." He quickly did as I asked, and I could feel his long erection pressing down against my balls. "Oh God, you feel good," I whispered to him. He pressed his hips into mine and his steel-hard dick rubbed against me. My whole body ached with the need of it.

I brought my knees up toward my chest and Damu leaned back on his knees, giving me some room. "I need, Heath Crowley," he rasped out, taking his erection in his hand and pumping it. "I need and I want, too much."

I reached down and slid my hand over his and together we lined the blunt head of his cock at my hole. I felt a hunger, a need, to have him inside me. "Push in, slowly. Nice and slow." My voice was strangled, desperate. "Damu, I need you."

He pushed forward, slowly breaching the tight ring of muscle, and he fell forward onto one arm. His eyes were wide and his lips parted as he entered me.

I burned with the stretch of him, and I buzzed. Like a junkie taking a hit, he was my high, he was everything. In that moment, he was all there was. He sunk inside me, slowly and surely, he filled me.

He gasped back a breath, and the look on his face was one of complete wonder with a hint of panic, and I was reminded that this was his first time. I put my hand to his face, swiping my thumb over his cheek, reassuring him. "Damu, so good. You feel so good."

He pulled out a little, only to push back in. He bit out a groan. "What is this?" he whined against my lips. His voice was tight and strained. "What is this dream?"

I smiled at him and leaned forward so I could kiss him. "This is no dream. This is perfect."

He thrust a little harder, causing me to moan and writhe. He was fully seated inside me now. Every inch of him was filling me completely, and yet I still wanted more. I put my hands to his face and brought our mouths together, knowing it would bring him undone.

I wanted him to unravel inside me.

I slid my tongue into his mouth, tasting his tongue, and he groaned into my mouth. His whole body surged; he kissed me deeper, he thrust harder, and he cried out into my mouth as he came.

His cock thickened and hardened more, and he flexed

taut and stilled. I could feel him release inside me, his cock jerking as it spilled his come in me.

Damu collapsed on top of me. I quickly wrapped my arms around him and pulled our shukas over him.

"You possess me," he murmured into my neck.

I chuckled. "In a good way, I hope."

"Very good way." He still didn't move, but his softening cock slipped out of me. I rolled us onto our sides and Damu's face was still buried in my neck. He seemed content to never move. "I have not known such a pleasure."

I rubbed his back. "Thank you."

He pulled back then. I could just make out the concern in his eyes by the flickering fire. "What you thank me for?"

I pecked his lips with mine. "For giving me what I needed."

He was confused now. "You not finish," he said, running his hand between us down to my still-hard cock.

"I don't need that tonight," I told him. "Tonight was for you."

His hand froze on my dick. "You not want?"

I kissed him again. "Maybe later. Sleep first." I snuggled down into him and he quickly wrapped me up in his arms, in his warmth, his security.

I WOKE up on my side, with my top leg bent out in front of me. Damu was behind me, covered by our shukas, as was the same when we woke up most mornings. Though this morning, Damu was kissing my shoulder, his morning wood pressing against my arse.

"Morning," I said gruffly.

"Thought you never wake," he replied, running his

hand down my side and over my hip. I rolled back against him and his hand on my hip stopped me. He slowly pressed his hips against my arse, rubbing his impressive erection between my arse cheeks.

Oh yeah. Now that he'd topped me, I doubted he'd ever want to stop.

"You want me again?" I asked gently. I pushed my arse back, a blatant offering, in case he was unsure of my compliance. Lifting my top leg off the ground, I reached down to feel my arse. I was still slick, with both lard and come from the night before. I slipped my finger inside of me, sparking my blood on fire. I groaned. "I can feel where you came in me last night," I whispered. "I want you to do it again. Just like this. I want you to finish inside me, just like this."

Damu whimpered as he pressed his lips against my shoulder. "I not want to stop."

"Then don't."

Damu's fingers replaced mine, just like I'd shown him the night before. Soon after, his fingers were gone, and I knew it wouldn't be long... His cock pressed against my slick and ready arsehole, and he pushed inside.

"Oh, fuck," I hissed. "Yes, God Damu, just like that."

He put his hand over my mouth and his lips at my ear. "Sshhh, quiet."

I froze, wondering if anyone might have heard me, but there was only silence. The sky was only beginning to lighten, we still had a bit of time before the kraal was awake and busy. I moaned at the feeling of being breached. I needed him to move...

Damu rolled his hips, sliding out a little only to push further back in. His hand still covered my mouth, his lips now tugged on my ear, his warm breath punctuated with soft kisses, and I was in heaven.

It felt so good. He was taking me, filling me and fucking me, as he wished. He was in charge of my body, and I gave it willingly.

I reached down and gripped my cock, already slick at the tip. I pumped myself in time with his deep thrusts. I was so turned on, being fucked like that, it only took a few passes of my hand and my orgasm uncoiled from deep in my balls. I arched against him, flexed taut as I came in strips into the dirt in front of me. Damu held on to me, pulling me hard against him, and giving me every inch of his cock. His fingernails bit into my hip and his teeth bit into my shoulder as he came. He groaned, long and low, his whole body shuddering as he emptied himself inside me.

It took a moment for us both to catch our breaths. He didn't pull out, and I didn't want him to.

"Heath Crowley," he murmured into the back of my neck. "You have possessed me. I not want to ever stop."

I half chuckled, half groaned as he slipped out of me. "You can wake me up like that every day." I sat up, and given we were a sticky, slicked mess, and that the sun was almost up, I said, "We better get to the river."

So we covered up with our shukas, pulling them high around our necks to brace from the morning chill, and went outside. Damu stood up to full height and shook his head as if to clear it.

"You okay?" I asked.

"My head spin, that is all," he replied.

I couldn't help but laugh quietly. "Dizziness from too much sex," I whispered.

He put his hand to his mouth to hide his smile, but he was totally proud of it. When we got out of the kraal gates and went toward the river a ways, he pushed my shoulder with a laugh. "You not say those thing to me! No talk of the... what you said."

There wasn't anyone near us for a hundred metres, but I whispered anyway. "What? Sex?"

Damu's eyes went wide and his dark cheeks flushed cherry red. "That!"

"Why?" I asked. "Because you're really good at it. What you did this morning was hot! Very good."

He stopped walking and put both his hands over his face. "Heath Crowley, stop that." He groaned, but eventually looked at me. "Was it? Good?"

I just laughed. "It was incredible."

He tried not to smile, but his whole face became a grin. It was adorable. He put his hands out, flat and final. "Okay. Now not talk of it," he said, taking a few long strides to catch up to me. "Talk of something else."

He was still smiling, and he had a spring in his step: he was the happiest I'd seen him, but he wasn't comfortable in talking about sex and that was fair enough. It was so new to him, and ultimately it was a taboo subject. Talking about it in the cold light of day made it real, and I could appreciate his reaction. "What did you want to talk about?" I asked.

"Tell me of your cities."

Oh, okay. Not what I was expecting, but whatever. "Well, I'm from Sydney. There are over four million people who live there."

"That is a lot, yes?"

"Well, compared to some cities, no. But compared to here," I swept my hand out to the open plains, "yes."

"And they all be happy there?"

"For the most part, yes. Every city has some problems, just like villages or even kraals do. Sometimes people argue, but mostly it is a happy place."

He seemed to think about that for a minute or two. Then he asked, "And your homes?"

"They're all different. Some people live in big houses, some in small houses. Some in units or flats, where there are lots of small houses in one big building."

"But not like our home?"

I almost laughed until I realised his question was a serious one. "No. Not like yours."

"Ours," he said, motioning between us. "Mine and yours."

I smiled at that and relished the warmth that spread through my chest. "Ours."

He beamed. "I have seen—" He seemed stuck for the right word. "—small picture of city."

"Like a postcard? Or a photograph?"

He nodded. "Very tall homes."

"Yes, the buildings are tall. Which city did you see?"

"Dar es Saalam."

"Would you like to go there?" I asked. "Not now, but someday."

He chewed on his lip and contemplated his answer. "I would. I would like to see it." I could see this was a brave decision on his behalf.

"Then I will take you. One day, we shall go. You know, Dar es Saalam is a bit like Sydney, where I am from."

"It is busy. Many people."

"Yes. Lots of people. There are shops for clothes and food, cinemas with huge screens and surround sound, clubs with music, libraries with thousands of books. Cities have many things."

He eyed me cautiously. "I not know those things."

I gave him a warm smile. "I will show you everything."

He smiled, and as we got to the river, he looked up at the sky. "We need to hurry. Rain will come."

I looked up at the blue, cloudless sky. "From where?"

"Listen."

I listened, and all I heard was the river. "Water?"

He tilted his head. "No. Tipitipi."

"What?" I whispered, trying to hear what it was he was hearing.

"Tipitipi is bird."

"Oh."

"Sings before rains." Damu unwrapped his shuka and edged down to the river. He filled the bucket first, then undressed fully and walked into the water. I undressed too and joined him, the cold water a welcome reprieve to my tender arse, though the cold water didn't help when trying to wash away our makeshift lube. I started to laugh. "The goat fat solidifies in cold water!"

Damu laughed with me, until he saw my shoulder. "What is that?"

I looked down at the red bite mark on my skin. "Where you bit me this morning."

He froze. "I did not, Heath Crowley."

I was going to tell him to just call me Heath, but I quite liked how he said my full name. It was endearing. I splashed some water over the offending mark and rubbed it with my fingers. "It's fine," I said. "It doesn't hurt. And actually, I liked it when you did it."

He still hadn't taken his eyes off the bite mark, and he stepped closer, gently touching the pink lines on my shoulder. "I did this?"

Standing in the water, I was reminded of how much taller he was than me when I had to look up to see his face. "Yes. When I possessed you, and you lost your mind."

"I am sorry," he murmured. "I know not what I do when I am with you like that."

"It's fine, Damu," I said as reassuringly as I could. "I liked it."

"They cannot see this," he said flatly. "No one can see this."

"No, they won't. I promise," I said, not breaking eye contact. I knew what the discovery of our secret would mean, so I needed to reassure him the best I could. "I will keep it covered."

He was a little quiet after that, pensive even, as we washed and dressed, and true to my word, I kept my shuka over my shoulders like a scarf. I collected some o'remiti leaves and Damu collected some berries, and we headed back to the kraal.

Damu told Kijani and Kasisi of the bird calls he'd heard by the river. Kasisi was grateful, and Kijani barely looked in our direction.

I wasn't sure if Kijani had stopped noticing us because his attentions were focused on Razina or if he'd just accepted me as part of his world now. But either way, it appeared I was no longer on his radar and that was more than fine with me.

But Damu's word of rain set the village in motion. Herding was kept short, the women secured their homes, and sure enough by mid-afternoon, it was pouring rain.

If these were the short rains, then that had to mean it was early November. I really had lost all sense of time. I probably should have been alarmed by that, being so removed from the outside world that days, and months could pass without a thought. But in fact, it was the complete opposite. I loved it. I had no other reason to mark the passing of time, because I was enjoying every minute. I was happy. Disconnected from everything I'd known, from the misery that had been my life, I was happy here in our dark little mud hut with no electricity or running water.

As the sound of the rain hammered the roof, I crept along the dirt floor to where Damu was resting on his bed. "You know what I like best about the afternoon rains?"

"What's that?"

"Being alone in here with you." I pressed my mouth to his, kissing him with a promise of more to come. I climbed on top of him, settling my weight on him. "How long will it rain for?"

"Every afternoon, for one moon."

Every afternoon of make out sessions for a month. My smile was slow spreading, and I kissed him again. "Perfect."

CHAPTER TWELVE

THE GREY CROWNED crane circles overhead, much like a vulture waiting for the last breath to leave the lungs of its next meal. Waiting for the tired and weakened body to be resigned to its fate.

The bird circles above, not silently, but with a mechanical roar. It's so absurd that the elegant crane would sound like an engine, but the noise belies its grace as it glides through the air.

It has something in its mouth. A stick, I think at first, as we all stand and watch. A crowd has gathered to observe it, though the women quickly usher their children into the safety of their homes.

No, the bird isn't holding a stick in its mouth. Is it a pen?

Kijani and the new warriors shake their spears at it, threatening it to dare land here.

Then the pen starts to leak, drops of ink fall like rain on the Maasai people. The ink is red, and as a drip splashes my face, I swipe it with my hand. Dark red stains my skin, with a metallic odour, so I put it to my tongue, only to taste it isn't ink at all.

It's blood.

As each drop of blood-ink drips from the pen the bird is holding, the drops fall like acid on the people below. Just one drop, hitting men, elders, warriors and the women and children, and they fall to their knees and without a sound, without a fight, they vanish from where they once stood.

I WOKE UP WITH A START. I wasn't sweating or thrashing like I sometimes did when my dreams were bad, and this dream wasn't particularly horrible, but this was by no means pleasant.

It was downright disturbing, and I had no clue what to make of it.

"Are you okay?" Damu asked.

I sat up and rubbed my eyes. "Bad dream."

"You not have bad dream for long time," Damu said.

I shook my head. "No. It was different. There was a bird. Like the ones on the Serengeti with the orange comb. Is it *n-káítōle⁻*?"

"N-káítōlē," Damu repeated. "Crane?"

"Yes."

He tilted his head, concerned. "And it was bad?"

"Yes. It was a crane, but it wasn't. It sounded wrong, like an engine, and it carried a pen that killed people." I shook my head, and my dream dissipated from my mind like smoke. I laughed it off. "It was weird."

Damu eyed me cautiously but never said anything more about it. We went about our day as normal, doing all our chores before the afternoon rains. I didn't think anything more about that dream, until I had the exact same dream the next night.

I woke up, my stomach turning with unease. I sat up, trying to get my breath.

"What is it?" Damu asked sleepily.

"I need to speak to Kasisi," I said, crawling toward the door. "Now, Damu. I need to speak to him now."

The sun was barely making an appearance, the sky was just starting to lighten on the horizon. The air was cool and I wrapped my shuka around my shoulders like a scarf. Damu quickly fell into step beside me, and when we got to Kasisi's home, Damu put his hand out to stop me from speaking. It had to be Damu who called his name.

The tribal chief witchdoctor came outside. He pulled his shuka around his ears and held his talisman that I now knew to once be a tail on an antelope.

"Alé wishes to speak with you," Damu said, slightly bowing his head.

"You dreamed of something," Kasisi said, matter of factly. I had no clue what his talents as a seer were, but he had visions of some sort. It was this talent that made him the witchdoctor or diviner.

I nodded to him. "I have."

"Tell of it."

I explained my dream to him, including the crane that sounded like an engine and the pen that dropped acidic blood and made the people of this kraal disappear.

"It makes no sense to me," I admitted. "Normally my dreams are exact and very vivid. This is like a puzzle. I don't understand."

Kasisi looked up at Damu, then back to me. "Dream has you worry?"

"I've dreamed the same dream twice," I said, holding up two fingers. "Two nights, exact same dream."

By this time, Kijani had come over. He was curious at

first, then he became concerned. "What it mean?" he barked at me.

"Um, *ma yolo*," I answered. "I don't know." I wanted to speak in Maa as much as I could to show these men that I'd made the effort to assimilate, to be a part of their people.

"That is all?" Kijani asked.

"*Ayeh*," I replied. *Yes.*

He shooed me away before turning to Kasisi and talking like I didn't exist. Damu grabbed my arm and pulled me away, and figuring I'd done all I could do, I went willingly. We took the bucket down to the river and went about our normal morning. We drank uji for breakfast and we watched the boys take the cattle out of the kraal to graze for the day. Damu and I waited at the gates for them to pass, and that's when we heard it.

An engine.

Someone was coming.

Makumu came running in through the fence, yelling for Kijani and Kasisi, and in no time every warrior filed out with military precision, spears at the ready. They were a sight to behold. Frightening and fierce, yet completely prehistoric, but incredible all the same.

Damu and I stayed back behind the acacia thorn fence, though Damu stood taller, prouder, his eyes wide, on keen alert. He also kept a hand on my arm. The women had taken the smaller children into their homes, though Amali and Yantai stood outside, too curious to stay hidden.

The vehicle came into view as it came over the crest of the hill. The loud roar of the engine was such a foreign sound.

I'd been here for eight or so months, and I'd almost forgotten what cars sounded like. Except for the one in my dream the last two nights...

It was a white Land Rover that approached the many-atta. It crawled to a stop, and two men got out. The passenger was an older man with greying hair and ruddy cheeks, wearing a suit straight out of the 1980s. The driver was a shorter, thin man who wore khakis, and he looked like a safari guide. The man in the suit waved nervously to the line of warriors. "Hello," he said loudly.

The guide man translated. "*Sopa*."

Kijani stepped forward, his spear held tight. "What you want here?"

"Ah, you speak English. Good, good," the man said. I wasn't sure if he was relieved by that or not. I got the feeling he was hoping no one would understand a word he was here to say. "I have come from government office in Arusha."

He handed over a folded piece of paper. Was it a letter? Any kind of letter from the government can't be good.

Kijani opened the letter and handed it to Kasisi. He turned back to the man in the suit and thumped his spear into the dirt. "What you want here?" he repeated. His tone and temper did little to hide his loathing.

The suit man smiled back at him. "Oh, can you not read English?"

He knew damn well no one here could read English...

"Alé!" Kasisi called. "Alé!"

I walked through the gateway, with Damu close behind me. We were a package deal: where I went, he went, and that was more than fine with me.

Suit man was clearly shocked to see another white man, especially one within the ranks of the Maasai. I went to Kasisi, and it was then I noticed the bird symbol on the side of the vehicle. I nodded toward it. "N-káítole," I said. "The crane I saw. It sounded like a truck."

Kasisi and Kijani exchanged glances.

"And it carried blood ink," I added, now looking at the letter.

Kasisi handed me the folded piece of paper. The Government of the United Republic of Tanzania was emblazoned across the header, and I read the letter aloud.

In a bunch of legalese, the letter went on to disclose how taxes were an important part of all contributing citizens, and then in the very next sentence it went on to spruik about the benefits of tourism, and how Maasai communities, who welcomed tourists, were a great benefit to the economy.

It said, in the interest of local tourism and subsequent economical benefits, the Government is taking the initiative to encourage local transient communities to engage in such developments.

Then the final paragraph was the real kicker. In the event such nomadic communities cannot contribute in accordance with the taxation legislation, as the Government is the rightful landowner, such transient occupiers will be displaced from such lands.

I looked at the man in the suit, who tried to look sympathetic, but the smug bastard couldn't quite pull it off. My hands started to shake and rage started to bubble and fester in my gut.

"What is it?" Damu asked. "Alé?"

Kasisi and Kijani were looking at me. Actually, everyone was looking at me.

"This letter"—I held up the letter in the direction of the suit man—"says your people need to pay tax or you'll be forced to leave."

There was complete silence.

And proving just how ill-equipped these people were to deal with white man's law, Kijani asked, "What is tax?"

Suit man choked back a laugh, and I glared at him. I took a step toward him and raised my finger at him. "You have no right! *Káíkínō ená kōp,*" I spat at him. "They are born unto this land. They have rights!"

Suit man would have probably laughed at me, if I weren't surrounded by Maasai warriors wielding spears and clubs. Damu stood on my right, tall and imposing, his rungu still holstered in his belt. Kijani and Kasisi stood on my left, both holding their spears with intent, and if Suit Man were a gambling man, he'd know better than to speak.

He simply scurried into the truck and they drove away.

We all stood in silence and watched as the cloud of dust disappeared, and the rumble of the engine finally faded, Kasisi turned to me. "Tell what this blood ink means."

Blood ink. My dream, the blood ink that made these people disappear, now made perfect sense.

AS IT TURNED OUT, Kijani knew what taxes were, just not what it meant in specific relation to his village. I explained that the local government was now seeking taxes for the land they occupied, which, of course, was not received well. I sat in a meeting of sorts with Kasisi and the other elders. Damu sat beside me, as always, and Kijani paced.

"This is Maasai land," Kijani said, shaking his spear at the sky.

"I know," I replied softly, trying to bring some calm into the equation. I was pissed off for these people, but me raging at them would only add fuel to their fire. "I told that white man you were born of this land, but he doesn't care. They just want money."

"You defend us to your people," Kasisi said, a smile pulled at his lips.

I met his gaze. "*They* are not my people." I left the 'You are my people' unsaid. Having them stand at my side when I yelled at the government official meant more than I could let on. I needed to be humble in my gratitude. "I will stand with you. As you have stood with me."

Kasisi smiled briefly. "Your dreams prove true."

I nodded. "Yes. It would seem so."

Mposi asked, "What of the blood ink that falls? We disappear now?"

"I think what my dream signified was the ink is our blood, and if we don't pay the taxes, we will be gone from this land."

Kijani growled in frustration. "We not be moved. We fight!"

"You can't fight this," I said gently. How could I explain that fighting the government with spears was like throwing rocks at a freight train? "They're too big. They don't fight battles with spears and shields. They fight with rules and laws."

"Not Maasai law!" Kijani cried.

I looked at him then. "I know! It's wrong and it's not fair. But they will do it anyway."

"You dream how we beat them?" Kasisi asked.

"No." I shook my head slowly. "I haven't seen."

"Then we wait until you dream," he replied with a hard nod.

What? "No you can't," I said. I felt Damu tense beside me, but I didn't dare look at him. "You can't wait, Kasisi.

You must act now. Don't wait. They won't give you a second chance."

Kijani stopped pacing and stared at me, and I wondered if I'd spoken out of turn, or if telling the chief *no* was some heinous crime punishable by god only knew what. Kijani took a step closer to me, and Kasisi put up his hand, stopping Kijani in his tracks. "What would you do?" Kasisi asked me. "You white man, what would white man do?"

Well, shit. *What would I do?* "I'd do what the letter tells us to do. They tell us to be a part of tourism, to earn money to pay the taxes. Many other Maasai tribes invite travellers to come and stay with them for money. People like me are very fascinated by the Maasai people, and they will pay to stay for a few days."

I had their full attention, though I didn't dare make eye contact with Kijani.

"If the government is asking you to pay taxes, they will have asked other Maasai tribes as well. Go and speak with them. Have a meeting, seek counsel. One manyatta is small in people, many manyatta is big in people. Gather knowledge from other elders, work together." I let my hands fall into my lap, hoping they understood what I was trying to say. "That is what I would do."

"We not take white man's money," Kijani said coldly. "We not take white man's law."

I supressed a sigh. "There is no choice." I stared directly at Kasisi. "There is no choice."

Kasisi stared back at me for the longest moment before his brow furrowed as he frowned. With a flick of his hand, I was dismissed. Damu was quick to his feet, and with his hand on my elbow, he led me toward the goat pen.

Without a word between us, we quickly herded the goats out. The animals were impatient to graze, and we hurried along with them to our familiar pasture. We wouldn't have long today—our morning had been cut in half by the visitors—and the afternoon rains wouldn't wait for anyone.

When we stopped walking, I stood in the warming sun, finally able to draw a breath. "Ugh. Kijani is so stubborn," I cried, letting out some of my frustration.

"He carries weight of all people," Damu replied, still defending the brother who despised him.

"Yes, I understand that," I admitted. And I *did* understand, but goddammit, Kijani's attitude would see the whole village evicted from their homes. "He is a good warrior, he is brave and fierce. But this is a fight he won't win with a spear."

Damu was quiet as he looked over the goats. He was clearly worried, and my heart hurt for him. "You are afraid for your people," I said softly.

"Yes."

"So am I."

He nodded and gave me a sad smile. "You tell them to speak with other Maasai people. Is good you say that."

"I hope Kasisi agrees. He is a very smart man." I tapped my temple. "And he thinks only of his people."

"You like him?"

"Yes. Your father is a good man."

Damu smiled genuinely now. My confession pleased him. "He like you."

"He does?" I asked, unable to hide my surprise.

"You have eyes of Kafir. You dream prophecy. He like you."

"Who was Kafir?" I asked. I'd forgotten that Kasisi had told them I had the same eyes as someone called Kafir. "Amali told me he protected the manyatta, but who was he?

The one with eyes like mine? Was he an outcast because of his eyes?"

Damu laughed loudly, making the goats all look at us. "Kafir was lion."

My mouth fell open. "A *lion*? I thought he was some nomadic warrior?"

"No warrior. Yes, brave lion. It is said that Kafir and Kasisi's father fought for much time. In the end, both be too tired to kill the other. Kasisi's father say Kafir is great warrior and let Kafir live. Then Kafir is grateful and honours Kasisi's father by protecting his people."

I was speechless. "Wow. That's a great story! Did that really happen?"

Damu nodded proudly. "Story all children learn."

"Your grandfather, your *nkoko*, fought a lion?"

Damu was grinning now. "Yes. Lion with two different eyes."

"Like me. That's why Kasisi let me stay here?" I asked.

He nodded. "And you dream."

"My dreams are both a blessing and a curse. Good and bad."

His smile faded and he deliberately looked over the goats instead of at me. "Do you dream of me?"

I wasn't sure why, but his question made my heart hammer, and the butterflies in my belly took flight. "Yes," I answered.

His eyes shot to mine. "Good dream?"

I grinned at him. "Very good dreams."

It took him a minute to get the innuendo. "Oh."

I laughed. "Not *all* dreams of you are about sex. Sometimes we just walk in the tall grass. Sometimes we sit and watch over the Serengeti. Sometimes you hold my hand."

His eyes were molten, and I could almost feel them

burning into me as he stared. He put his hand to his chest, as if to tame his heart, and I knew then it wasn't just me who felt this way.

His voice was just a whisper. "Have you dream of me not here?"

I wasn't sure I understood his question. "Have I dreamed of us together when we're somewhere else?"

He nodded. "You see us be somewhere else?"

I wasn't sure how to answer... I didn't want to upset him, but the truth was, I hadn't. "Only here."

He blinked a few times, his disappointment written on his face.

"Did you want to be somewhere else with me?"

His eyes met mine for a brief moment before he searched the horizon. "Future. Not for now, but future."

Oh, he wanted to know if I saw us together, not in another place, but in another time. "Do you want to know if we're together in the future? If I've seen that?"

He didn't look at me, but he nodded.

"I haven't seen it in my dreams," I admitted. "But I feel it here." I put his hand to my heart. "For the first time in a long time, I have hope in here."

He smiled the most beautiful smile. "As do I."

IT WAS DECIDED KASISI, Kijani, and Makumu would walk to a neighbouring manyatta. Our closest neighbours were a full day's walk away, and by the time other elders were called upon and travelled back, they would be gone for a week.

It wasn't the best of circumstances, but I felt a great relief. There were no watchful eyes, no one trying to glare a hole into the side of my head. The first afternoon they were gone, our chores were done when the rains started, so I fell back on the thin mattress with a sigh.

"Care to join me?" I asked Damu.

He chuckled. "Yes, but someone may see or hear."

"I'll be very quiet," I goaded, suggestively running my hand down over my dick.

His eyes darkened and his voice dropped. "Heath Crowley, I have no power to stop. You know this."

I bit my bottom lip, trying not to smile. "That's why I suggested it."

He scoffed, but quickly crawled over me. He pinned my wrists to the mattress and brought his lips to mine. I leaned up and stole a kiss, making him laugh. "You have no power either, it seem."

"I want you," I whispered. I was suddenly vulnerable and exposed, being honest with emotions was never easy. Especially for me, especially after Jarrod... "I feel alive when you are with me. When you are inside me."

Damu closed his eyes slowly. A shiver ran up his spine. I spread my legs and hooked my ankles around the back of his thighs, keeping him right where he was. I could feel how much he wanted this; his erection pressed against my own.

The storm picked up outside, winds swarmed, and the rain fell at an angle. No one would be out in this weather.

"Please Damu," I whispered, rolling my hips into his.

When he crashed his mouth onto mine and kissed me like he owned me, I knew I would get what I wanted. He wasted no time in grabbing the last of the makeshift lube, and I quickly rolled over onto my stomach. We'd never had sex in this position—we'd only ever done missionary—and he stopped, unsure.

I lifted my hips and pulled my shorts down to reveal my arse. "Lay over me," I whispered. "Quickly."

He did just that, pulling up his shuka and pulling his loin cloth down. Then I felt his long erection in the crease of my arse. "You are not ready," he murmured in my ear.

"Please Damu, just do it."

The head of his cock slid over where I needed him most. He was slicked up, but still unsure. I lifted my hips and spread my thighs, out of patience. He put his weight on my back and pushed his hips into me. I felt the pop as he breached me, the burn and ache was everything I needed. "Oh yeah," I gasped.

He groaned in my ear as he pushed all the way in, and when he was fully seated inside me, he stopped. "What you do to me?" he asked, his lips teasing the back of my neck. "I cannot resist you."

I raised my arse, urging him to please, *please* move. "Don't resist me," I whispered.

"*Kayieu...*" he murmured, his voice strained. "*Kayieu...*"

I want... I want...

"Have me, take me," I bit out.

And so he did.

Damu pulled out to his tip then slammed all the way back in, causing me to cry out in pleasure. He dug his fingers into my hips, then slammed into me again, making every nerve in my body sing. He ran his hands up my sides, along my arms, to entwine his fingers with mine. His thighs were between my spread legs, his hips at my arse as he hammered into me. He kissed my neck and whispered my name. He was everywhere, all around me, inside me, fucking me exactly as I needed. In that moment, he was everything. He was everything.

Any sounds we made were drowned out by the storm

outside, and as the wind howled and the rain poured down. He thrust into me one final time before crying out; his whole body jerked as he came. His orgasm rippled through him, and I could feel the swell and surge of his cock as he emptied himself inside me.

I didn't need my own orgasm to feel sated. I felt relieved, the desperation had eased; I felt wanted and needed. I felt... part of something bigger than me.

Damu slowly pulled out of me and rolled me onto my side to face him. He kissed me softly, adoringly, his gentle fingers traced lines through my hair. I closed my eyes and relished the familiar warmth of his arms. He pulled my shuka over me like a blanket, and I dozed.

It was dreamless, though something was knocking on the periphery of my subconscious mind. I didn't know what it was, but there were whispers, like the wind through the Serengeti grass. I couldn't touch it, I couldn't chase it, I couldn't explain it, but I woke up certain of one thing.

There were changes coming.

EVERY DAY that week in the afternoon rains and as evening fell over the manyatta, Damu and I fell onto our bed and fooled around. We'd run out of our makeshift lube, so while we were limited as to what we could do, it certainly didn't stop us from doing everything else.

It was easy to forget we were in the middle of a world that would have us dead for doing what we did. Well, for me it was easy to forget... Damu, on the other hand, seemed to be constantly on guard.

One day, we'd brought the goats back early and I was in the classroom with the kids and a few of the women. We'd progressed to basic sentences and math sums now, and I was distracted by the sound of Damu laughing.

He was helping Amali carry the leather hides out to dry in the sun. The sight of him with his head back, laughing with abandon at something Amali had said, stole my breath.

He was everything good in my life. When everything had been dark and cold, he was the sun and warmth. I couldn't take my eyes off him.

"Alé!" Momboa had called, snapping me out of my thoughts. He giggled, and the children made fun of me for staring at Damu.

It would have been cute, if not for the curious looks some of the mother's gave me and the furious glare Damu had shot in my direction before he disappeared. A nervousness twisted in my belly, but I laughed it off and went back to repeating the sentences about lions and zebras.

When the afternoon storms rolled in, I ran to our house to find Damu sitting by the fireplace. His arms folded across his chest, his brow creased.

"What is it?"

He shook his head, still not looking at me, he spoke to the dying embers in the fireplace. "You should not look at me with those eyes. Not where others can see."

Those eyes? "How was I looking at you?"

He whispered, "*A-sanja*."

"What is a-sanja?" It wasn't a word I'd heard before...

"Lover. That is man."

Oh. "Did I look at you that way?" I asked, though I knew I did. I sat on the dirt floor, with my feet tucked up underneath me, feeling the weight of his anger on my shoulders. "I didn't mean to. But you laughed in the sunlight, and it was so beautiful."

His shoulders fell, and he slowly closed the distance

between us. Kneeling before me, he put his hand to my cheek, his long fingers lifted my chin. His face was an inch from mine, a dozen emotions swam in his eyes. "Heath Crowley, you look at me with those eyes in here, not out there," he whispered, and the rain began to fall. "They are not to see that."

"I'm sorry," I whispered.

"They cannot know."

"I know," I murmured, unable to stop the tears pooling in my eyes. "I forget where I am when I am with you."

He kissed me softly. "I wish it were not this way. I wish to be free with you."

I looked up at him then. "What?"

He sat back on his haunches, and I held his hands on his knees. "I am never free here. Only with you. I am free with you."

My heart squeezed with the pain of his words. "I am only free when I'm with you too."

"I wish to be free with you always," he murmured. "Not in our home, but in daylight as well."

I knew exactly what he was saying. He wanted to be free to be himself, not just in the privacy and darkness of our hut. But this country, this culture, was unforgiving of homosexuals. He wanted to come out in a world that would have him executed for doing so. It just wasn't possible.

And it broke my heart.

"I wish for that too." I squeezed his hands. "Damu Nkorisa, look at me." I waited for his gaze to meet mine. "I am sorry for what happened today. I told the children I looked at you because it made me happy to see my brother happy. They understood that. But I'll be mindful next time, and I won't do it again."

He gave me a sad smile. "I worry, that is all."

"I know. And rightfully so. I'll be more careful next time."

He seemed mollified and eventually he smiled more genuinely. "You say I was beautiful again."

I laughed. "Yes. You are. Handsome and beautiful. I couldn't help but look at you."

Damu chuckled, embarrassed. I truly do think I am the only person who had ever given him a compliment. He liked to hear it but didn't know what to do with it. Knowing Damu, he probably felt narcissistic because it made him feel good about himself. He was a paradox, for sure. He was proud of who he was, yet unable to see his own worth.

I put my hand to his face. "Am I forgiven?"

He nodded, and I drew him in for a kiss. Our kiss deepened and we were soon on our bed, me on my back and Damu lying between my legs. He pulled his mouth from mine. "Is it wrong to be impatient for next feast?" he asked, kissing along my jaw. "Not for eat meat, but for the fat."

I chuckled and ran my hands down over his arse, pulling him hard against me. "I am impatient for that as well."

He hooked my left leg over his hip and ground his steel-like erection against me. His other hand pushed my hair off my forehead and his eyes searched mine. "I want inside you again."

Oh, fuck. "I want that too," I whispered, barely able to speak.

He crushed his mouth to mine in an all-consuming kiss. I brought my knees up toward our chests, and Damu rutted against me. I held onto his arse, keeping him right where he was, grinding our cocks together through our clothes.

In no time at all, he stilled over me, his head thrown back in ecstasy as he came. The sight above me and the feel of his cock pulsing and spilling was too much. I came with him, shooting between us, both of us collapsing in a heap of tangled limbs and mingled breaths.

As the rain hammered down the most soothing lullaby, and with his weight on top of me, I dozed again.

Not quite awake, not really asleep, a familiar dream played through my mind. The winds blew through the grasses, though the sun shined. This time Damu was there, looking as he had in the sun earlier that day. He held his hand out to me, I had no clue where he was leading me, but I entwined my fingers with his anyway. Because I knew, even in subconscious thought, I'd go with him anywhere.

I WAS WOKEN by a tap on the leg, and Damu whispering, urging me to get up. When I sat up, trying to clear my sleep-fogged brain, I heard the commotion.

Kasisi, Kijani, and Makumu were back.

I followed Damu out, just as the three men came back. They were welcomed with offerings of beans, rice, and milk—a hero's welcome—and as the sun set, the weary travellers sat by the communal fire and told their people what they knew.

Kasisi spoke in Maa, and although I didn't catch everything, I understood most of it. "Other tribes had received the same letter," he said. "All Maasai people were to start paying taxes on the land they occupied. Many other tribes, like them, had no income to do so. Some clans welcomed tourists for short visits, as the government had suggested—" Kasisi looked at me then. Kijani glared at me. "—and it is something this tribe should consider."

Kijani still stared at me, like I was personally responsible for their current situation. I had no doubts on his stance on this tourism idea. The way his nostrils flared and his jaw bulged told me all I needed to know.

Kasisi raised his hand. "More talks to come," he said. "For now sleep."

Everyone dispersed in whispered conversations. Whatever decisions the elders made for this tribe, would affect each and every one of the people in it. Damu was quick to take my elbow and ushered me to our hut.

The fire was going inside, and I could see his expression. He was worried. "You okay?" I asked.

He spoke so softly, I barely heard him. "I not like how Kijani look to you."

"He's angry and defensive," I replied. *My God, now I was defending him?* "I think he blames me for the white man taxes."

Damu's brow furrowed. "You are not for blame."

"We know that," I said gently. "Kasisi knows, but Kijani needs someone to blame, and I have the right coloured skin for his anger."

Damu's eyes flashed with something I hadn't seen in him before. Was it anger? "You be white man or not, make no different to me."

That made me smile. I squeezed his hand. "And that's what makes you a good man."

Damu didn't reply to that. Instead, he said, "You not be near him."

"Kijani?"

He gave the smallest nod. "I not like his eyes for you."

He was worried for me, and that pleased me more than it should. "And you not be near him either," I countered. "If he blames me, he might think you know something."

He shrugged one shoulder. "He not like me."

"He blames you for something that was not your fault, just like he blames me for this government tax. He might mean well, but he doesn't see clearly. His temper clouds his judgement."

Damu sighed. "Kasisi will see truth."

"He will," I agreed. I ran my thumb over the back of his hand. I hated seeing him so down. His usual happy, peaceful aura was gone. "You know, I dreamed of you this afternoon," I said wistfully.

His gaze shot to mine, then to my smile. "You did?"

I nodded slowly. "Yep."

"Good dream? A dream of future?"

My diversion tactic worked, because he smiled. "It was a good dream. Peaceful. We were walking in the grass. You looked so happy in the sunlight, and you held out your hand to me."

"It will happen?" he asked, hope brightened his eyes.

"I think it will."

His smile became a grin. "Let us eat," he said happily. He scooted over to the stove and heated bean stew and potatoes. We'd eaten the same thing for a week, but I was still grateful for every meal. We ate in companionable silence, and after we'd rinsed out our bowls, we lay down on our bed.

I made myself the little spoon, using Damu's arm as my pillow, and he covered us with our shukas. He settled his arm around my waist, his lips at my ear. I felt the weight of sleep taking me under, when Damu murmured, "Did you hold my hand? In your dream? Out in the sun, where someone would see? You take my hand?"

I pulled his arm tighter around me and sighed. "Yes. Of course I did."

WE SPENT the next week under the watchful eye of Kijani. As much as we tried to avoid him, he was there. When he wasn't in meetings with the other elders and warriors and when he wasn't courting around Razina, he was never far from us.

Even as we did our chores and when we herded the goats, I could feel his eyes on us, and sure enough, every time I looked for him, he was watching. It seemed I was his new focus. His new role was to be a pain in my arse.

Damu and I kept a platonic distance from each other, always mindful not to touch, not to even look for longer than would be deemed respectable.

But the nights were ours. I'd suggested that we should sleep apart, my little corner of dirt floor wasn't that far from him, after all. But Damu frowned. "It is the only time I have you near, in the night. My true self is when I lay with you," he whispered. "He not take that from me."

It was such an honest response, I wasn't sure what I could say. So I simply slid over to him, cupped his cheek, and kissed him. I lay down next to him, and I certainly never questioned it again. Once night fell and the stove fire was out, inside our hut was so dark, even if Kijani looked through the door, he wouldn't be able to see us.

The Maasai had a saying, Damu told me. "Eyes cannot pierce the darkness." He kissed the back of my head and tightened his arm around me. "Yet I dream of days when I hold you in the sunlight."

I turned in his arms and kissed his lips. Neither of us moved to deepen the kiss before I snuggled back into his neck. "One day, Damu. I promise you."

CHAPTER THIRTEEN

I WOKE IN A PANIC. My ears still rang with the sound of thundering hooves that echoed the hammering of my heart. The bed was empty, Damu was gone, and the sun was already over the horizon.

I'd overslept, and I'd dreamed the most frightening thing... Adrenaline still pumped through my blood, my fear on high alert.

I raced out of the hut, looking for Damu. He'd never left the hut without me before, and I needed to find him.

"Damu!" I called out. "Damu!"

Yantai turned to face me, alarmed at my urgency, and pointed toward the cattle pens.

I ran past Yantai's hut and saw Damu being spoken to by Kijani. It didn't look too amicable, but I didn't have time for that right now.

The cattle pen was empty...

"Damu!" I called again as I ran towards them, and both he and Kijani stopped and stared. "The cattle?"

"Momboa and Jaali take them early," he said, a mix of confused and cautious.

Oh no...

"We must go," I cried. I started to run toward the gate in the acacia fence. "I dreamed of this. We must run!"

I didn't wait to see if anyone followed, I just ran. I ran as fast as I could in the direction the boys had taken the cattle every day that week. It was toward the ridge line, a long way down, then into a valley. The rains had brought fresh grass shoots there.

Damu was soon running alongside me, his long legs and lean body outmatched me, and soon he was in front of me. He didn't even know why he was running. He didn't question me, he trusted in my judgement, he trusted me, and he simply ran.

My God, he was fast.

He reached the crest of the valley before me and he stopped. Down the slopes and leading out toward the plains of the Serengeti basin, was a herd of cattle and two small boys.

Damu turned to face me as I got there. "They are there," he said, his brow furrowed. "What is wrong?"

Then we heard it.

The same sound that woke me from my nightmare. It was the sound of a hundred hooves. In my dream, the thunderous sound trampled the bodies of two small boys...

Damu turned, like in slow motion, just as the first of the wildebeest broke through the valley, and they were headed straight toward Momboa. He was just a boy, no more than five years old, too damn young to be out here. Too damn young to die.

I'd started running down the slope before I knew what I was doing. Damu called out to me, but I wouldn't stop. I had to do something.

The stampede of wildebeest looked like a brown tumultuous river, flooding down through the valley, destroying everything in its path. Adrenaline overruled my fear, though my brain was screaming at me to stop. I ran anyway. I saw a flash of red flanking my right, and I knew it was Damu.

I ran directly toward the boys, who were now standing stock still, staring at what was coming toward them. Damu ran wider, I realised, to try to sway the wildebeest to change course, running at them from the side with his herding stick held high. Jesus, he was so much faster than me.

I reached Momboa first and scooped him off his feet. We landed near Jaali, and I cradled them, shielding them the best I could, as the first of the stampede ran past.

The boys' screams were drowned out by the rumble of hooves and bellow of wildebeests and cattle and by the sound of my pulse booming in my ears.

I had no idea where Damu was. He was behind me somewhere, in the throng of unstoppable wildebeests. I tried to turn my head to find him, while keeping the small boys against my chest, but just as I looked, a huge beast brushed past me, almost colliding with me. I quickly ducked back down, trying to keep the boys safe. It seemed a thousand of them ran past us, on both sides, a never ending flow of wildebeests, each animal twice the size of me.

The noise was deafening. The smell was rank. The fear was debilitating. I couldn't move. I didn't know whether to expect a hoof to crush my skull, or if a horn would spear my spine. But I kept Momboa and Jaali in my arms, shielding them. They were quieter now. I could hear them crying, sobbing against my chest. But the animals racing past us got fewer and fewer, and I eventually—finally—dared to turn around.

I needed to find Damu.

He was about forty metres away. I just saw that he was

on the ground, and I didn't hesitate. I stood, leaving the two small boys, and started to run over to Damu. "Damu!" I called as I ran.

He put his head up, then looked behind him for any more rampaging wildlife. Seeing nothing but a few straggling wildebeests, he slowly got to his feet, just as I got to him.

"Are you okay?" I asked. I scanned his body and found a gash on his side. "You're hurt!"

He touched the wound gingerly. "It is fine."

It didn't look fine. It was bleeding and looked wide and deep. "That's not fine."

Damu looked up then, at something over my shoulder. I turned and followed his line of sight. Kasisi and Kijani stood on the ridgeline, no doubt having seen the whole ordeal. Damisi and Amali were running down the slope toward Momboa and Jaali, quickly scooping them up in their arms. Mposi and Lommuuyak had run farther down, and Mposi threw his hands up in the air, clearly not happy with something.

"The cattle," Damu whispered. "They are gone."

He was right. The stampeding wildebeests had run right through the herd of cattle, and the domestic beasts had run with the wild. It was basically the entire manyatta's wealth, their pride and joy, gone.

But in that moment, I couldn't care less. "We need to get your cut looked at," I said, touching his wounded ribs. He looked at me, like I didn't understand the significance at the loss of cattle, but that wasn't true. "We can get the cattle back. We *will* get them back," then I whispered, "but I care more about you than cattle, Damu. You are worth more than *a thousand* cattle."

He almost smiled, until his eyes darted to the ridgeline, to where his father and brother looked on. "Come."

He started back toward them, and Amali and Damisi were walking back, ushering Momboa and Jaali.

"En-ashê, en-ashê," Amali said, bowing her head. "Thank you, Alé, thank you, Damu."

Damisi put her hand to my arm. "En-ashê oleng!"

"You're welcome," I replied. Then I looked to the two small boys. "Momboa, Jaali, *imuy?*"

They nodded that they were fine, but they looked a little scared. I decided then that I would give them some time before I asked if they were okay again. I assumed they felt bad for the now-missing cattle, and as we climbed the embankment to the ridgeline, the two small boys put their heads down, not wanting to make eye contact with Kasisi or Kijani.

I didn't blame them. I didn't really want to either.

The two women took the children back home, while Damu and I stopped. Kijani pointed to the general direction the cattle had gone and yelled something so fast and angry in Maa that I didn't catch it. All I heard was cattle and responsible, and I didn't really need to translate any more to fill in the blanks.

Kasisi put his hand up, silencing his angry son. The chief looked at me for a long moment. "You run for children."

"Yes," I answered. "We both did," I included Damu. "He is injured and I would like to have him seen to. A doctor?"

Damu frowned, trying to downplay his injury. "It's nothing."

I lifted his arm so they could see the cut. "It's not noth-ing. It needs cleaning and sealing or it could become infected." Before Kijani could open his angry mouth, I looked him right in the eyes and added, "We will retrieve the cattle. We will get them back, but first Damu gets treatment."

I didn't leave any room for argument, and it probably didn't help in his justifications in hating me, but I took Damu's elbow and led him away. It was probably disrespectful to treat these two clan leaders as such—first demanding something, then turning my back to them—but I was well past caring.

Maybe it was the crash from my adrenaline-high from running all that way and saving those boys, and maybe it was relief that no one was killed, but mostly it was anger. I was pissed off that we'd risked our own lives to save those two small boys and our only reward was more loathing.

As we made our way back to the manyatta, when we were alone and out of earshot from any of the others, I stopped walking.

Damu eyed me cautiously. "Heath Crowley?"

His use of my full name twisted my heart. "Are you okay?" I asked, fighting tears.

He was immediately concerned. "Yes. Are you?"

I nodded. "I am angry. And exhausted. I'm hungry, and I was so scared. All I could think, the whole time, was about you. I didn't know where you were or if you were hurt. I was scared for you." I wiped at the tears, smearing dirt and salt water across my face. "You could have been killed, and we don't even get a fucking thank you!"

Damu stared into my eyes, and he lifted his hand a little, as though he had to stop himself from touching me. "We are not harmed. Kijani speak in fear. Give our actions time in his mind. He be grateful."

I sighed. I understood what he was saying, but I was still

pissed off. And now the adrenaline had gone, I felt kind of sick.

"Come," Damu said. "You need rest and food."

We started walking back, and I had to admit, my body was starting to quit. The lack of calories, the constant use of energy with so little intake, was starting to take its toll.

Back in our hut, Damu quickly fixed some ugali with berries and nuts, and I ate more than my usual share. When I was done, I could barely keep my eyes open. I'd overslept that morning, ran a kilometre at full speed, almost died in a stampede, had a belly full of polenta porridge, and felt like I could sleep for a week.

"Lie here," Damu said softly. He took my bowl, and setting it aside, he patted the thin mattress. "Rest. I will seek Amali to tend my wound. Rest."

I couldn't even argue. I was done. I closed my eyes, wondering if this was the beginning of the end of my stay with Damu and his people. I'd been here for almost a full year, and I had to wonder if my body had had enough. My heart squeezed at the thought of leaving Damu.

I wondered whether it was physically possible for me to leave him. I'd been broken when I came here. Incomplete. And he had healed me in ways I never thought possible, and the mere thought of leaving him broke my heart all over again. I closed my eyes, unable to stop the tears that fell, and too tired to fight it.

Damu put his hand to my face. "Sleep, Heath Crowley. I not be far."

I knew my dream would not be pleasant. The events of the morning were too fresh, the exhaustion in my body too heavy, and the pain in my heart was too real.

I wondered what nightmares would come for me.

Instead, I dreamed of nothing, just a black void of...

nothing.

I wasn't sure what was worse.

———

I WOKE UP RESTLESS. Unsettled was probably a more apt description. I'd probably napped for an hour, but I woke up feeling more tired than when I'd lain down. I felt disconnected, almost in a daze.

The manyatta was quiet. Eerily so. The only people who remained were Amali and Damisi, who were minding all the children, and Kasisi and Damu, who sat outside the chief's hut. It seemed they were waiting for me.

"Hello," I said, sitting my weary body in the dirt next to Damu. We both faced Kasisi, but I spoke to Damu. "How is your wound?"

He lifted his arm, and I could see the dark but clear, sticky stuff pasted over the gash. "It will heal."

"What is that? Is it tree sap?"

"Medicine," he answered.

"Medicine?"

"Yes," Damu replied. This whole conversation was taking place in front of Kasisi like he wasn't there. Damu put his head down and spoke to his lap. "Leaf and herb medicine is natural doctor fix."

Kasisi was looking between us, and I was reminded to avoid such scrutiny. I looked around, again noticing the quiet. "Where is everyone?" I asked.

"They go look for cattle," Damu said quietly.

"Everyone?" I couldn't hide my surprise.

Damu nodded. "Yes."

Realisation crept over me then, of the significance of their loss. If even the women had left the manyatta to go in search of the missing cattle, then it was serious. Not just the women, but all the warriors, the guards, the elders, everyone.

"I'm very sorry about the cows," I said.

When Kasisi never replied, I met his gaze. He was smiling at me. "You dream of stampede?"

I nodded. "I dreamed it too late. If I'd seen it sooner, we could have saved the boys and the cattle."

"You save two boys," Kasisi said. "Bravery not taken like feather."

"It was not me who was brave. I knew what was coming," I said. "Damu didn't, yet he ran with me anyway."

Damu's gaze shot to mine. "No."

Ignoring Damu's rebuttal, I smiled at Kasisi. "He is too humble and modest. Damu didn't know what I'd dreamed, yet he ran into the valley with me. Actually he ran ahead of me."

"You mention Momboa, and your eyes were big with fear," Damu explained. "I knew where they take the cattle, so I run there. I tried to stop at hilltop, but you kept going down. So I go with you."

"I just collected the boys and shielded them. You ran into the wildebeests, so they didn't trample us." I looked from Damu to Kasisi. "He was braver than me."

Kasisi nodded slowly, then he looked at Damu. "Tell me his dreams?"

Damu stared at his father. "What do you mean?"

Kasisi looked between us again. "You share house, you must see and hear."

Damu swallowed hard. "Very troubled dreams at first. When he arrive, he would yell and fight in his dreams. Now he sleeps with peace."

I stared at Damu. I didn't know it was that bad in the

beginning.

Damu looked straight ahead, not at me. "He would speak a name, but not anymore."

I blinked and my heart hammered and felt it would break at the same time. I was too tired to go through this right now.

Kasisi asked, "Name?"

"Jarrod."

I couldn't swallow or even think. I sure as hell couldn't speak. I didn't want to talk of Jarrod. It was a personal matter I'd shared with Damu in private, and it hurt my heart to hear it now.

Damu looked at me. His eyes flashed with recognition, apology, and understanding. "His brother."

Brother?

There was no way Damu could tell Kasisi the truth. A truth that could not ever be uttered to these men. If they knew Jarrod was my boyfriend, my lover, I could expect a rather unpleasant death. I guessed Damu wanted Kasisi to know I loved Jarrod, but not in the way he expected.

"What of Jarrod to send bad dreams?" Kasisi asked.

"He died," I whispered. "He was murdered."

"And you not dream to save him?"

I shook my head. "No dream."

"You not see his danger? Not save him?"

"No."

"And it troubles your mind and heart."

I swallowed down my emotions. "Yes."

The old man looked back to Damu. "But he's not troubled dreams now?"

Damu paused before answering. "Not for many moons."

Kasisi nodded thoughtfully. "Good it is here for you.

The earth and sky, our God Enkai, heal your heart."

I nodded, though truthfully, it was the man who sat beside me that had done most of that.

"You come here to save my sons," Kasisi said. The gentleness of his voice surprised me, and there was a humbled gratefulness there now. "Your purpose for being here was not to learn our ways. Your purpose, your dreaming, was to save my sons."

I bowed my head, in recognition of his kindness. "It was my duty, my honour. I'm very happy they were not harmed." When I looked at up at him, I realised he wasn't just talking of Momboa, but of Damu as well. It went unsaid, but it was in his eyes when he looked at us both.

Did he know? Had he seen something, had visions of mine and Damu's relationship?

Surely not. He couldn't have. He wouldn't be sitting there smiling at us if he knew…

Kasisi looked over the manyatta and smiled. I could tell by his eyes we was remembering something. "When Damu be born, his mother die. Yet I see, I dream, he be saved by Kafir. But Kafir was dead. It make no sense to me, until I see you. Eyes of Kafir, I knew you be here to save him."

I didn't know what to say. My heart was thundering in my chest, my mouth dry. I was so damn tired, my mind was foggy.

"Damu, leave us," Kasisi said.

My blood ran cold, and I tried to steady my breathing as Damu silently got to his feet. Only when he'd walked a few yards did he glance over his shoulder at me, and the worry on his face told me his thoughts were the same as mine.

I thought my heart would beat right out of my chest while I waited for Kasisi to speak. Eventually he said, "I have many sons."

I bowed my head. "You are a great leader. Your people are lucky you are their chief."

"Yes," he said without doubt. He also said it without a hint of arrogance. He *was* a good leader, and he knew it like he knew the sun would rise in the morning. He led with a fair mind and ruled with a level head. Which was more than I could say about his eldest son, Kijani.

"First son, Kijani be strong warrior."

Even though I didn't like the guy, I couldn't deny the truth. "Yes, he is."

"Second son..." Kasisi shook his head. "Damu born with two hearts."

"I don't know what you mean," I admitted quietly. Damu had mentioned this story of two hearts, but not even he knew what it meant. I took a guess. "He is very brave and very kind."

Kasisi held up two gnarled fingers. "Two hearts. He not be warrior."

I was so confused but wanted to see where this conversation was going without pushing. "No. But he has the courage of a warrior. He admires Kijani."

Kasisi nodded thoughtfully. "He show bravery today."

"Yes. I feared he would be killed."

"You were afraid?"

I nodded quickly. "Very."

He was quiet then for a long while. "I decide to do tourist money for taxes."

I blinked back my surprise. *Why was he telling me this?* "I think this is wise and for the good of your people."

Kasisi gave a nod, though a frown marred his brow. "We lose cattle, have no money."

"We'll get them back," I said firmly. "And then we can start to build a house for the tourists to use. They can sleep separate. You don't need to do anything else to accommodate them, no fancy beds, no white man lifestyle. Let them come and stay here as real Maasai do."

Kasisi's lips twisted in an almost smile. "Like you do."

I assumed explaining my job with a travel company would be lost on him, so I stuck to the basics. "I know what people will pay money for when they travel," I furthered. "Tourists will pay money to come here for a few days and learn your ways. Cook a feast for them, show them how you dance and sing and jump. Sell beads and bracelets. They will buy them."

Kasisi nodded more enthusiastically now, but before he could say anything, Damu ran over with a smile. "Mbaya return with cattle!"

And sure enough, Mbaya, one of the junior elders, was walking back to the manyatta with four cows in front of him.

And by evening, three more had returned.

The next day, five more, and the day after that, another four. By the end of the week, all but three were returned. Whether those three cows became dinner for lion or crocodile, I could only guess, but the mood in the manyatta was high.

It was so high, in fact, Kasisi called for a feast. A celebration.

It was the new moon, the short rains were passing, and spring had finally settled over the Serengeti. There were baby goats, and the returned cows wouldn't be long from calf.

It was almost like a Maasai version of New Year's Eve. A time of new beginnings and a celebration of new things to come.

I knew changes were coming, my dreams for the last

few nights had made that clear, but apart from that, my nights were blessedly dream free.

The gash on Damu's side was healing nicely, though he acted like it was no bother at all. The truth was, he'd earned respect for saving the lives of Momboa and Jaali, and it had lifted his spirits tremendously.

He'd smiled more in the last few days than I remembered ever seeing. The village men, elders and warriors, only acknowledged him a nod, but that was more than he'd had his entire life.

And when Kasisi announced that Damu and I were to go with the warriors and help with the killing of the goat for the village dinner, Damu was so damn proud he could burst.

Kijani, on the other hand, wasn't amused.

The celebration was a great opportunity for Kijani to reinforce his desire to take Razina for a wife. I assumed after tonight, there would be no more doubts and their intent to marry would be official. It was sweet really, knowing their forbidden love would be tolerated, forgiven even. It was also bitter, because I knew mine and Damu's would *never* be allowed. But this new affection kept Kijani distracted, and for that I was grateful.

We still earned ourselves a hateful glare from him every chance he got, but for the most part, he only had eyes for Razina.

"We must hurry," Damu said. His grin was wide and he buzzed with excitement. He ran to our hut and I followed quickly. Damu knelt at the extinguished stove and collected our bowls and two empty gourds. "We not be late."

I knelt beside him. "Stop for one moment," I murmured. He turned to me, and kneeling before him, I took his face in both my hands. "Your happiness makes you beautiful." I leaned in and brought our lips together for a tender kiss. "I just needed to kiss you."

He sat back and laughed, before giving me a quick peck of a kiss. "Come! We go now!"

I took the bowls from him and we ran to where the young warriors were leading an older goat out of the kraal. I wasn't sure how I'd feel about witnessing it being killed and butchered, but Damu's excitement was contagious. He'd never been included with the warriors before, and he was beaming.

The killing of the goat was a profound moment, and one I was not expecting or prepared for. Each warrior touched the goat's forehead and thanked the animal for giving its life so the men would be strong and women and children would have food in their bellies.

They bowed their heads and acknowledged the living creature was a gift from Enkai and how the goat's life was not taken in vain. They acknowledged the earth and the sky and all living creatures and gave thanks to Enkai for being a merciful god.

One warrior held the goat's head, someone else held its body and they stretched the animal's neck. Not to harm it, just to have better access for the jugular. Then, with deft fingers, Kijani felt along the animal's neck for a pulse and with a sharp stick and a quick jab, he pierced the skin. Dark red liquid streamed out like a jet stream, and gourds were quickly in place to collect the blood. The goat was let go, and it did no more than shake its head, seemingly unfazed by the bloodletting.

The gourds were passed around, everyone taking a sip. When it was my turn, I bowed my head in thanks and let the still-warm liquid pass my lips. I'd drank goat blood before, so at least I knew what to expect, but it didn't make it any easier. The younger warriors laughed at me, and I handed the gourd onto the next person, wiping my mouth with a smile.

When it came time to kill the goat, Damu and I stood back. The warriors circled the animal, and I was glad not to be able to see. The men sang a song of praise and thanks to an otherwise silent affair.

Nothing was wasted. Everything would be eaten, used for soups, the skin turned to leathers, and the bones used as tools or left for other animals. Sections of meat were bundled up and taken back to the manyatta by the leading warriors.

Damu and I were left to bring back the remains and entrails, which wasn't the most glamourous job, but when it was only he and I, he scooped the fat into a bowl. "For later." He bit his lip and chuckled.

I groaned freely, knowing damn well what he wanted to use it for. And I couldn't wait. "It's been a long time. You better get double. I've missed you inside me."

He swallowed hard. "You not speak of it to me, and you not make that noise, or we not do dinner."

"Promise?"

He laughed now. He didn't answer me, but he took as much fat as he could.

I burst out laughing, and had to give my dick a squeeze to keep it under control. "If we could miss dinner and spend the whole day in bed, I wouldn't mind."

"Heath Crowley, you tempt me," he said, his voice a low rumble. His eyes were molten onyx, and my blood warmed at the promise of what the night held.

We carried our parcels of goat meat back to the many-atta, where the celebrations were already starting. Women danced and sang, the children played games, the men jumped, and the smell of roasting meat filled my nose. We drank some type of tea that gave me a pleasant, warm buzz.

It was the best I'd felt in a week.

I was still tired, but the excitement was contagious. I hadn't stopped smiling yet.

Just before the meat was ready, Kasisi stood before the fire and called for his people to listen. He told them the manyatta would build a house for the white people to pay money to stay. It was a new direction for his people, he said. A new direction, for new times. Then he announced that Kijani would have Razina as his first wife, to which everyone clapped and sang, myself and Damu included.

But then Kasisi raised his hands, and a silence fell over the crowd. "We celebrate new life of the earth," he said, referring to the seasons. "New life for Kijani, in which he will have many sons and cattle." I raised my bowl of tea, all the while mumbling under my breath about the misogyny of it all, and when Damu eyed me, I realised I'd probably mumbled a little too loud.

I tried to speak quietly, but my head buzzed. "I think I shouldn't drink this tea," I said. "Feeling a little drunk."

He laughed quietly, just as Kasisi called his name.

"Damu, come," Kasisi ordered, and my heart suddenly pounded in my throat. I had no idea what was about to happen. Damu stared, frozen like a deer in headlights, before he handed me his drink of tea and walked through the silent crowd to his father.

Makumu handed Kasisi a spear, and I almost dropped the gourd cups I was holding.

"Damu show great bravery," Kasisi said. "He ran against wildebeests to save Momboa and Jaali. I award him this honour spear," he said, handing over the spear to Damu.

Damu took the spear and bowed his head. The crowd

was quiet, clearly stunned at this proceeding. Damu, still speaking to the ground, said, "I am only happy my brothers were not harmed."

Amali and Damisi, mothers of the boys we'd saved, both sang their praises, which started everyone singing.

His father had acknowledged him, for the first time. And publicly! Damu found his way back to me, holding his first-ever spear. He looked about ready to burst. He was shocked, that much was clear, but he was proud and so fucking happy.

I wanted to take his face in both hands and kiss him until he broke for air, and I was grateful for the two cups I was holding, otherwise I probably would've done just that.

He somehow looked flush and pale at the same time, if that was even possible for someone with his skin colour. But his eyes... wide with pure joy.

"Did you see?" he asked, obviously still in the not-believing stage.

I snorted out a laugh. "Yes, I saw. Everyone saw."

He looked over the spear. It was dark wood with some carvings, and a metal tip. He was still grinning as he admired the details, and I was reminded of a kid who got the one thing he wished for on Christmas morning. "It's an *esururu*. Spear for not warriors."

So they gave him the equivalent of a participation certificate. Didn't win anything, but thanks for trying. It should have pissed me off, but the look on Damu's face told me all I needed to know.

"I'm so proud of you," I whispered. "And I'm so happy for you."

He gave me a grinning-nod. "Thank you." Then he pointed to the carvings near the tip. "Look at this."

It was beautiful, I had to admit. But it wasn't really the spear I was so thrilled about but what it represented.

"Your father said you were very brave," I reminded him.

Damu's gaze shot to mine, like he still couldn't believe it. "Yes, he did." Then he laughed. "He did."

Some of the younger warriors came and asked him if they could look at his spear, and he proudly showed them. As he talked and laughed, I caught the eye of Kasisi and gave him a smile and a nod of thanks. He returned the unspoken gesture. A silent discussion passed between us before he turned away, and I could feel eyes burning into the side my head.

Kijani. He'd obviously just witnessed the gesture between myself and his father, and he didn't seem too pleased. And of course, Damu—the brother he despised—had just received praise and a gift from his father, which had to have gotten under his skin.

In Kijani's eyes, it would never matter how much praise he got from Kasisi. He could have, and probably did, sing Kijani's praises every day of his life, but it was all for naught if Damu was praised just once.

Damu didn't seem to notice it, or maybe he was just used to it. But we ate our meat, as always, away from the men and away from the women, as we, in their eyes at least, didn't quite fit in to either box.

Maybe it was the buzz from whatever kind of tea we were drinking, but it annoyed me more than it did before. Though Damu's happiness couldn't be dampened, and I certainly didn't want to see that smile leave his face, ever.

Knowing no one could hear us, I said, "I can't wait until later. When we're alone." Then I leaned in, "I've never lain with a man who had a spear before."

Damu burst out laughing, but quickly looked around us.

When he was sure we were out of earshot, he reprimanded me. "Not speak of such things out here," he said.

"No one is listening," I said quietly. "But I still can't wait. If I close my eyes, I can imagine the feel of you."

He pointed his finger at me, a glint of daring in his eyes. "Stop, Heath Crowley. You make me think of such things."

Now I laughed. "That was my intention."

He shook his head at me and finished eating his meat. "You are bad."

I probably would have been offended if he weren't smiling when he said it. "I mean it though, Damu. I am proud of you. As is your father. You deserve it."

He stared into my eyes and whispered, "I owe it to you."

"No. You earned it on your own. You're a good man, Damu. It's just a shame it's taken until now for your father to see it."

"Kijani not think so."

Ah, so he did notice. "He's just jealous. Ignore him. And anyway, I think his anger is directed at me. He thinks I'm the reason the tax man came. He blames me for your father wanting to make an income from tourists."

Damu finished his meat and sipped his tea. "Kijani not like you because you dream."

"Oh."

"Do you not see?"

I shook my head. I had no idea what he meant. "Because I dream?"

"You are like Kasisi. Prophet."

I shrugged. "Not really. I don't choose it."

Damu smiled. "Heath Crowley, you would be Diviner."

My eyes almost fell out of my head. "I would what?"

He chuckled. "You be chief. Not Kijani. Chief is not warrior. Chief is one who sees."

I shook my head vehemently. "Oh no. No I wouldn't be."

"This is why Kijani not like you. When Kasisi and he go to elders meeting with other tribes, Kasisi tell them all you dream of tax man visit. Then it happen. Then you dream of stampede and it happen."

Was he fucking serious? There was no way. Just no, no way. "I don't mean for it to happen. And I wouldn't want the responsibility of Kasisi. Kijani can have it. I would never want that."

"Kasisi tell me the other day. When I talk to him, he says you have divining dreams. You be sent here to save his sons."

"He said that to me too," I admitted. "And my sole purpose wasn't to come here and save Momboa."

"No?"

I shook my head. "It was to meet you."

A shy smile quirked at the corner of his lips. "You believe this?"

"I know it. I dreamed of it. Of meeting you. I didn't know it was you at the time, but looking back, I can see now it was."

We were both quiet for a while, and with food in my belly and a buzz of tea in my brain, I felt great. I held up my now empty cup. "What is in this tea?"

"You like?"

"I'm kinda drunk."

"It is honey ferment and leaf." Damu said with a tipsy smile. "We only drink on special celebration."

I couldn't help but laugh. "The stars are really pretty here."

He laughed and stood up, holding his spear. "Come. We sleep."

I remembered the makeshift lube waiting for us in our hut and certainly didn't need telling twice.

MY HEAD WAS SWIMMING with the alcohol buzz, and I crawled on all fours from the small door to the thin mattress along the far wall. It was pitch black inside, there was no fire for light, and given there weren't any windows and the ceiling was five foot off the ground, I had to go by feel.

Which wasn't all bad.

Damu was already on the bed. I felt up his calf and trailed my hand up his thigh. "I can't see a thing," I mumbled, leaning in for a kiss. He tried to deepen the kiss but I pulled away. "I wish I could see your face when you're inside me."

Damu moved so quickly, somehow manoeuvring me so I was on my back and he was above me. "Whoa," I said, the dark room spun around me. "I think I'm drunk."

Damu pressed his weight between my open legs, rubbing his long erection, hot and hard against me. "Do you wish for this?"

I bucked my hips into his and moaned. His mouth crashed to mine, silencing me. "No sound," he murmured against my lips.

I writhed underneath him, every nerve ending alight with desire. I was drunk, for the first time in over a year, and I was desperate to feel him inside me. Desperate to feel him want me. Desperate to feel alive.

"Yes, I want you," I said, barely breathing the words. "I need you inside me."

My words sparked something in him, and he kissed me

deeper and ground himself against me, like he was trying to crawl inside me. He kissed down my jaw, and with his lips at my ear, he whispered, "Need you now, Heath Crowley. I cannot wait. You possess me in ways my body does not understand."

God, if he doesn't fuck me soon, I think I might die.

I pulled at my shorts, trying to get them down, which wasn't easy given he was between my thighs. Damu sat back on his haunches and dragged my shorts and underpants down, pulling them off one leg. He leaned over, I assumed, to grab the bowl of makeshift lube, and I pulled my shorts off the other leg, leaving myself naked from the waist down.

I lifted my hips in anticipation, so keen for what was about to happen. When Damu's slicked fingers found my arse, I couldn't help but moan. He leaned over me, his fingers pushed inside me, and his lips were soft against mine. "No sound," he murmured.

I whined as he stretched me, needing more and running out of patience. "Please Damu," I whispered. I didn't care how desperate I sounded.

His fingers were gone from my hole and I was fraught at the loss. Okay, this was more than desperate, this was frantic. I felt shattered and splintered in all the wrong directions, and only when the blunt head of his cock pushed against my entrance, as he leaned down to kiss me as he entered me, did I feel centred again. I felt whole again.

He slid into me slowly. His tongue filled my mouth as his cock filled my arse. My knees were up at our chests, giving him full access, and only when his balls pressed against me did he breathe.

"This is..." he started to say, but stopped. His mouth found mine again, and he shuddered as he pulled out and thrust back in. He slid his arms under my shoulders and held me as tight as he could, and he rocked into me over and over. Our tongues slid together and I touched his face, his neck, ran my hands up his back and over his arse, pulling him closer every time he thrust into me.

He felt just as good as I knew he would. It had been weeks, and this was worth the wait. This was everything.

A groan strangled in his throat as he buried himself in me, rocking his hips into me before pulling back only to slide right back in to where he belonged. "You are..." he mumbled into my neck. "You are..."

I could barely form coherent thought, but I needed to know. "I am what?"

He pulled back a little, stilling his cock inside me. "You are..."

I could see his face in the darkness, the warmth in his eyes. "Tell me."

"*Képer áinéi*," he murmured. "*Képer áinéi*."

My heaven. My heaven.

I couldn't help it. With both hands on his face, I brought his mouth back to mine and angled my head to consume him with a kiss. It was enough to bring him undone. He thrust into me sharply, deeper than he'd ever been, and groaned into my mouth as he came.

Only this time he didn't stop. He kept fucking me, leaning up off me and taking my cock in his hand. He pumped my dick and slammed into me until he ripped my orgasm from my bones.

Trembling, unable to take anymore, but not wanting it to ever end, I came hard. Damu collapsed on top of me with a sweaty, sticky mess smeared between us, and I held him as tight as my leaden arms would let me.

I was exhausted, sated, and I didn't want him to ever move. The fractured feeling was gone. I felt whole again, and I knew without doubt it was Damu's doing. He'd put me back together again. He hadn't just fixed me, he'd *saved* me.

I tightened my hold on him and kissed the side of his head, unsure of where we would go from here. For the first time in almost two years, I was now thinking about my future. I didn't know where or even how, but I knew it involved Damu.

He stirred on top of me, but I held him right where he was. He was still inside me, and I couldn't bear the thought of him being anywhere else. He mumbled into my neck, "Képer áinéí."

I closed my eyes, unable to hold sleep at bay any longer. I repeated his words back to him. "My heaven." And he nuzzled into me.

Drunken sleep curled itself around me, like smoke, pulling me under until there was nothing but darkness.

I STAND BACK in the shade of the trees, a good forty metres from the graveside, while the funeral procession goes on without me. Jarrod would have hated that. He would have hated his parents for not letting me be there, for forbidding me to be there. They were angry, I was angry, everyone was fucking angry.

I was angry at the world, I was angry at God, I was angry that the sun still shined. Didn't it know it was supposed to rain the day he was buried? Wasn't the sky supposed to fucking weep?

No, I wasn't allowed to attend his funeral. They'd made it very clear when they told me. Unable to comprehend the loss, and without the will to fight, I had simply nodded that I understood.

I'd always understood. It was me and Jarrod against the world, our families refused to accept what we were...

Now he's gone. It's me against the world, alone. No Jarrod, no family. He was too young to be gone, and I was too young to have my heart ripped out of my chest.

All our friends are there, some stand with his family, some must have felt bad and come over to stand with me. They hug me, not knowing what to say... Not that it matters. There are no words that can fix this.

I'm still banged up, stitches and a cast on my arm, physical reminders of my failure to save him. I relish the pain of my injuries. I deserve them.

I say nothing. Even as they lower him into the ground, I say nothing. I want to scream and cry, but I can't let the floodgates open. Because don't they know? How could they not see? It wasn't only him that died that day...

"HEATH, WAKE UP, BABY," Jarrod whispered.

It had been almost two years since I'd heard his voice. I'd yearned to hear it, I'd have given my life to hear him speak, just one more time. I started awake, my heart thundered in my chest. He was there, Jarrod was there, sitting on the dirt floor in front of me, in the darkened hut.

I was so confused, I couldn't make sense of it.

"How are you here?"

He threw his head back and laughed, and my heart soared and broke at the same time. It was then I realised Damu's arm was still around my waist, his lips at my ear.

"You always liked being the little spoon," Jarrod said, his eyes smiling and warm.

"Jarrod," I whispered. I wanted to tell him it wasn't what he thought, it wasn't what it looked like, but I couldn't.

Because it was.

Jarrod chuckled, then said, "You came here to find him. It was always meant to be. He loves you, Heath. And you love him. Allow yourself to feel it."

I tried to sit up but somehow couldn't... "But I love you," I reasoned.

"You always will," he replied simply. "But you have a life to live yet, and it is with him."

I didn't understand. I'd waited two years to hear Jarrod's voice, and he was telling me to love someone else. "What?"

"You need to leave here," Jarrod said. There was a seriousness to his voice now. "Take him from here. You will save him." Then Jarrod ran his fingers over my eyebrow and down my jaw. It wasn't his touch as I remembered but something ethereal. "You need to wake up now," he said sternly. "Heath! Wake up, wake up. Heath!" I could have sworn a hand on my shoulder shook me, but there was nothing there. I woke with a start, my heart hammering, and my dream so was real. The feeling of being watched was like needles into my skin, and I expected to find Jarrod sitting in front of us.

But it wasn't.

It was Kijani.

The sky outside was darker than it had been in my dream, and I tried to distinguish what was a dream and what was real... First Jarrod's funeral, then Jarrod sitting in the hut and talking to me and me *finally* hearing his voice, and now Kijani. I tried to blink myself awake...

Then Kijani, with the rage of hellfire in his eyes, reached over and grabbed Damu's arm and dragged him out of the hut.

CHAPTER FOURTEEN

I WAS STUNNED, frozen with fear, and not really understanding what the fuck just happened. Kijani had grabbed Damu's arm, the one draped over my waist, and literally dragged him over me, from his house.

Damu woke up of course, startled, but he only resisted until he realised who it was who had hold of him.

I scampered to the door, only to realise I still had no shorts on, and I became acutely aware of just how much Kijani had seen.

Two men, mostly naked, wrapped around each other in bed.

I fumbled to get my shorts on, my hands were shaking so badly, but I pulled them up and scampered out of the hut. I raced around the corner and saw a crowd had gathered in front of Kasisi's house. Men stood in a circle, the women stood back, children hiding in their skirts. Damu was on the ground, his shuka barely covering his hips, and I ran towards him just as Kijani's fist struck his face.

Kijani roared words of abomination and disgrace, and I flew between the men trying to protect Damu with my body. Kijani struck the side of my head, knocking me sideways, and I fell into the dirt.

There was no pain. I knew it would come later, but right now there was only fear. Fear and memories, because there in the dirt under the Tanzanian morning sky, my memories took me to that darkened alley beside the pub in Sydney... Of Jarrod on the ground, of him being punched and kicked, and even as they beat me, I couldn't look away from the man I loved as they pummelled him... Only now it wasn't Jarrod. It was Damu.

"Leave him alone!" I cried.

Kijani ignored me and struck Damu again. I knew there was no reasoning with Kijani. I couldn't beg, plead, or stop him, so I looked around for the only man who could.

The Chief sat, as he always did, with his back against his house. He was watching, Kijani had, after all, brought Damu to him so he could witness. "Kasisi, please!" I scrambled to my knees, tears streamed down my face. "Tell him to stop. Please."

Kasisi's face remained neutral as he studied me for the longest moment, but he slowly raised his hand. Kijani stood back, his chest heaving and his eyes wild. A picture of pure rage.

Damu sagged into the dirt, his hands out, his head down. I couldn't see his face, but I could see drops of blood as they spilled into the dirt. I scrambled on my hands and knees to him, needing to touch him, needing to protect him.

The whole manyatta was silent, everyone was watching. Even the cows and goats were quiet. I couldn't hear anything but my pounding heart and the blood rushing through my ears.

Kijani pointed at us and spat in the dirt. My God, he was livid. He paced like a lion, opening and closing his fists, never taking his eyes off Damu. He bared his teeth at him. "*Il-mínoŋîn!*"

I'd never heard that word before, but by the reaction of everyone standing around—the gasps of shock and horror—I could guess what it meant.

I looked at Kasisi, my eyes pleading. "It's not what you think," I said lamely. I didn't care if I lied. I'd deny everything. I'd tell them anything they wanted to hear, just to save Damu.

Kijani came back with his rungu, a wooden club, and aimed it at Damu. "*Káɨbárbar*," he ground out through gritted teeth. "I kill him."

"No!" I cried, jumping to my feet. I stood between Kijani and Damu, my hands out. "No!" I turned to Kasisi. "I beg of you, no."

Kasisi stood up and walked into the centre of the circle. Without taking his eyes off Damu, who was still kneeling on the ground with his head down, Kasisi raised his hand toward Kijani. "Enough."

I sagged with relief, though I knew the danger wasn't over. "Thank you."

Kasisi eyed me with passive eyes. "Kneel."

Fuck. I was quick to comply and went to my knees next to Damu. It felt like an execution, and I wondered if I'd read Kasisi wrong. I wondered if this was my last day on earth. I didn't want to die, not today, not here in the dirt. But more than that, I didn't want Damu to die either.

Damu finally sat back on his knees, and it was then I saw his face. His eyebrow was swollen and split, blood streamed down his chin. His cheek was cut, as was his lip, but it was his eyes that broke me.

He was defeated. He was resigned, and he was ashamed.

I shook my head, as an irrational anger seeped through my veins, and my head started to throb where I'd been struck. I took a deep breath and spoke as evenly as I could to Kasisi. "I have a request. A favour to ask, with respect." I looked up to find I had everyone's full attention. "I seek permission to leave, to go back to my people."

Damu's gaze shot to mine, but he schooled his reaction quickly.

Kasisi's voice was calm and measured. "You not need permission."

I lifted my chin. "I wish to take Damu with me."

All eyes went to Kasisi, a few muttered wonderings went around the people, but it was only Kasisi's permission I needed.

Kijani's nostrils flared. "No. Damu stays here."

I shook my head. "No. He is to come with me."

Kijani's anger was immediate. He lunged at me and shouted insults at me, his club turning over in his hand.

As scared as I was, I never flinched. I had to hold my nerve. Damu's life and mine depended on it. "You don't need Damu. You need money and cattle. I can give you that. I can give you money to buy cattle and goats."

Kijani stopped and stared at me. I was now speaking a language he understood. It might have been a low blow—his first concern was for his people. He would do anything to keep them safe, to ensure they survived and thrived. And I was no different. Except my people was Damu.

He sneered at me. "You buy him like bride?"

I resisted the urge to grit my teeth. I let out as steady a breath as my anger and fear would allow. "Not bride. A trade. What price?"

Kasisi raised his talisman. "You offer this?"

"Yes." I swallowed hard. "I give you money, and Damu and I can leave."

I could feel Damu staring into the side of my head, but I didn't dare look at him. I wasn't exactly buying his freedom, I was buying *him*.

I felt sick to my stomach. And if I'd had food in my belly, I'm sure I'd have vomited. My eyes welled with tears, but I blinked them back and swallowed the bile in my throat.

Kasisi gave a pointed nod to Makumu and Mposi, the other senior elders, and they stood to the side and had a whispered conversation. While they discussed our fate, Kijani came to stand in front of us. He taunted us with the wooden club, without a word, letting it swing near our faces. I half expected him to lose patience with the discussions and just swing it at us anyway, though I doubted he'd ever defy his father. Well, I hoped he wouldn't.

After what felt like forever, Kasisi turned to face us. Everyone waited, I didn't even breathe, and Damu kept his head down. "You say money?" Kasisi asked me.

He wanted me to make an offer. Jesus fucking Christ. Was I bidding for a human life? My stomach rolled. "You can have all my money," I told him. I wouldn't put a dollar figure on it. I couldn't.

"Get it and show us," Kasisi said.

I didn't want to leave Damu, but I had no choice. I got to my feet and raced to our hut. I grabbed my backpack and ran back to where Damu was still on his knees. It didn't look like Kijani had touched him in the moments I was gone, but I glared at him anyway as I went back to my knees.

I ripped back the zipper and fumbled through the contents. There wasn't much left in there now, hardly any of it recognisable as what I had come here with. I pulled out the waterproof insert and opened it. Ignoring my passport, I grabbed the folded wad of money.

I'd separated all my cash when I'd first come to Africa, keeping stashes in different places, and this was all the cash I had left. My emergency fund that, as a tour organiser back in Sydney, I had spent years telling people to have. Sure, I had credit cards I presumed still worked, though after a year of being completely off the grid, I really had no way of knowing.

All the notes I had left equated to about one million Tanzanian shillings. It was more money than Kasisi had seen in his lifetime, and more than enough to buy a hundred fucking herds of cattle. But to me, it was about six hundred Australian dollars.

I was buying a human being for six hundred bucks.

I felt nauseous. And dizzy. And scared. But mostly I was fucking angry.

I handed the money over, and Kasisi snatched the notes with eyes as wide as his smile. There was much excitement around the people who stood in the circle and watched, like they'd all just won the lottery. Kasisi shushed them. "Leave us!" he demanded.

Kijani never moved, and when Kasisi nodded for him to leave as well, he put his knee into Damu's shoulder, and when Damu put his hands instinctively out to stop his fall, Kijani stomped down Damu's hand.

His right hand.

I heard the crunch of bones breaking, and Damu bit back a cry as he brought his hand back to his chest. Kijani simply walked away.

When I looked back up at Kasisi, he was no longer holding the money. I didn't see who took it. I didn't care.

"You not dream of this," he said. It wasn't a question. "Like you not dream of the death of your brother."

What? Before I could reply, it dawned on me. "No, I didn't see this coming. But you did."

His eyes met mine, and I knew I was right. He'd seen this would happen.

"Why didn't you send us away earlier?" I asked quietly. "You could have told us to leave yesterday, and this wouldn't have happened."

"When you come here, Alé, you not care if you die," Kasisi said. "You want death. Now you want life." He shrugged. "One cannot wander from path life has you walk. True for Damu also. Before this day Damu not leave for no reason." He put his gnarled hand on Damu's head. "This gentle son with two hearts. One heart for this land, one heart for another land. Now is free to go."

I blinked. Then I blinked again. I was trying to make sense of it, but like trying to hold a fistful of sand, I couldn't grasp it all.

Damu looked up at his father, his expression one of pain and such deep sadness. "*A-isirái.*"

I'm so sorry.

Kasisi leaned in and whispered to Damu. "The wind has ears. To admit regret means to admit guilt. No let him hear you."

Oh my God. I got it now. Kasisi was protecting him. He knew this would happen, but it was the only way Damu could leave without his brother killing him.

Then Kasisi stood back and said, "Go."

Picking up my backpack, I pulled Damu to his feet. He still cradled his right hand, but I quickly led him back to our hut. "Get everything you want to bring with you."

Damu knelt in his darkened hut, his shoulders sagged. I put my hand gently to his face and lifted his chin. His eye was badly swollen, there were streaks of blood down his face, and his eyes were so full of sadness. "We have to leave."

"Where I go?"

"Anywhere that isn't here. You're not safe here. Kijani wants you dead." My heart broke at the look in his eyes. "We'll work it out on the way. Please, Damu."

He shook his head. "I do not know."

I fell to my knees in front of him and rested my forehead against his. I couldn't fight the tears any more. I simply let them fall. "You can't stay here. It will mean your death." I put my hand to my heart. "And that would mean mine."

"You will stay with me?" he whispered.

"Always."

He sobbed but quickly composed himself. "Okay."

I looked around the small hut that had been my home for a year and Damu's his whole life. "What will you need to bring?"

He reached over and grabbed his spear from where he'd put it down last night. Then he lifted up the corner of the thin mattress and grabbed something. He held his hand out to me, and on his palm was the small paper origami crane I had given him so many months ago. I had no idea he'd even kept it. I carefully slotted it between the pages of my notebook, trying not to dwell on the fact that for twenty four years of life, all he was taking with him was some folded paper I'd given him six months ago and the spear he'd been given the night before.

The only two gifts he'd ever received.

And right there in our humble hut, my heart shattered into a thousand pieces. But I refused to cry. I shoved our two bowls into my backpack and wrapped my shuka around my shoulders before bending over to fit through the door of the hut for the final time. Damu followed me, and as we stepped away, Amali grabbed Damu.

The woman who had more or less been the only mother he'd known pulled him against the wall where no one would see. Amali handed me a pouch of seeds and berries, then she looked up at Damu. "May Enkai guide your feet," she whispered. She put her hand to his banged up face. "Wherever you go." Then Amali looked at me with fierce eyes. "Keep him safe."

"I will."

And with that, she was gone.

"Come on," I urged him, walking around the hut toward the gate that would be our freedom.

Kasisi stood at the exit, along with the other elders. The warriors stood back, Kijani amongst them. They would watch us leave, but no more. When Kijani saw Damu was holding his spear, he called out that it should be taken from him.

Kasisi shushed him. "No one takes another man's spear," Kasisi said with finality. I had to wonder if Kasisi had given that spear to Damu last night knowing he'd be leaving the next day; a parting gift, if you will.

Kijani mumbled something about Damu's cut face and laughed with his friends like a bully in the school yard, and I'd had enough.

"Thank you, Kasisi," I said. Then, because Kijani was an arrogant prick, I added, "Your son will be great chief. I have seen it."

Confusion crossed Kijani's face, but he soon preened. He reminded me of a hen house rooster.

I smiled as I found Momboa, the Chief's five year old son, standing in front of Amali. I waved to him and the small boy waved back. "Momboa will be a very good chief."

The look on Kijani's face was worth it. His mouth was open, and realisation dawned on his features. Superstitious by nature, the Maasai lived by the guidance of their visions. And if I just placed a seed of doubt as to Kijani's role in this tribe, then it was worth any beating he could give me.

Damu gave his father a final nod, and together we walked out of the acacia thorn fence, into the Serengeti plains and the vast unknown.

WE HEADED in the direction of the Ngorongoro Conservation Area. It was the huge building on the edge of the Serengeti I had passed when I arrived in a car with three strange men and some goats.

There was a hotel there, from memory. Buses too, and with a bit of luck, a ride back to Arusha.

We walked for what must have been hours, and Damu was quiet, and he favoured his injured hand, keeping it against his chest. His eye was almost swollen shut, and I imagined his pain wasn't only physical but emotional as well.

"We'll be okay," I told him. I wasn't sure who I was trying convince, him or me.

He gave me no more than a nod.

"There's a creek up ahead. We can stop for a drink and rest awhile. Do you feel okay?"

He nodded again, and I didn't push him. He'd just lost everything he'd ever known, been kicked out of his tribe, lost his family, disgraced.

I stopped walking. "I'm sorry," I said. "I'm sorry this

happened to you. I'm sorry Kijani saw me in your bed. If I'd slept on my own bed, he wouldn't have reacted that way."

Damu frowned. "Are you sorry?"

"I'm sorry you're hurting."

"Are you sorry to meet me?"

"What? No!" I shook my head and put my hand to his cheek. "Never. Meeting you saved me." He looked like that made no sense to him, so I said, "Last night I dreamed of Jarrod."

He pulled his face back a little, like my words added another wound to his list of many.

"No, listen," I said softly. "He spoke to me. He hasn't spoken in my dreams since he died, but he did last night. He told me it was my destiny to find you. He said you were my path. He told me to take you away, that I had to leave with you."

"He saw this would happen?"

I shook my head. "He urged me to wake up. He shook me awake, and when I opened my eyes, Kijani was there."

Damu's face fell, and his shoulders sagged. I put my hand around his neck and brought him against me for a hug, and Damu simply allowed himself to be held. I kissed the side of his head and realised something.

"See this?" I kissed his not-swollen cheek. "In the sunlight, and I am free to kiss you, touch you."

The corner of mouth curled upwards, but his whole side of his face was swollen and bruised, his lips included. Again, he nodded, but seemed content just to have me near. Eventually we started walking toward the small river again, and after a long silence, he said, "Did you really see that Momboa would be chief?"

I snorted out a laugh. "Nope. I said that just to mess with Kijani. Did you see the look on his face?"

Damu finally smiled, then winced as his face pulled.

I lifted my hand, but wasn't sure where I could touch him that wouldn't hurt. "Come on, let's drink some water."

As we sat by the river, I pulled the pouch of berries and nuts that Amali had given us. I was so hungry, having missed breakfast completely, and my body was letting me know it. I was getting weak, and although the circumstances of us leaving were horrible, the timing was right.

I wasn't sure how much longer I could have stayed there. I felt like I was wasting away, my energy levels were depleted, and my stomach felt empty ninety percent of the time.

I tipped some of the nuts and berries into my hand and held them out for Damu. He laid his spear on the ground, and I expected him to use his good hand to eat with, but he didn't. He reached with his injured hand. His right hand.

And my heart broke all over again. I hated Kijani with the power of a thousand raging suns. He'd stomped on Damu's right hand, deliberately, so he couldn't eat. In Maasai culture, it was a great disgrace to eat food with your left hand.

I took the nuts and berries and lifted them to Damu's mouth. "I'll feed you."

He ducked his head, ashamed.

"Hey, look at me," I said softly. I waited until he did. "Remember when I was sick and you took care of me?" Recognition flashed in his eyes, so I said, "Then let me feed you. Let me take care of you. It's what we do, we take care of each other. Okay?"

Eventually he nodded and let me feed him the berries and nuts. He ate them one by one, without a word between us. It was a quiet moment, a profound and gentle moment. I knew then, without doubt, that we'd done the right thing by leaving. When he was done, I leaned up and gave him a soft kiss.

He pulled back and quickly looked around, as if someone might have seen.

I laughed. We were standing in the middle of the Serengeti. "I'm pretty sure the water buffalo and flamingos don't care," I said with a smile. I stood up, slipped my backpack on, and picked up his spear, then I held out my hand to him. "Remember when you said you dreamed of holding my hand in the sunlight?"

His gaze went from my eyes to my outstretched hand, and a smile pulled at the corner of his lips. He slid his left hand into mine, and I pulled him to his feet. And we walked, hand in hand, in the sunlight through the tall grasses of the African plains.

Spring had definitely arrived. There were zebras off in the distance and some giraffes near far-off trees. Birds flocked, gazelles grazed, and the irony of new life spawning out before us wasn't lost on me. As the biorhythms of the animals and land thrummed and thrived, new life beckoned on the horizon—and Damu and I walked towards it.

WE WALKED, our pace careful and slow, until evening, away from the river and the danger of animals who patrolled it, waiting for thirsty prey. "Shall we start a fire?" I asked, looking for a suitable location. "No fire," Damu said. "Attract lions who come for meat."

Instinctively, I looked around. "Lions?"

He chuckled at my expression but quickly recoiled and put his hand to his cut lip and swollen face. "They not worry us here."

"Your lip is sore," I noted, gently touching his face. "And your eye."

"Not so bad," he replied.

I put my hand on his chest. "What about your heart?"

He sagged a little and he looked toward the ground between us, but eventually he nodded. "Sadness."

Sliding my hand around his neck, I gently pulled him against me. He came willingly and sighed against me. "I'm sorry they hurt you," I whispered. "I wish I could heal that pain."

He breathed in deep. "But you do, Heath Crowley," he replied. He pulled back and his eyes met mine. "But you do."

His words warmed my heart. "Like you healed me."

He kissed my forehead before stepping away. "I look for o'remiti. You stay here."

I didn't really have the energy to argue. We'd walked so much slower than normal, our bodies too weary, so I found a spot and flattened the grass the best I could. I laid my shuka out like a picnic blanket and sat on it, watching Damu seek out the plants he was after.

He was a striking figure. Tall, dark, and handsome was so cliché, but he was every sense of the word. He was also hurting, dealing with the rejection of his family, and having to leave behind the only world he had ever known.

I knew tomorrow would be the day that everything changed. Tomorrow we would walk into Ngorongoro National Park base camp, where there were buildings, cars, and people.

Given Damu had never left his manyatta before, he was in for one helluva culture shock. I was reminded of the movie *Encino Man*, and Damu wasn't much different. As the rest of the world sped through the twenty-first century,

Damu had been living in the 1700s. Not only had he never seen the Internet, he'd never actually seen a light bulb or a flight of stairs.

As I watched him, this tall and gentle man, scouting through the long grasses, I wanted to both show him the wonders of the modern world and shield him from it at the same time.

I had no clue what tomorrow would bring. I didn't know how he would react or if he'd cope at all. But when he came back over to me, holding some different plants and smiling so beautifully, I made the decision right there, to only do whatever he wanted to do.

"Here," he said, handing me some long, seeded strands of grass. "Eat."

I took them gratefully. "Thank you." The grass and grass seeds tasted bitter, but I ate them anyway. My body needed all the fuel it could get.

Damu took what looked like some kind of aloe vera plant and, with his left hand, rubbed the gel on his swollen eye, then dabbed some on the cut on his lip.

"We'll find a doctor tomorrow," I said. "For your hand." Then I remembered. "How are your ribs?"

He pulled his shuka up, revealing where the wildebeest had scratched his side. "Better." He looked over the egg-sized lump on the side of my head. "And you?"

"I'm fine." And I was fine. I was more concerned for him. The wound on his ribs did look better, but not completely healed. He dabbed more of the aloe onto that wound as well, and it made my heart ache and my bones weary.

"I'm tired," I admitted, lying down on my side. Ignoring the pangs of hunger in my stomach, I patted my bicep. "Your pillow tonight."

Normally he was the big spoon, but after his terrible beating and eviction from his people, I figured he could use the comfort tonight. He lay down gingerly, like his whole body ached, and rested his head on my arm. I slid my arm gently around him and watched as the sun performed its last curtain call on this day. Pinks and oranges became purples, and eventually blackness blanketed us with the most amazing display of celestial brilliance. "The sky is amazing," I whispered. "Look at the stars. I've never seen anything like it."

Damu was quiet, and I thought he may have fallen asleep. But then he asked, "What do the stars look like in Australia?"

"I've never noticed them before," I admitted. "Why?"

He pulled his shuka up over our shoulders and sighed. My question went unanswered.

I WOKE WITH THE SUN, to an early morning sky boasting a dozen different shades of blue. It was cool, but with Damu's back at my front and our shukas over us, I was toasty warm.

I craned my neck to look around and saw a herd of giraffe walking silently, no more than a hundred metres from where we lay. I tapped Damu on the arm. "Wake up."

He startled, and I quickly remembered how Kijani had violently woken him the day before. "Shh," I urged him to calm down. "You're fine."

He relaxed back into me. "What is it?"

"Look over there," I said, and we both sat up.

Sure enough, the giraffes were walking fluidly through

the grass, like windsurfers on the water. It was a beautiful sight.

"And there," Damu pointed further east. There were impalas heading toward the river, and further out—maybe five hundred metres from where we sat—was a herd of elephants. "They come for water in early morning."

"That's not a bad view," I whispered, taking in the whole scenery before me. It was so perfect, it looked like a postcard or a jigsaw puzzle.

"And after today we see it no more," Damu said with a sigh.

I rubbed his back. "We can stay if you want?"

He glanced at me, and he shook his head. "My father was right. My heart does not belong here."

I leaned in and kissed his shoulder. "He said you have two hearts. One for here and one for somewhere else. You will always be from here. One heart will always belong here. We will find where your other heart belongs."

His eyes glistened, and he looked away to scan the landscape in front of us like he was seeing it for last time. And who knew, maybe he was. "Where do you see my heart belong?"

"I don't know," I answered. "But we will find it together, yes?"

He glanced at me and almost smiled. "Yes."

I scanned his face, taking in the extent of his injuries. It was better than I was expecting. "Hey, your eye is much better. And your lip."

He smiled, and at least his cut lip didn't reopen and bleed. "O'remiti plant is good."

I got to my feet, and taking his left hand, I pulled him to his. "Come on, the sooner we get there, the better."

I could almost feel the hot shower on my skin, and my

stomach grumbled for the food it would get. I wrapped my shuka around my shoulders and collected my backpack. Damu applied some more of the aloe-like gel to his eyebrow and lip. I held some of the edible grass to his mouth, which he ate with a smile.

And with upbeat spirits, we walked the final leg of the path I'd walked a year ago. Only this time, I wasn't lost and in search of something to make me feel alive. I was leaving, with hope in my heart, and with that *someone* by my side.

CHAPTER FIFTEEN

AS THE BUILDINGS came into view, Damu got quiet. And as the buildings got closer and their height and size became apparent, his steps became slower.

"It's a double storey building," I explained. Then I realised that would have meant nothing to him. "That means there's one level of house, then another level of house on top. But it's not really a house. This is a hotel, a big hotel. Where people pay money to stay in a room with a bed and a bathroom."

Damu looked at me like I'd spoken in tongues.

"A bathroom is a room with a shower and a toilet."

He stared at me, unblinking.

I smiled and put my hand on his arm. "I'll explain it all when we get there."

THE NGORONGORO NATIONAL PARK was a large white building with a thatched looking roof. After seeing nothing but loaf shaped huts, no taller than four feet, this building, and those surrounding it, were monstrous.

The building fronted the road, but the view was at the back, the side facing the Serengeti. Which was the side we walked in from. There were buses and safari trucks and people.

People who literally stopped and stared.

Damu ground to a halt and grabbed my arm with his left hand. "Heath Crowley," he mumbled.

I stopped and turned to face him. I took a deep breath and smiled. "I know you're scared, but it's okay. No one here will hurt you." I looked around at the tourists, who were watching Damu, with wide smiles and fascinated eyes. "In fact, I think they're very happy to see you."

He glanced around and saw that people were staring at him. He took a step back and shook his head.

I turned to the small crowd and raised my hand. "He is not used to such attention."

An African man wearing a National Park uniform walked around the corner and stopped when he saw us. I smiled at him and waved. It was ridiculous how nervous and excited I was to see other people. "Hello."

He came toward us, and the second he saw Damu's spear and rungu, he stopped. "Can I help you?" he asked cautiously. Then he looked me up and down. "Are you injured?"

"I'm not, but my friend here has hurt his hand. I think it's broken. Is there a doctor? And possibly some food and water?"

He took another step forward. "How long have you been out there?" he asked quietly.

"What month is it?"

"January."

I'd thought as much, but still, hearing it made my head swim. "A year."

The guide's eyes went wide. "A year?"

"Yes, but my friend has broken his hand. Is there a doctor?"

"Come, come," the guide said, ushering Damu and I over to a bench seat in the shade of the wall. I fell onto the wooden seat like my bones were made of lead. I leaned against the wall and let my head rest. Whereas Damu sat beside me, still holding his spear, his back ramrod straight, his eyes taking everything in. He looked like a rabbit in headlights. "Wait here," the guide said before he raced away.

I put my hand on Damu's arm. "Everything's fine, Damu. This man will get help. Relax, you're safe here."

The tourists hadn't moved an inch. In fact, there were now more of them, all standing there, watching. I lifted my hand and waved at them. "Hi."

A man stepped forward. He was about fifty, with greying hair and ruddy cheeks. He wore long cargo pants and sandals, and even though it was a pleasant day and he was in the shade, he was sweating. And he was staring at Damu. "Is he a Maasai warrior?" the man asked, his accent American.

"*He* speaks English," I said, not meaning to sound rude, but I was exhausted and he spoke to me like Damu wasn't even there. "His name is Damu, and yes, he is Maasai." I wanted to add on that yes, the six foot black man wearing a red shuka and holding a spear on the Serengeti was probably a bit of a clue that he was Maasai, but I refrained. I was defensive of Damu. I couldn't help it.

"Oh," the man said, blushing. "Of course."

Still resting my head on the wall, I turned to look at

Damu. I deliberately spoke in Maa. "He is curious and excited to see you."

Damu blanched. "Why?"

I smiled at him. He really had no idea. "Because you're incredible."

"Can we have photograph?" the tourist asked, but before I could answer, the guide and another man came around the corner of the building. The man with him was about sixty, with wiry grey hair and glasses. He was a little pudgy, but he had a friendly smile.

"This is Doctor Tungu," the guide said. "Tanzanian doctor. He very good. He help you."

I got to my feet wearily. "Thank you." Damu quickly stood behind me, and I gave the doctor the friendliest smile I could manage. "My friend has injured his hand. I think it could be broken."

Doctor Tungu tried to look around me at Damu, but then he studied me for a long moment instead. I gathered that Damu and I were a bit unkempt, but seriously, these people just stared. "You been living out in the manyattas for a year?" he asked. He spoke perfect English.

"Yes."

"I can tell," he replied, with a nod and a smile. Then he pointed his chin toward Damu. "Come on then. I'll need a closer look at that hand."

We followed the doctor along the footpath around the front of the hotel. There were signs to the administration office, but Doctor Tungu walked straight to the door with a red cross, and a sign with a dozen different ways to say doctor. Once inside, it wasn't the furniture, or even the overhead lighting that struck me. The first thing I noticed was the air conditioning. I'd gotten so used to the heat that the controlled climate made me shiver.

"Come take a seat in here," Doctor Tungu said, opening another door to a small examination room.

I knew this had to be all so foreign for Damu, so I took his arm and gave him a smile. "It's okay."

I sat with him on the examination table, knowing he'd find my proximity reassuring. "Damu has never left his manyatta before," I explained. "This is all very new to him."

Doctor Tungu's gaze shot to mine. "Oh."

Damu was staring at the ceiling light, and I couldn't help but smile. "Damu, the doctor is going to need to touch your hand and feel along where it hurts."

Damu nodded, so while the doctor felt the back of his right hand, I held his left. If the doctor thought it was odd, he never let on.

"Tell me," Doctor Tungu said. "How did you find yourself here?"

I almost laughed. "It's a long story, but I left Australia last January and literally walked into their manyatta. Damu was like my guide."

"You've had no contact with the outside world for twelve months?" he furthered.

I shook my head. "I wouldn't know if World War III broke out." I thought about that and what it meant. And how being oblivious wasn't a bad thing. "And to be honest, I don't want to know."

The doctor smiled as he continued to inspect Damu's hand. "Can I ask how this happened?"

Damu swallowed hard. "My brother..."

Doctor Tungu nodded slowly. "And the eye?" Damu nodded, and the doctor sighed. "Brothers. There's nothing quite like them."

Just then there was a knock on the door, and the guide from before appeared, holding a bowl of fruits. Apples, bananas, grapes, and cut watermelon had never looked so good.

He walked in and handed the bowl to me and said, "For you."

I almost cried. "Thank you," I choked out, surprised by the sudden emotions to overcome me.

The guide then handed over two bottles of water, and with a smile, he disappeared through the door.

"Are these for us?" I asked the doctor, trying to blink back tears.

He frowned. "Yes, eat, please."

Damu was staring at me, concerned. "Are you sad, Heath Crowley?"

I wiped at my eyes, smearing stupid tears across my cheeks. "No, very happy. I don't know why I'm crying."

The doctor put his hand on my knee. "Exhaustion, malnutrition."

"Malnutrition?" I asked.

"Eat first, we'll talk after."

He walked over to a cupboard to get something, and I picked up a piece of watermelon and groaned when I bit into it. The sweet and juicy fruit was the best thing I'd ever eaten. I picked up the second piece, and knowing Damu still couldn't use his hand, I put it to Damu's mouth. "Try this watermelon. It's really good."

Damu took a small bite, and his eyes lit up with delight before he took another bigger bite. "I like this," he said with his mouth half full.

I laughed and popped a grape into my mouth. Man, fresh fruit was heaven on a plate. "Here, try this. It's a grape."

I fed him that, then realised the doctor was watching us. "Maasai will only eat with their right hand," I explained.

"And he can't use his. He looked after me for a year, it's the least I can do for him."

Doctor Tungu nodded again and shut the cupboard door. Whether he read more into my protective tone, I wasn't sure. I was too tired to care.

"I don't have x-ray machines here," he went on to say. "But from the swelling and bruising and from what I can feel, I'd say these two metacarpal," he showed us on his own hand just below his index and middle fingers, "are broken, or have hairline fractures at least. He has some movement but not without pain." He held up what looked like a plastic splint with straps. "This will keep the hand stable. He'll need to keep it on for a few weeks at least and limit the use as much as possible."

As the doctor fitted the splint and fastened it, he asked Damu, "Are you going back to the manyatta?"

Damu shook his head. "No."

Doctor Tungu didn't press the issue, thankfully. "If you're going to Arusha, I can write a letter to the hospital for x-rays. Just to be sure."

I gave him a genuine smile. "Thank you. We really appreciate it."

Then the doctor turned his attention to Damu's cut eyebrow and lip and said they looked almost healed.

"He has a scrape on his ribs too," I added. "That was from a wildebeest stampede where we saved two small boys."

The doctor stared at me, then blinked. "You're serious?"

I couldn't help but smile. "Yes."

I broke off some banana and fed it to Damu, and after that he put his hand up and patted his belly. "Too much."

The doctor now focused on me, shining his light into my eyes. I expected him to mention my heterochromia, but he didn't. Instead, he asked, "Tell me, how long have you been tired for?"

"Since we saved Momboa and Jaali in the stampede. We must have run a kilometre at full speed, and I have been lethargic since."

"Hmm," the doc hummed thoughtfully, then patted my knee. "I want to show you something." He walked to the door and nodded for us to follow. Putting the bowl on the seat, I took the bottled water and Damu grabbed his spear, and we followed the doctor into another examination room. The doctor opened a cupboard door to reveal a full length mirror. "Come take a look."

I couldn't believe what I saw.

Staring back at me was not the man that left Australia a year ago. I was filthy dirty, my hair was sticking up in dusty clumps, my shirt was threadbare with holes, and I could see my toes through my joggers. But it wasn't that... it was my body.

My face was gaunt, my teeth looked too big for my head. I could see my collarbones, my shoulder bones. My elbows were knobbly, as were my knees. I didn't need to lift my shirt up to see my ribs: I could see them through the thin material of my shirt.

I leaned in to the mirror. If it weren't for my different coloured eyes, I would have sworn it wasn't me. I put my hand to my mouth and couldn't stop the tears. "Holy shit."

Doctor Tungu nodded. "That's what I thought."

Damu was alarmed. He put his hand up, as if to touch me, but stopped himself. "What is it?"

I shook my head. "I just look so different. I'm fine."

"You look malnourished," the doctor said. "The Maasai people are used to such restrictive caloric intake. You, are not."

"I've been fine for a year," I reasoned. "It's just been these last few weeks that I've struggled."

"It's probably just as well you left when you did," Doctor Tungu said, softer this time. "I need to ask. What are your plans from here? Where are you going?"

I shrugged. "I don't know. We hadn't really decided."

"I'd like you to stay here tonight," the doctor said. "I can't make you, but I'd like to see you eat a proper meal. I can give you electrolytes and a dozen different shots and pills, but how about we start with a hot shower and a clean, soft bed."

I had to fight back tears and could barely manage a nod. Once the floodgates were open, I didn't think I'd be able to stop. "Sounds great."

The doctor clapped my shoulder. "I'll see the staff about organising a room and some new clothes."

"I have money," I said. I pulled my backpack off and rummaged to find my clip seal bag with my passport and travel documents. I found my credit card and showed him. "I know it's been a year, but I assume these still work."

He grinned. "Not that much has changed. Come on. Follow me."

***

THE HOTEL itself was a four-star place, fancy as hell compared to what we'd lived in for the last year. The poor girl behind the counter, with her perfect hair and make-up and neatly pressed uniform, looked at me like I was some hobo off the streets. . I made a very quick phone call to my bank back in Australia to make sure they hadn't frozen any of my accounts, which they hadn't. Thank God.

Luckily for us, Doctor Tungu did most of the talking to

the hotel reception. He asked for some clothes from the gift shop, all extra small in size, and he even ordered room service to be delivered. He didn't ask what we liked, he just ordered a range of nutritionally balanced food. I didn't argue. I didn't have the energy.

"Are there personal products in the gift shop?" I asked.

Doctor Tungu nodded. "Go ahead and get what you need."

I took Damu with me into the small souvenir shop. There was a small range of personal hygiene items; this place was, after all, the only convenience store for miles. I grabbed toothbrushes, toothpaste, a hairbrush, shampoo, deodorant, soap. There wasn't any lube, but there was a small tube of 100% aloe gel, and figuring it would be good for Damu's eye as well, I grabbed two.

Damu was quiet, taking everything in with wide eyes, and I had to keep reminding myself that this was all new to him. Not just the products on the shelves and the artificial lighting, but the procedure of buying goods. "Remember when I was teaching the kids and we would pretend to buy rice with rocks as money?"

He nodded.

"Well, this is kind of like that. Except my money is in this card." I held up my credit card. "Well, the money is in the bank, which is a place that holds all the money. And when the lady behind the counter puts my card into the machine, it tells the bank to take the money from me and give it to her."

I figured that was the easiest way to explain electronic funds transfer. I gathered I'd be explaining a lot of things to Damu in the future, much like how he explained things to me when I first arrived in his world. He wasn't stupid, far from it. It's just that he was learning new things. Like I'd literally landed him in a different world and had to explain things from scratch.

I handed over my purchases to the lady behind the counter, and sighed with relief when my card worked. If my bank had frozen my accounts or cancelled my card sometime in the last year, I'd have been screwed.

She handed me the room key, and Doctor Tungu seemed pleased. "I'll show you to your room." We followed him to the furthest room in the complex. He smiled as I slid the key card into the slot and the door pushed open. "This room is one of the older ones, but I figure you won't mind. And there is just one bed. It's a double. I can organise a pull-out cot if you prefer, but something tells me it won't be necessary."

"Oh, I um..." Shit, I wasn't sure how to answer.

The kind doctor just smiled. "I'll come and see you in the morning. Your food will be delivered on the hour, shower, eat, sleep." He gave a bow of his head to Damu before walking back the way we'd come.

"Doctor Tungu," I called out. He stopped and turned. "Thank you. For everything."

He waved me off. "Don't mention it," he replied.

Damu and I watched him walk away, then we went inside. It was a small room, but huge in comparison to Damu's hut. It was about four metres squared, with a double bed, a small round table with two chairs, and a glass sliding door that opened onto a patio overlooking the Serengeti.

I threw my purchases onto the bed and let my backpack slip off my shoulder. Behind me was a door that led to the ensuite bathroom. But the wardrobe door was a full-length mirror. I stood there, staring back at the strange reflection, still not fully believing the man looking back at me was actually me.

I had to wonder what my doctor back home would think if she could see me now. Actually, what anyone from back home would think if they could see me now…

I pulled my shirt over my head and tossed it onto the bathroom floor. The bones in my shoulders stuck out, I could see my collarbones, sternum, and ribs. My skin was ingrained with dirt and my hair was filthy.

Damu stood beside me. "You are sad?"

"No. I'm just really tired," I replied weakly. "I've lost a lot of weight."

Damu stared at me in the mirror. "You look the same to me."

I smiled and toed out of my joggers and unrolled the waistband of my shorts, letting them slide right off my hips. I kicked them onto the tiles as well, standing completely naked in front of the mirror. I stared at how my hip bones jutted out, how my thighs were almost as thin as my calves.

I noticed Damu staring at my naked reflection. His eyes raked over me. "Heath Crowley, what are you doing?"

"I'm going to have the longest shower in the history of the world," I said, collecting my toiletries off the bed and stepping into the small bathroom. Then I remembered… "Oh." I threw the soap and shampoo onto the shower floor and pulled Damu into the ensuite with me. "This is called a basin or a vanity." I turned the tap on and smiled at his expression as he watched the water run. "This is a toilet. You pee and poop and the toilet paper is to wipe your arse when you're done." I lifted the toilet seat and started to urinate, and the look of shock on Damu's face was almost comical.

"You not do that inside! In the water!"

I smiled as I flushed the toilet. "Yes, you do."

He stared as the water flooded the bowl, swirled, and disappeared, completely amazed. "Where does it go?"

"I'll explain all that later," I said. "I want to show you the best part." I turned to the shower and turned the taps. "This is called a shower. And dear God, I've missed this."

He watched the water cascade from the shower rose and how it ran down the drain and slowly put his left hand into the spray. I took his right hand and gently unclasped his splint, then pulled at his shuka, letting it fall from his body. "What are you doing?" he whispered.

"I want you to join me."

"In the shower?"

I nodded, then pulled at the material straps of his cod piece. I stepped into the shower, letting the warm water hit my chest and then my face. I groaned. "God, that feels so good."

When I turned around, Damu was behind me. I'd never seen him unabashedly naked in the daylight before, nor him me. Sure, we'd seen each other's bodies at the river, but this was different. This was close up and personal, with no fear of being seen.

There would be time for closer inspections later, for now, I needed to scrub my whole body. I moved aside and pulled Damu under the shower spray while I soaped up.

I scrubbed the cake of soap up my arms, over my chest and down my legs; the bubbles on my skin were a dirty brown. The water at my feet swirled brown, and I scrubbed and scrubbed at my skin. When I looked up at Damu, he stood under the water, seemingly not interested in the shower at all, because he couldn't take his eyes off me. "Let me wash off," I said softly.

We traded places again and I rinsed the soap off. Then I

put my head under, lathered up shampoo and scrubbed my fingers into my scalp. I could literally feel grains of dirt lifting from my scalp and groaned again as the water rinsed me clean. I had my eyes closed and my head back under the water, letting the shampoo rinse out, when Damu's hand touched my chest.

I opened my eyes, but his eyes were transfixed at the bubbles running down my skin. It was like he just had to touch them.

I took the soap and ran it over his chest, down his arms, and I turned him around so I could wash his back. His skin was so dark, so beautiful in the daylight, I couldn't help but press my lips to his shoulder. Then I went to my knees and washed his legs. "Turn around?" I asked. My voice was thick with desire.

He did as I asked and gasped when he saw me on my knees. I was looking straight at his cock. He was half-hard. His shaft was dark and long, thin and perfect. His balls were up tight, and my mouth watered with the need to taste him.

"Heath Crowley," he whispered, and his voice hitched. His left hand threaded through my hair, and I looked up at him. His eyes were black, his lips parted, and just when I was about to lean in and take his dick into my mouth, he lifted me to my feet and crashed his mouth to mine.

He pressed me against the tiles, his left hand cradled my neck, lifting my jaw so he could kiss me properly. He kissed me so deeply, so thoroughly, my eyes rolled back in my head and my knees went weak.

Then I remembered that the doctor had ordered room service. Reluctantly, I pulled my mouth from his. "Our food will be here soon. I don't think they should find us like this."

Damu took an immediate step back, out of the stream of

water, but I slid my hand around his neck and drew him in for another kiss. "After we eat, you can have me in bed. I want you inside me tonight."

He gasped out a groan. "Heath Crowley, you should not say such things to me."

I smiled at him and handed him the soap. "Wash my back for me?"

I turned around, and he washed me like I'd just washed him. His hands ran over my arse, and I heard his breath hitch.

"You like taking showers?" I asked.

He barked out a laugh. "I'm not sure if it's very good or if it's torture."

I laughed at that and turned around to wash the soap off my back. I let my head fall back into the water once more, before trading places with him again so he could rinse off. "We can shower together again later tonight if you want."

He nodded keenly. "I want."

I reached past him, our bodies close, and whispered, "Then you shall have." I shut the water off. He let out a rush of breath over my neck, making me shiver. "We better get out of here or the food service people will be in for a shock."

Reaching out, I grabbed two towels and handed one to Damu. I dried myself, and he followed my lead, using the towel as I did. When I was dry, I wrapped the towel around my waist, then I helped Damu tie his off in the same fashion. The white terry-towelling looked remarkable against his smooth and beautiful skin.

Before I could get carried away in admiring his body and wondering what his skin tasted like after a shower, I held up the toothbrushes and toothpaste. "Remember when you first showed me how to clean my teeth with o'remiti?"

He smiled warily. "Yes?"

"Now it's your turn."

His eyes went to the tube of Colgate. "Oh."

I chuckled, and after ripping open the toothbrush packages, I squeezed a small amount of the toothpaste on each. "We wet it first. I don't know why. We just do," I said, holding it under the tap for half a second. "Then we do this." I started to brush my teeth, and although it wasn't a taste I'd had in what felt like forever, it was a familiar comfort. "This is good," I said with my toothbrush still in my mouth. "Come on, your turn."

He held the toothbrush like it would electrocute him, and after watching me for a little while, he tried it. He only did about three rotations before his whole face contorted like he'd sucked on a lemon. "Bad, bad, bad."

I couldn't help it. I laughed. I pointed to the mirror. "Is that what my face looked like when I tried o'remiti?"

He glared at me, which made me laugh some more. I spat and rinsed in the sink, then Damu did the same. "Not good. How is it a cold spice?"

I chuckled. Cold spice was actually a pretty good way to describe toothpaste. I pecked my lips to his and hummed. "Mmm, minty."

I unfolded the shirt on the bed and pulled it over my head. It was still too big, but it was new and clean, and it felt nice. I pulled on the new shorts, two sizes down from what I used to wear, and they buttoned easily. I looked like a walking advertisement for the hotel, but I was scrubbed clean and I was warm, and I was with Damu. Nothing else really mattered.

A knock on the door startled Damu. "It's just room service," I said. "They're bringing food."

I went and opened the door and was met with a smiling

lady holding a tray of covered plates. "I bring in for you," she said, her English just fine.

I held the door open for her, and when I followed her in, I found the room empty and the bathroom door half-closed.

When the lady had gone, I slowly opened the ensuite door. Damu, still wearing just a towel, tried to look around me to see if anyone was there. "It's fine," I told him. "It's just us now."

He breathed in a visible sigh of relief, and it made my heart hurt. I understood it. I just didn't like it.

"From now on, Damu," I said, taking his injured hand. I gently refixed the splint and tightened the straps. "From now on, you don't need to be afraid. In this country, we still have to be careful, of course, but no one knows us. To the outside world, I'm just a tourist and you're my guide. That's all they need to know, and what we do is just between us, okay?" I leaned up on my toes and pressed my lips to his.

He gave me a small smile and nodded. "Okay."

"You hungry?" I asked. "Because I am." I didn't wait for him to reply. I took his left hand and led him to a chair at the table. I pulled my seat right in close to him, my knees on the outside of his, and took the lid off the first plate. It was grilled chicken and salad, and it smelled incredible. I cut into it and stabbed a piece onto the fork and put it to his lips. He slowly opened for me, and I slid the fork inside his mouth and watched as his lips closed around it. He chewed slowly, his eyes never left mine.

"Is it good?" I asked.

He nodded.

I tried a small piece of the chicken and groaned as the burst of flavour hit my tongue. It'd been so long since I'd tasted anything like it.

Damu's eyes were trained on my mouth, and when I

swept my tongue across my bottom lip, he opened his lips like he wanted to taste...

Every bite of chicken, every taste of salad was foreplay. His eyes darkened with each mouthful, and by the time we started on the fruit salad, I was turned on.

I fed him a piece of cut apple, and as soon as the fork left his lips, I leaned in and kissed him. The faint taste of apple, as I drew my bottom lip between my teeth, made me hum.

"I've never seen you like this in light before," he murmured. "Only darkness."

It was true. I'd only ever been intimate with him in the darkness of our hut. Now, I could see everything. "Same. I had no idea your eyes gave so much away."

He swallowed hard. "How you mean?"

"You want me. I can see it in your eyes."

"Heath Crowley," he breathed my name. I wasn't sure if it sounded like a warning, or a prayer.

I slowly slid a slice of strawberry into my mouth and moaned at the sweetness. Damu's eyes went straight to my mouth and his nostrils flared. I stabbed a piece of strawberry for him and traced it across his bottom lip. "I like feeding you," I said gruffly. "I like watching your face when you taste new things."

He took the fork from me and set it on the table then slid his hand around my neck and drew me in for a bruising kiss. He tasted like strawberries and melon, and needing to taste more, to be closer, I climbed onto his lap.

Straddling his thighs, I ground against him. The towel he wore did little to hide his desire, and I rubbed against him without shame.

I wanted him.

Needed him.

"To bed," I murmured against his lips. Managing to stand, I drew him to his feet. "Lie down."

He did, and I made sure the door was locked before stripping naked. I considered turning the lights off, but decided not to. I wanted to see everything.

I crawled over him. His long and lean frame looked divine against the white of the bed. "You're injured, so let me do all the work." I undid his towel to reveal my prize. He was hard, his cock pointed up to his belly. I leaned in and licked him from base to tip.

He hissed and raised his injured hand, only to let it fall back onto the bed. I did it again, and this time his left hand found my hair. His touch was gentle; it always was.

In this light, I could see all of him now. His cock was dark, the head a lighter pinkish brown, and he was circumcised, as I knew he was, but I could see the scars now. It was a crude surgical job, a little jagged, but he was still perfect. I tongued his cockhead, eliciting a moan from him.

"You're so beautiful," I whispered. I licked up his stomach, making him hiss and squirm, and when I rolled his nipple between my lips, he bucked his hips into me. I kissed him, giving him my tongue. His left hand held my jaw, and he pulled me back a little, he searched my eyes—what he found I don't know—but he brought our mouths together again, deeper and softer this time.

I was aching with need, craving him to be inside me. I leaned back on my knees, now straddling his hips. I took a second to catch my breath before reaching for the aloe gel. I poured a generous amount onto my fingers of my left hand and applied the cool liquid to where I needed him most.

Damu's eyes raked over every inch of me, taking in every glimpse they'd been deprived of in the darkness of our hut. "I understand now," he murmured. He trailed his hand over my chest. "When you say I am beautiful. It is what you are." He swallowed hard. "You are..." He shook his head, like words failed him.

"*Túan.*"

Beautiful.

I gripped his cock and slicked it before pressing it to my entrance, and slowly, deliciously, I sank down onto him.

Damu's mouth opened and his left hand gripped my hip. I leaned forward and kissed him as he filled me. When he was fully seated inside me, I pulled off only to slide back down. Damu gasped, a desperate sound, and I answered by kissing him deeper.

His back arched, deepening his reach inside me. I couldn't stop the groan in my throat. I leant back, and still rocking with him buried to the hilt in me, I pumped myself. Damu sucked back a breath as he watched, and his fingers on his left hand dug into my hip. He arched a final time as he came inside me.

The swell and release of his cock pulsed through me, drawing my own orgasm to the surface. I rolled my hips and with a final pull of my dick, came onto his belly and chest. Spent and boneless, I fell forward on him. His arms quickly encased me, my face buried in his neck. The rapid rise and fall of his chest was comforting, and he kissed the side of my head.

"We need another shower," I said sleepily.

Damu sighed and nuzzled his nose into my hair. He never spoke, and I assumed he was dozing. I was slipping into sleep myself when he said, "I want to be with you, always."

I pulled back and rested my head on my hand and stared into his eyes. "I want that too."

"You show me the real me."

I swallowed thickly. "And you healed me."

His eyes searched mine. "Before, you say we must be careful in this country."

"Yes. Parts of Africa don't understand us."

"Then take me to your country."

Wait, what? "You want to go to Australia?"

"Yes. I want to see where you live. I can't stay here. And I want to be free."

"Australia isn't perfect," I said, running my fingers down the side of his face. I didn't want to remind him that Jarrod and I had been attacked because someone took offense to us. But it was an unfortunate, random act of hate. I wouldn't let that stop me from living again.

"Can we be just us there?"

"Yes."

"Then that's where I want to be. With you."

I kissed him softly. "Then that's where we'll go."

CHAPTER SIXTEEN

AFTER A BREAKFAST OF PORRIDGE—THE oatmeal kind, not the uji kind—I'd come to realise there were three things Damu loved of this new and much bigger world: watermelon, hot showers, and brown sugar.

Once we'd agreed to leave for Australia, we had a newfound determination. We packed up early and booked our tickets on the next bus. I wore new clothes, except for my worn and busted joggers, but Damu still wore his red shuka and sandals made from tyres, and Doctor Tungu was surprised when he saw us. He'd met us near the administration office with a doctor's certificate, a bag of malaria tablets, and vitamins. "Well, don't you look different! All clean and well-fed," he said. "I trust you slept well."

"The bed was divine," I answered. "Though I woke with a backache. Twelve months of sleeping on the ground ruined me."

Doctor Tungu laughed at that. "Are you leaving now?"

"Yes, but I can't thank you enough for everything you did for us yesterday," I told him. "It was a great kindness."

He smiled. "You are a strong one. Many a man wouldn't have survived what you have." His words surprised me. Little did he know all I'd survived. Then he turned to Damu and gave him a nod. "You take care of him."

Damu bowed his head. "I will."

He left without saying goodbye, while Damu and I stood there, neither of us sure what to say. Eventually, Damu said, "Does he know?"

"About us?" I clarified. "Yes."

"He does not care?"

I shook my head. "No."

Damu was still staring at where the doctor had disappeared around the building, a look of wonder and disbelief on his face. I smiled at him. "Come on, the bus will be here soon."

DAMU HAD NEVER SEEN A BUS, let alone been on one. The driver stared at him, taking in the six-foot-three Maasai holding a spear, with an almost comical expression. I smiled at him. "We need to get the airport in Arusha."

He nodded silently, and Damu and I sat at the front. Other passengers got on, all of which I assumed were tourists, and they all stared too. "Here," I whispered, "let me take your spear. I'll put it in the overhead compartment where it will be safe." He didn't seem too keen to let go of it, so I added, "I think you're scaring the other people."

He shot around to look at them, horrified at the thought. I mean, it was funny: Damu was the most peaceful person I'd ever met. He reluctantly handed the spear over to me, and when I put it away, I think everyone on the bus let out a collective sigh of relief. I gave them a wave before falling back into the seat next to Damu with a laugh. When the bus started, Damu tensed, but as we started to move, his grin got wider. He took in the scenery, the passing farmland, seeing this new world for the first time. And as we neared Arusha and the wilderness gave way to houses, he watched it all in wonder. As Mount Kilimanjaro got closer, his excitement grew.

No one on the bus spoke to us, which I was grateful for. But when he arrived at the airport and got off the bus, a few tourists approached us. "May we take photograph?"

Damu looked to me for guidance, and it occurred to me he probably didn't know what they were asking of him. "It's fine," I reassured him. He awkwardly agreed, and people stood around him while others snapped pictures on phones. Afterwards, they showed him the images, and his grin was immediate. "Heath Crowley, look!" he called.

His excitement was contagious, and I found myself smiling with him. "Very good pictures," I said. It was pretty clear it was very foreign to him, and the tourists were gracious and kind. "We best go inside and book a flight," I said, slipping my backpack on.

The truth was, if a mobile phone was foreign and digital images were mind-blowing to him, I knew I should take some time to tell him about aeroplanes. And the enormity of what Damu was doing hit me. He was taking an absolute leap of faith by coming with me, and it strengthened my resolve to do right by him.

Sure, it was hard for me to go from the twenty-first century to the seventeenth, which was effectively what I'd done when I'd walked into that manyatta. But it was, fundamentally, just a case of going without.

Whereas Damu was bypassing the last few hundred

years of technology and leaping feet-first into the current world... the term *culture shock* was a gross understatement.

I put my hand on his arm. "Are you ready for this?" I asked.

He nodded. "Yes."

"If at any time you feel it's too much, if you start to feel like you've taken on too much, just say the word. We can go as slow or as fast as you need, okay? Take as much time as you need."

"I want to go now."

I laughed. "Okay then. Now it is."

We walked into Arusha airport and headed straight for the one and only check-in desk. It wasn't a big airport, by any stretch of the imagination. It was just one large rectangular room with a small cafeteria at one end with the arrivals and rows of chairs in the departures. There were two screens that showed a flight to Dar es Salaam left at 1:00 p.m., which gave us one hour. I just hoped there were two available seats on it.

The man behind the check-in counter balked at the sight of Damu. "Hi," I said cheerfully, getting the man's attention. "I need to book two tickets to Dar es Salaam." I slid my credit card across the counter.

"Of course, sir," the man said dutifully, taking my card. Though I noticed a security guard was now watching us.

I figured friendly and ignorant was my best bet of avoiding an incident. I gave the man behind the counter my best smile. "How can we get this spear on the plane?"

The man blinked a few times. "Oh, no weapons to go on the plane. It can only go with cargo and luggage."

Damu tensed beside me, and I turned to him to explain. I smiled and spoke quietly, doing my best to reassure him. "It can go with us, but not where we sit. They'll hold it with the bags. It'll be fine." I turned back to the clerk and laid on the friendly Australian charm. "That'll be fine. It will be looked after, right mate?"

The man nodded, relieved. "Yes, yes. We could wrap it for you."

"Yes!" I said. I pulled my old ratty shirt out of my backpack and wrapped it around the pointy end of the spear, and the clerk wrapped tape around the shaft, holding it in place. I was happy with our makeshift efforts. "Much better."

"Yes, yes," the clerk said, much happier now too. Then he went back to the computer screen. "Names?"

"Heath Crowley and Damu Nkorisa." I smiled at Damu, only to find him worried. I took our boarding passes and took my passport out of my backpack before checking my backpack in. I could have taken it as my carry-on, but I wanted to show Damu that it was okay. We watched as they tagged the only things we owned and took them away, and I led a very quiet Damu over to the seats near the window.

I rubbed my thumb on his arm. "Your spear will be waiting at the other end with my bag, okay?"

He nodded but said nothing.

Needing to distract him, I pointed out the large glass window at the plane being taxied in. I explained what the planes were like inside and what to expect. Taking off, landing, and how planes flew. I'm pretty sure the tone of my voice and his own curiosity made him forget about his spear for the moment.

"Are you hungry?" I asked, nodding toward the cafeteria. It was technically lunchtime, but I'd gotten used to only having two meagre meals a day. "Thirsty?"

He finally smiled. "No."

"Are you nervous?"

He let out a laugh. "Yes."

"It's perfectly normal to be nervous," I said. Then in another attempt to distract him, I nodded toward the mountain in the distance. "Mount Kilimanjaro is impressive, yes?"

He nodded quickly. "*Oldoinyo Oibor* is important to Maasai people," he said. "Not just my people, but all." He waved his hand across the horizon. "I not seen it before this. Only what we are told by our fathers." He then proceeded to tell me the story of how Enkai, the Maasai God, created the lands, making them brown and green but the peak of the mountain was white. This symbolised the beard of Enkai, a holy place from which water came.

The story itself didn't make a great deal of sense to me, but I was so intrigued by what he was telling me, by the sound of his voice, that I didn't hear the first boarding call.

I could listen to him speak all day long. Some words were in English, some in Maa, but I understood every single thing he told me.

It was only when I noticed other people walking toward the gates, that I realised we had to go.

I handed Damu his boarding pass. "This is yours. You'll need to give it to the lady over there," I said quietly. "Just do what I do."

He managed it perfectly, all while the lady collecting the boarding passes gave Damu the serious once over. Oblivious, he just smiled politely, thanked her twice, and followed me out of the small-town airport onto the tarmac. We had to walk out to the plane, then up a long flight of steps to board, and when inside, I gave Damu the window seat.

His splinted hand was on the window side, and it allowed me to slip my hand over his left one. "It's going to get loud," I told him. "And then we'll take off, and it will feel like you're being pushed back into your seat. That's normal. Then you can watch out the window as we get higher."

His fingers tightened around mine. "Yes."

"You'll be fine," I said.

"You've done this many times?" he asked.

I nodded. "Many."

This seemed to pacify him a little, and when we actually took off, I expected him to panic. But he didn't. He just grinned. He watched out the window, and his eyes nearly fell out of his head as we lifted through cloud cover and above it.

He grinned the entire way. When he noticed my passport in my hand, he asked, "What is that?"

"My passport," I answered. I showed him the stamps from the different countries I'd been to.

"I will have one of those?" he asked innocently.

"Yes. You'll need one of these."

He went back to looking out the window, like getting a passport was as simple as walking into a store and picking one from the shelves. I guessed to him, it was. But I knew different. And getting Damu a passport wasn't going to be easy. After all, he had no papers, no birth certificate, in fact, he had no identification, at all.

I realised then, that getting Damu out of the country might not happen.

We'd fought to get this far. He'd been beaten, had his hand broken, and I'd begged and paid money for his life. We'd walked for two days through the Seren-fucking-geti to leave the manyatta behind. We'd taken a bus and now a plane to fly half way across the country to get this far.

Yet, it only just occurred to me that the real fight, hadn't even begun.

DAR ES SALAAM reminded me a lot of Sydney. It was a harbour city with a few million people. The city centre was modern and bustling, with tall buildings and busy roads where the traffic pulsed through the streets. We'd caught the shuttle bus from the airport into the city, and to give Damu credit, he took it all in stride.

Sure, he was wide-eyed and mostly disbelieving. But he was much more relaxed when he had his spear back, and I told him I thought it best to leave the shirt wrapped around the bladed tip. City folk didn't tend to appreciate being confronted with weapons. Neither did the police or government officials.

I'd grabbed a tourist map from the airport and decided a hotel closer to the government offices and financial district was a better idea, so we could walk everywhere. I was hoping we wouldn't be staying more than a few days, but my gut told me otherwise.

The thing was, the embassy buildings and banks were all on Msasani Peninsula, which was clearly where the wealthy professionals lived. And that meant the hotels close by were all five-star, sharing views with yacht clubs and golf courses, with the price tag to prove it.

But, hoping the address would work in our favour with getting Damu's passport, I happily handed over my credit card.

The woman behind the reception desk, a strikingly beautiful lady whose name tag declared her to be Kele, smiled graciously when I told her I didn't have a reservation. Damu stood back in the foyer, wearing his red shuka and looking three hundred years too late surrounded by the pristine marble floor and walls, tall glass windows, and expensive décor. Yet, there he stood, taking one helluva leap of faith, just to be with me. It made me smile.

Kele eyed him cautiously. "Is your... friend staying also?"

"Yes," I said without missing a beat. "His name is Damu Nkorisa. He's... my personal guide. He'll be staying with me."

The twinge of her eyebrow told me she obviously thought this was a little a strange, but out of professional courtesy, she smiled while tapping away at her computer. "The only room we have without a booking is a family room. A king bed and one single. It is... an executive suite."

That was a polite way of saying it was expensive and asking if I was sure I could afford this. I smiled right at her. "Perfect."

"And how long will you be staying with us?" Kele asked.

"Truthfully, I'm not sure at this stage. Three days, maybe a week?" I gave her my best stupid-tourist smile. "Can I pay for the three days now? And if we need longer, I'll let you know in plenty of time."

She nodded with a smile and processed the payment. "Of course."

She handed over the key card, gave us directions to the room, then ran through a brief detail of room service, the pool area, security. There was even a courtesy bus that would take us around the city and bring us back, if required.

The room was huge and extravagantly furnished. Everything was brand new, in shades of creams and browns. The view over the water was ridiculous. What it cost to stay here now made sense. "Wow," I said, walking inside. "We're not used to this."

Damu lay his spear on the single bed and looked around the room like he couldn't believe his eyes. "What is that?"

He was staring at the large black, wall-mounted rectangle on the wall. "That is a television." I picked up the remote control and pressed the on button. The screen blinked once, then what looked like a news program came on, a woman reporter took up most of the screen with a parkland behind her.

Damu gasped and quickly tried to look behind the screen, making me laugh. "It's just images projected through the screen," I explained. I hit the channel button letting him see a few different shows. "I used to watch a lot of television, but truthfully I haven't missed it at all."

Damu was squinting at some talk show. "Why do they yell?"

I snorted. "God only knows." I clicked the TV off and tossed the remote onto the bed. Nope, I hadn't missed it all.

Damu took in the room around him. "Is this like your home?"

I barked out a laugh. "Uh, no. Not like this. My whole flat would fit in this room."

"Flat?"

"Sorry, my home. A flat is a small house with other small houses." I figured that explained it well enough. "It was not as nice as this place."

"You have not been home for a long time."

"No, I haven't. I put all my furniture into storage before I left. I technically don't have a home anymore."

Damu's gaze shot to mine. "What will we do if we not have a home?"

I rubbed my hand up his arm as I walked past him.

"We'll find one together." I sat on the huge bed and fell back, sinking into the cloud-like mattress with a sigh. "This bed is awesome. Want to see how we fit on this big bed together?"

I expected him to reply, but when there was only silence, I turned to look at him. He was standing at the glass sliding door, looking out over the ocean.

"Damu?"

He half-turned his head to glance at me, but went back to looking at the water, and that's when I realised something...

"You've never seen the ocean," I said, rolling off the bed. I stood beside him and kissed the top of his arm. "Come on, I'll take you down there. Passports can wait until tomorrow. Today we add another first to your list. Buses, planes, cities, television, and beaches."

THE THING about Tanzania was that the beaches were beautiful. Blue sky, white sands, and aqua coloured water. Damu looked stunning against the Indian Ocean, but his smile... his smile was something special. There were people who stared at him, though it was something we were used to now. It wasn't every day you saw a Maasai man at the beach, or down the street for that matter.

We'd left our shoes in the hotel room, and the sand was warm between our toes and the water was cool. As the tide rushed in to wash over our feet, Damu put his good hand on my arm and laughed. And even though not getting Damu a passport weighed on my mind, for the rest of the afternoon, at least, we didn't have a care in the world.

THE NEXT MORNING, right after our breakfast of porridge with brown sugar, we went shopping. I needed better clothes for where I was going today, and the tourist-style Ngorongoro National Park outfit just wasn't going to cut it. I mean, Jesus. If my old friends back home could see me now... The fashion conscious, coffee-sipping socialite they knew was a distant memory.

The man they once knew, before Jarrod's death, no longer existed. Hell, even the shell of a man they knew before I left for Tanzania was long gone.

I was so different now. Jarrod's death had changed my life completely, in ways I couldn't have imagined. If someone had told me three years ago that Jarrod would be gone and I'd be in East Africa trying to save the life of a man who had saved mine, I'd think that person was insane.

Yet, here I was, walking into a clothes store in Tanzania, looking for a suitable outfit to wear to get an appointment with the Australian Consulate.

I picked a shirt off the rack, when it occurred to me that I'd thought of Jarrod and how he'd died, and although my heart ached with the loss of him, it didn't wreck me like it once did.

"Heath Crowley," Damu whispered beside me. "Are you sad?"

God, I loved his perceptiveness and his gentle way with words. I looked up at him and smiled. "I'm fine." I held the shirt against my chest. "What about this one?"

It was just a simple blue button down shirt, and I highly doubted Damu cared either way. To him, clothes were not important. "Yes," he agreed.

So, some tan dress pants and a blue shirt, and a pair of brown dress shoes later, which the woman behind the counter charged me an obscene amount of money for, we found a supermarket and grabbed some fresh fruit, rice crackers, and bottled water. It really was remarkable how my entire diet had changed along with my life. Gone were the superfluous food and material things, and in its place were the bare essentials. It was eye-opening what was truly important when the bullshit was stripped away.

It was liberating and gave me a clear perspective of what I needed to do.

I had to get Damu out of the country.

WHEN WE'D GONE BACK to our hotel room, I changed into my new clothes, shaved, and did my hair. I walked out and held my arms out, giving Damu a full view. "How do I look?"

He was sitting on the bed and looked me over from head to foot and frowned. "Not like my Heath Crowley."

I laughed and leaned down to kiss him. *His Heath Crowley.* It gave me a thrill to hear that. "Well, it's not for long. I need to make a good impression and to meet them on their terms." The truth was, I felt constricted and stuffy. "So I can get *my* Damu to Australia."

He grinned, but then it slowly faded. He stood up and looked down at his shuka. "What of my clothes?"

I leaned up on my toes and kissed him. "Perfect. Don't you change a thing."

The truth was, I wanted them to see him in his traditional Maasai clothes. I wanted them to see that this was not a normal case. "Come on then, let's get this over with."

The Australian Consul in Tanzania wasn't what I expected. It looked like a house with a security gate. We literally just walked straight in. A young man behind a glass office wall came out to greet us. "Can I help you?" It was the first Australian accent I'd heard in a long time. A lump formed in my throat.

"Yes. I'm an Australian citizen," I said. "I need to speak to someone about getting an extraordinary circumstance passport for my friend here." I motioned toward Damu.

The guy, no older than me, blinked and frowned. It was clearly not a standard request. "If you can take a seat here." He waved his hand at the three chairs to our left. "And I'll see if someone can help you."

So we waited. And we waited.

People were busy, walking from office to office with files in their hands. Other people came in and were seen to—they'd made appointments, and we hadn't—so I didn't begrudge them that. But after two hours and just when I got up to ask someone if there were bathrooms we could use, a woman came down the hallway.

She was possibly fifty, with blonde-grey shoulder length hair. She reminded me oddly of Hillary Clinton. She smiled right at me. "Sorry to keep you. There's more paperwork than hours in the day," she said. "My name is Susan. Please, come this way."

Susan led us down the hall she'd come from, and I had hope, maybe foolishly, that this would be easier than I'd been dreading. I smiled at Damu as we sat in the two chairs across the desk from her.

"So tell me, what can the Australian consulate do for you?"

Right. Here went nothing. And everything.

"My name is Heath Crowley. I'm from Sydney. I've spent the last year living in a remote manyatta with the Maasai."

She blinked. "Is there someone back home I can contact for you?"

I shook my head. "No." I focused on Damu and smiled at him. "This is Damu Nkorisa. We'd like him to come back to Australia with me."

"Okay," Susan said slowly. "How does that involve the Consulate? That is an issue of the Republic of Tanzania."

"He has no passport," I explained. "In fact, he has no form of identification, at all."

"Oh."

"The Maasai don't register births or deaths. There are no such things as birth certificates and certainly no photo ID." I smiled at Damu. "In fact, Damu had never left his village until two days ago."

Susan nodded slowly, looking between us, then tilted her head. She had the diplomatic smile down pat. "I'm still not sure if this is a matter for this office."

"He can't stay here," I said, getting to the point. "I fear for his life if he does."

Now she frowned and shifted in her seat. "Should this be a matter for the police?"

"No. We've done nothing wrong, we just want to leave. I have a current passport, Damu needs one. He needs a visa or something. Isn't there an extenuating circumstances under the Australian Government's refugee status? Or mitigating circumstances?" I couldn't remember what it was called. "There has to be something that can make this happen."

This had her attention. "Possibly. Though he—"

"Damu," I corrected her. "His name is Damu."

She smiled at Damu. "Sorry. You will still need a Tanzanian passport, and I can't help with that." Her eyebrows knitted together and she took a deep breath. "What is the real reason he must leave?"

I took a deep breath and let it out slowly. "He was in

danger amongst his people. They were beating him. I have no doubt if we hadn't left, they would have killed him. He's been displaced, his life threatened because of his sexual orientation."

She pursed her lips and spoke carefully. "Don't tell anyone that. Not here."

"This is Australian soil, yes?"

"Yes," she answered. "But out there, with the Republic of Tanzania deciding if Damu can leave or not, they will not take kindly to this news."

"That's *why* we have to leave."

"I can't get a passport for him. It's not within my power."

"Isn't there a refugee travel clause or something? If he stays here, he will die."

"I can't get him a passport," she repeated.

I was so frustrated and angry, it brought tears to my eyes. "I won't leave without him. I can't. I've lost one partner to a hate crime, had him ripped from my life too soon, and I refuse to lose another. He was cheated out of his life because of fear and hatred, and I can't..." My voice croaked and tears welled in my eyes.

Damu was obviously confused by everything we'd talked about, but his worry for me was evident on his face.

Susan took a notepad and started to scribble something down. I assumed we'd been dismissed, like our lives weren't worth her time.

I wanted to rage at this woman. I wanted to reach across the table and shake her. How dare she decide Damu's life wasn't worth anything! But I knew landing myself in a Tanzanian jail wouldn't help Damu's cause. I stood up and looked to Damu. "Let's go."

She put her pen down. "Mr Crowley, I said *I* can't get

him a passport..." She slid the piece of paper across her desk and she whispered. "But I know someone who can."

I picked up the post-it note and read the name and address. When my eyes found hers, she added, "Speak only to him. You'll need to pay, and it won't be cheap."

The tears that had been threatening, finally spilled down my cheeks. "Thank you."

Susan looked at the slip of paper in my hand. "You didn't get that from me."

"No, of course not."

I turned to walk away, and she said, "Mr Crowley, Mr Nkorisa?" Damu and I both stopped and waited. She gave us a small but warm smile. "Good luck."

<hr>

WE HAILED a taxi and I gave the man the address Susan had given me. The trip took no more than ten minutes, and when the driver stopped the car, he put his hand out. "Fifty dollar."

I stared at the meter. "The meter says ten." I'd quickly learned most places here worked with Tanzanian Shillings and the equivalent in US dollars, so that was fine. But this was blatant robbery.

He turned the meter off and tapped the top of it. "Broken."

First the clothes were overpriced, now this. Needing to keep my cool but not giving in completely, I threw the equivalent of about thirty dollars at him. "That's all I have," I said, and nodded for Damu to get out of the car.

The taxi driver didn't argue as we got out, just drove off with a smile. I tamped down my frustration. "What was wrong?" Damu asked.

"He charged me too much money," I said. "Like in the clothes store."

Damu frowned. The value of money was something foreign to him, and I envied him that. "Why do they not be truthful?"

"Because in their eyes, I'm a white tourist, and that makes me rich. They think I have lots of money."

"Do you?"

"Kind of." I breathed in deep and let it out slowly. "It doesn't matter." I looked at the building we'd arrived at. The Immigration Department of the Republic of Tanzania was a large, modern building, and looking at the name Susan had given me one more time, Damu and I walked inside. The man behind the reception window smiled politely at us.

"We need to see George Palangyo," I said.

"Do you have an appointment?"

"No. But we're happy to wait."

"Your names?"

I told him.

"And what is it in regards to?"

Oh nothing much, just wanting to buy a forged passport. "I have some questions on passports and visas, and I was told he could help me."

The man stared at me for a long moment, and I knew he knew what we were here for wasn't strictly legal. I quickly deduced that George Palangyo was a popular man for such requests. I half expected him to call security or the police, but he didn't. "Take a seat."

I walked to the furthest row of chairs and sat in the last chair. Damu sat quietly beside me. My stomach was in knots and my palms were sweating. The closest thing I'd ever done to breaking the law back in Australia was a parking fine. Now, I'd paid cash for the life of another person, and I was about to ask a government official to forge legal documents, which could probably land me in some forgotten Tanzanian rat-hole jail cell forever. I let out a slow breath, trying not to think about the worst that could happen.

Instead, I wanted to concentrate on the positive. "There's so much I want to show you when we get to Australia," I said. "What do you want to do? Do you want to go to school? To university?"

"I can do these things?"

I smiled at his expression. "Anything you want."

He was grinning now. "I do not know," he said, like the possibilities were endless.

"You don't have to decide right now."

"I think I would like to go to school," he said, with wide, bright eyes.

"Then that's what you'll do."

He sat back in his seat, sitting taller and smiling, when our names were called.

George Palangyo was about fifty years old. His hair was cut in a short afro style and greying at the sides. He wore grey trousers and a pale green, button-down shirt. We followed him into his office and he closed the door behind us. He walked around to his side of the desk, and when Damu and I sat in the two seats across from him, he took off his reading glasses and threw them onto his desk. "So, you have questions on passports, yes?"

I swallowed hard. "Yes. Damu needs a passport, but he has no forms of identification. I was hoping you might be able to help us with that."

"The passport or the identification?"

"Both."

George eyeballed me for a good twenty seconds. If he

was waiting for me to crumble, I wouldn't. I held my nerve and never broke eye contact.

He spoke like he was discussing the weather. "Birth affidavits aren't difficult. If no records of his birth exist, then someone who was present at this birth needs to verify."

"There are no family members to verify," I replied.

George nodded, more to himself than to us. "Maasai, see? They have no authority in this world." He looked at Damu like he was a piece of shit. He sighed dramatically. "Passports are not as easy."

"I'll pay."

His eyes gleamed. "Passports are not cheap."

My nostrils flared. I'd had just about enough of this man as I could stand, but I couldn't blow this. This was our one and only chance. What I wanted to do was drag this piece of shit over his desk and punch the living crap out of him. He had no clue what kind of man Damu was. His strength against adversity, the pain and torment he has endured his entire life. Always on the outside, always told he was never worthy, yet still proud of who he is. And above everything else, whether he was Maasai, a great warrior or not, he was a fucking human being. Instead, I nodded compliantly and asked, "How much are the fees?"

I was at the point where bribery neither offended nor surprised me. I had expected it when Susan had given me this guy's name as one who was known to get documentation others couldn't. I also expected my fees would be exponentially higher because of the colour of my skin.

"Three thousand American dollars."

I stared at this piece of shit, my urge to break his fucking nose bubbling just under the surface. But in spending the last year with Damu and his people, learning their quiet ways and cohesiveness with their environment, I took a deep breath and smiled. "Fine."

He smiled, surprised and victorious. If he expected to me to barter for a man's life, he was more despicable than I first thought. "Come back tomorrow. Have money and photos for passport and proper clothing." He shook his head at Damu like he was a disgrace. "He not go anywhere looking like that."

I could barely contain my disgust at this self-righteous prick. "I assume that is to include a permit to get Damu's spear and rungu through customs in Australia."

"Oh yes," he said, and I had the feeling he was already wondering how much he could sell them for.

"I want them registered with the Australian consulate for cultural significance and certified through the proper authorities," I said, my tone leaving no room for doubt.

Now he nodded a little more seriously. "Tomorrow. Ten o'clock."

"We'll be here."

WE FOUND a bank in the financial district where I could withdraw a large sum of money. Then after that, a store that did passport photos, and after that, we needed to get Damu some different clothes. He could wear his shuka all he liked with me. In fact, I loved it on him. It showed off his body in all the right ways, and it spoke of his culture and heritage without having to say a word.

But the arsehole at the government office was right. Damu needed to look the part, he needed to blend in and not get flagged through the whole process. A normal guy going to Australia was no big deal. A Maasai wearing a traditional shuka, holding a spear and rungu, wasn't going to happen.

We picked out some jeans and dress pants and some button-down shirts. I couldn't help but get him a red shirt, which I hoped would allow him to keep a little of himself. I thought getting him socks and shoes would be another challenge, but he went along with everything without argument. In fact, he was quiet and compliant the entire time.

"It's not permanent," I said to him. "It's just to get the passport. When that's all over, you can wear your shuka."

His only response was a slight nod.

When we got back to the hotel room, I put his new clothes in the wardrobe and found him sitting on the end of the bed.

"You okay?"

He nodded, then shook his head, and ended with a shrug.

"What's wrong?" I asked gently. "Damu, if you don't want to go ahead with this, just say. We'll do something else. We'll find another way."

He frowned. "Why me?"

"Those government people don't know you. And they fear what they don't know. You're a Maasai, and that strikes fear into a lot of men."

"No," he shook his head, like I'd misread his question. "Why me? Why you do this for me? You fight them with words, and you give money. I have no money, but you give yours."

I knelt before him and took his left hand in mine. I swallowed hard, not having said any of this out loud to him before. "Damu, do you know what you are to me?"

He shook his head.

"You are the warmth of sunshine on my skin when all

there was before you was darkness and cold. You surround me with warmth I thought I'd never feel again. You brought new life to my heart, like the rains to barren soil."

Damu stared at me and put his injured hand over his heart. "That is what I feel here."

I breathed out a laugh. "That is love."

He whispered, "Love..."

I nodded, still smiling. "Damu, I want to be with you always. It doesn't matter where we are, as long as we are together. I love you." A slow smile spread across his lips, and his cheeks tinted pink. I leaned up and kissed him. "That is why I'm doing this. For you. I'm doing it for you, because you're worth it. I don't care what it costs, I don't care if the world is against us."

He slid his left hand along my jaw and drew me in for a kiss. "You say the words like they come from my heart."

I rested my forehead against his, but I needed to be closer. I pushed him back on the bed and crawled on top of him. I lay over him, and simply put my head on his chest. He wrapped his arms around me. It wasn't sexual; it was intimate and lovely. He kissed the top of my head, and I closed my eyes, feeling loved and safe.

Then Damu chuckled, and the sound reverberated through my ear. I lifted my head to look at him, and he was staring at the mirrored robe door. "What's so funny?"

"Look at us," he said, still smiling. He turned back to the mirror. "This is why they called you Milk."

I could see what he meant. I was ridiculously pale, especially compared to him. It was really apparent when we lay like this, him rich and dark, me pale and white. I chuckled with him. "I'm not that white."

He put his fingers to my chin and made me look at him.

"You are perfect. With your skin of milk and different coloured eyes."

"The eyes of Kafir," I said wistfully.

He sighed and touched my hair. "When I was a boy, Kasisi told of a dream that I would be saved by Kafir the lion. He said it make no sense, Kafir was dead."

"He meant me?"

Damu nodded. "I think so."

I kissed him softly. "I think your father knew. I think he saw you would be with a man, not a wife. I think he knew you would leave." I ran my thumb over his cheekbone. "I think he gave you that spear because he knew you would be leaving soon, and he wanted you to take it with you."

Damu searched my eyes. "Why would he do this?"

"Because you're his son, and he loves you."

Damu's eyes glistened before they slowly closed. I rolled us onto our sides so I could hold him properly. I kissed the side of his head, hoping he felt as loved and as safe as he made me feel.

After a quiet few minutes, he said, "You not dream lately."

"No. Dreamless is sometimes good."

"You not see if we are doing the right or wrong thing?"

"Sometimes I don't need the dreams to know." I took his left hand and put it my chest. "I can feel it here."

He smiled at that and sighed contentedly. "I think I dream of what will happen?"

"Really?"

"Yes. I dream of our feet in the ocean, and having watermelon to eat."

I barked out a laugh. "Is that right?"

He nodded. "Yes."

"Well, then," I said, rolling off the bed. "We better make sure it happens."

WE WERE SITTING in George Palangyo's office at five to ten the next day. Damu looked different in jeans, but the red shirt suited him so well. Even George seemed impressed. I handed over the passport photos, and citing Damu couldn't write because of his hand, I filled in the forms. I didn't want George to know Damu couldn't write that well, but we'd practised his signature and he nailed it, even with his sore and splinted hand.

One thing we hadn't even thought of was Damu's date of birth.

I spoke to him in Maa, so George wasn't privy to the conversation. "What's your birthdate?"

"Don't know," he replied in Maa.

"Do you know the month?"

"No."

Jesus. "The season? Was it hot or cold?"

"*Oltumuret.* Short rains."

Okay, the short rains were August. "What about the first of August?"

Damu nodded, like I'd asked him if he wanted a drink of water, not pick your own birthday. I already knew he didn't know his exact age, so I took the liberty of making him twenty-three.

I slid the completed forms across the desk, and George gave me a smarmy smile. "Money?"

I pulled the two rolls of bills from my pocket. I had no idea how this would go, but I needed to gain some kind of control in this whole shitshow. "Half now, half when we collect."

George smiled like he accepted the challenge, or maybe he found my shaky attempt at bravery amusing. "Fine. One week."

I stared at him. "Four days."

He shook his head. "One week, that much I cannot change."

"Fine," I said, rising to my feet. I wouldn't thank him until I had that passport in my hands, but I offered him a nod before we turned and left.

WE SPENT the next week enjoying the beach, the pool, the room service, and that king-sized bed. The full length mirror made it all the more fun, and there was nothing hotter than watching our love making. Damu could hardly tear his eyes away.

We went to the museum as well. I figured it would give Damu a better grasp on world history and developments, and the extensive Maasai exhibition was incredible. We lost a whole day in the museum, though it was a day well spent.

Over the week, Damu never complained. Not once. He took everything in stride, his placid and gentle nature was a joy, and his sense of humour really started to shine.

After spending a few hours in bed one afternoon, we ordered room service of grilled meat and vegetables, and I turned the TV on for something to do. I rolled my eyes as the 80s movie *Police Academy* started, and I was appalled that Damu found it so damn funny.

He was in hysterics, laughing so hard he had tears in his eyes.

I mean, I laughed too, but I was only laughing because

he was laughing. It was a contagious sound, and one I wanted to hear a lot more of.

As the days crept on, our troubles of the past few weeks seemed a lifetime ago. Where my life with Jarrod had been busy and loud, a fast pace of work and social life, Damu was calm and peace. He was the place my soul had longed for, had been homesick for, where I was centred and everything in my world wasn't broken anymore.

If this was how my life with Damu was going to be, then it only made me more determined to make it happen.

STRANGELY, I wasn't nervous the morning of our meeting with George. It was going to happen, I could feel it. I wasn't nervous. I wasn't even worried that some federal agent was going to haul my arse into custody as part of some crackdown on crooked government officials. I was just excited to finally get Damu his damn passport.

George wore the same clothes he'd worn before. There was a photo frame of him, a woman, and three kids on the window sill behind him, which I hadn't noticed last time, and upon closer inspection, George had worry lines on his face I hadn't noticed before either. If he was having money issues, I hoped, probably naively, that the money I paid him today went to support his family.

Well, that's what I told myself to justify paying this guy three large for a passport which, through the proper channels, according to the poster in the waiting room, cost fifty bucks.

"Money?" he asked, cutting right to the chase.

"Passport and visa?" I countered.

He pulled a yellow envelope from his desk drawer and

slid it across the desk to me. I opened it and took out the contents. Republic of Tanzanian passports were green, and to my very untrained eye, this looked like the real thing. Damu's name, photograph, and new date of birth were printed inside. The pages were watermarked and had the proper electronic markings. The next item was a permanent visa approval for Australia, stamped and dated three days ago. In all my years with a flight company, I'd seen a lot of these, and this one was legit. I had no clue how George had made this happen—I didn't want to know. I simply took out the roll of money and put it on the desk, collected our documents and stood up. "Thank you," I said. Despite the cost and this guy's general shitty attitude, he had made things happen, and I was grateful. I also couldn't get out of there quick enough.

Everything after that happened very quickly.

I had Kele at the hotel's reception book two tickets to Sydney, handed her my credit card, and she printed off the booking confirmation for me. We were leaving in six hours.

She very kindly organised the hotel courtesy bus take us back to the Australian consulate office so they could organise the proper shipping of Damu's spear and rungu. It was, as she'd explained, highly unlikely a taxi would let us in while we were carrying such weapons.

At the consulate, I handed over the paperwork George had given us to Susan. She helped package the items and addressed them with official Australian Consul stickers. The only catch was, the items would need to be held by the Australian government in quarantine for a few months, but given the alternative of losing them for good, we had little choice. Damu was apprehensive, understandably, but he trusted me to know what was protocol.

When we were done, Susan asked quietly, "Can I ask how much George charged you for these?"

"Three thousand."

She flinched. "I'm sorry."

I looked at Damu, then smiled at Susan. "I'm not. I'd have paid him ten times that."

Susan nodded. She was impressed by the paperwork, that much was clear. "Well, everything's legitimate. I guess that's the going price. For what it's worth, I'm glad it worked out." She smiled at us. "Good luck."

"I owe you everything," I told her.

"Send me a postcard when you get there," she said. "And I'll call us even."

I shook her hand. "Deal."

I turned to Damu. "You ready to go to Australia?"

He grinned. "Yes."

"Then let's go."

CHECKING in and getting through to the boarding gate was horrendously stressful. I swear I didn't breathe the entire time. Damu was great though, like everything else, he took it all in stride and went with the flow.

Even the flight was stressful, because I knew we still had to go through customs. And I couldn't go through with him. If they pulled him out and questioned him, he'd be on his own. By the time we landed in Sydney, I was almost sick with worry. I was hoping to arrive rested and happy, but truthfully, I was a nervous wreck.

"If they ask you what you're doing here," I whispered to him, "tell them you're here to work and study. Your visa permits this. Tell them you study history of the Maasai people, and you wish to study at Sydney University."

"Why my people?"

"Because you're an expert, and they're not."

As I handed over my passport and medical certificates from Doctor Tungu, the lady simply stamped and wished me good day. I moved on, standing and waiting... I waited for Damu to come through, then I waited some more. My heartrate was hammering, and I could feel my blood pounding in my ears. I felt sick to my stomach and had visions of them interrogating him and him not under-standing their questions and panicking, and then I started to panic.

"Sir? Are you okay?" a security guard asked me.

"Yes, well, no, I'm waiting for my friend. He hasn't come through yet."

"You can't wait here. You'll have to move on."

"But he won't know where I am," I said, my panic rising even further. Just when I thought this security guard was going to haul my arse for acting suspiciously, Damu came through the line. He saw me, and his grin was instantaneous.

I cannot describe the relief I felt. There are simply not the words.

"Oh, here he is now," I said to the guard, a wave of emotions washed over me. I looked up at Damu. "I was worried."

We walked through the concourse to where people were waiting for their friends and loved ones, though no one was waiting for us. I had all I needed right beside me. And I was so overwhelmed, I couldn't walk another step. I had to sit down.

Damu put his hand on my shoulder, his eyes wide with worry. "Heath Crowley, what is it?"

I looked up at him, at his beautiful and serene face, and couldn't stop my tears. "We did it. We made it."

Damu smiled and put his left hand to my face and wiped the tears away. "You did it."

I took a steadying breath, and my tears finally gave way to a smile. "Are you ready for this?"

He looked out the glass walls to the traffic and to the new life that waited for him. "If I'm with you, I be ready for anything."

EPILOGUE

WE DIDN'T last long in Sydney. I showed Damu as many touristy things as I could think of. He loved it all, but his heart wasn't in it. He longed for a quieter life, out of the hustle and bustle, where there were wide open spaces, much like that of Tanzania.

I couldn't blame him. He'd been ripped from the only world he'd known, and thrown into the twenty-first century. He loved his new life in Australia, but something just wasn't quite right.

And for the first time in months, I'd dreamed of where our lives would take us. It was an absurd dream, abstract but real at the same time. There was a flood of butterflies, but they weren't really butterflies. I knew, in that weird dream kind of way of knowing, that it was Jarrod. And when they swarmed and fluttered their wings, it was the sound of Jarrod laughing. As he took flight, the murmuration shimmered away and the name of a town remained.

Blakeford.

I looked it up on a map the next morning. It was a smaller town, about six hours drive from Sydney. A small farming community hit hard by the drought but soldiering on. There was a population of eight-thousand people, a few stores, a few schools, and not much else.

"What are you looking at?" Damu asked, handing me my bowl of porridge.

I pointed to the screen. "I dreamed last night," I said, "that we moved here."

Damu studied the pictures on screen, taking in the dried off pastures and the wide main street. He kissed the side of my head. "Then that's where we'll go.

And so we went.

And I knew that fate had the last say when we got out of the car in the main street of Blakeford, and the local police officer who just happened to be walking out of a shop, stopped and stared. "Heath Crowley," he whispered. He looked at my odd eyes, my most distinguishing feature. "Oh my God, it is you."

Detective Don Walmsley. He was the policeman who was there when Jarrod and I were attacked. He was the one who had stayed with me in the hospital corridor when Jarrod's parents kicked me out. He sat beside me when my own mother told me, just minutes after Jarrod died, that now this gay-nonsense was over, I could live a proper, normal life.

I hadn't seen him in over two years. "Detective Walmsley," I said, shaking his hand.

"Please call me Don." He swallowed hard. "I thought about you often. Wondered how you got on."

I shook my head. "Well, the last two years... jeez, where do I start?" I turned to Damu. "This is Damu, my boyfriend." I didn't need to hide anything in front of Don. He already knew I was gay. He took in the six-foot-three black man and never missed a beat.

He went to shake his hand, but seeing it was still in a splint, he clapped Damu on the shoulder instead. "Nice to meet you."

"I've spent the last year in Tanzania, living with the Maasai actually," I said. "Which is where Damu is from."

Don looked twice at Damu. "Really? Wow!"

Damu nodded graciously. "We not expect to know anyone here," he said.

"Yeah, fancy us meeting again here, of all places." Don looked up the street. "Not much happens here. It's why I chose to be transferred here. I have to say, Heath, after what happened to you, I... well, it stayed with me. Never much fancied the city after that."

I wasn't sure what to say to that. "Oh, same."

He brightened and changed subjects. "So, what brings you here?"

I wouldn't go explaining the whole dream thing to him. Not yet, anyway. "We've come to check Blakeford out. We might move here, actually."

He grinned. "Well, I'd like that."

He told us where the real estate office was, the post office, the library, and the supermarket. "Police station is down the end on the right. Call in and see me anytime, you hear?"

"Sounds good," I said, shaking his hand again. "And, Don. I never did thank you, for staying with me that day."

His face softened, and he smiled. "Just seeing you alive and well is all the thanks I need."

We watched him walk away, and after a long silence, I turned to Damu and said, "Fate sure is a funny thing."

THE HOUSE we ended up getting was a run-down old

farmhouse. Set on thirty acres of drought-stricken land, it was flat and dry, much like the lands we'd left behind in Tanzania.

The real estate agent had been professional, but it was clear she thought the place was a dump. "The house is old and the kitchen and bathroom are original. Built in the 20s I think," she said, looking around the dusty room. "The owners couldn't afford to stay on. The drought was too much, and they simply walked out."

The living room had a fireplace and hardwood floors, leading to an old kitchen with a large window and faded yellow curtains. Yes, the house was old, but if I tried to picture us living anywhere else, I couldn't. Sure, the fancy hotel rooms had been nice but too modern and sleek. I tried to picture Damu living in a new place like that, but I just couldn't. He belonged somewhere with history, with character, somewhere earthy and warm.

Damu walked through the house, taking it all in. "What do you think of it?" I asked.

He looked at me and smiled.

"*Enk-âŋ.*"

Home.

I turned to the real estate agent. "We'll take it."

I'D ORGANISED ALL my stuff to be taken out of storage and delivered, and I knew going through the boxes of mine and Jarrod's life together wasn't going to be easy. But I was ready. It had been over two years, and I had a different life now. Damu helped me, sitting with me and letting me tell stories and laugh and cry as I unpacked Jarrod's favourite coffee cup, the photos, the clothes. And those damn abstract canvases that I'd hated, but Jarrod bought them anyway.

Rich coffee colours, reds, and golds were spread across three tall frames, and it was funny how they now reminded me of my time in Tanzania. I had to wonder if it was Jarrod's way of telling me of what was to come.

I hung those three canvases above the fireplace. The mantle proudly displayed the gourd bowls Damu and I had used every day, and the small paper crane I'd given Damu, alongside a single framed photo of Jarrod. It was Damu who put it there, telling me his life should be remembered, and it was, after all, Jarrod who led me to him.

I kissed his cheek and whispered, "Thank you." He understood and accepted my past, he never questioned my ability to read dreams. Not that I'd dreamed anything in months, which I took to be a good sign. Though, dreams or no dreams, Damu accepted all of me.

I surprised him with five goats a week after we'd moved in. He was so excited, so moved by what it meant. Back in his manyatta, for him to have his own goats was simply not fathomable. He wasn't wealthy enough. He wasn't *worthy* enough. But here he was, and I'd make it my life mission to remind him every day if I had to.

When the truck had gone and the goats were bleating in the small paddock near the house, watching Damu made everything worthwhile. He could barely stand still, and he almost cried. We spent that afternoon checking the fences and water troughs in the first few paddocks, and I happened to find a long, thin branch that had fallen from one of the trees. I pulled the smaller branches off it, so all that was left was single long staff. I handed it to Damu and leaned up to kiss him. "Here, now go tend your goats. I have work to do inside."

I left him grinning in the middle of the paddock. And I would watch from the kitchen as he herded the goats. He had plans for more goats, making goat's milk products, like soaps and cheese, to sell at the local markets. I had no idea if it was doable, but he was adamant and determined to make it work. He wanted to contribute some income, to be equal, and that was something I couldn't argue with.

I was doing some research on soap making when I heard a car approach outside. I looked through the front window to find a police car coming down the drive. It was Don Walmsley and I felt a stab of dread on what his visit could mean... until he pulled out a long white tube with Australian Consulate stickers on it.

It'd been three months since we'd arrived in Australia. There had been delays because of the change of address, but finally—finally—Damu's spear and rungu had made it.

I greeted Don at the door with a welcoming smile. "This is gonna make someone very happy."

Don obviously had no clue what was in it. "You know what it is?" he asked. "Not every day we get special parcels from Tanzania with Consulate labels. Came to the station because it's listed as "dangerous weapons" but when I saw where it came from, I knew who it belonged to."

"Don't imagine you'd get many Maasai weapons out here," I said with a smile.

He barked out a laugh. "Uh, no."

"Come through here," I said, leading the way through the kitchen. "He's outside."

Don carried the long tube and put it on the dining table. "I like what you've done with the place," he said.

"Thanks. It's a lovely house. Old, but a palace compared to where I spent the last twelve months. I slept in the dirt and the only thing I owned was that bowl," I said, nodding to the mantel.

Don shook his head in disbelief, and he looked me right

in the eyes. "Did you find what you were looking for in Tanzania?"

"I did." Then I grinned. "He's out with his goats."

We walked into the backyard, and Damu was in the middle paddocks, some four hundred metres away. With his real shuka packed away for safe keeping, he wore a red shawl over his jeans and shirt. It was really just a red picnic-style blanket we found at the store, but his eyes lit up when he saw it. It was a lot like the shukas worn by his people, and now the weather was cooler, he wore it most days when he was outside. And I had to admit, I loved it on him. I called out and waved for him to come in, and as soon as he saw there was someone with me, he started to walk toward us.

"He's a quiet fella, isn't he," Don said. It wasn't really a question.

That made me laugh. "He is. He's the most peaceful person I've ever met. He's calming and gentle. Dressed in his Maasai clothes, he looks kinda intimidating, but he's anything but."

He studied me for a long moment. His voice was quiet when he said, "You went through something over there, didn't you?"

I smiled at him. "I went there not caring if I lived or died. And I found my reason to live, in the unlikeliest of places." I looked back to where Damu was walking toward us and took a deep breath and sighed. "One day I'll tell you the story of a guy who purchased another human being to save his life, then had to bribe government officials to get him out of the country."

Don blanched, his eyes wide. "Jesus."

I smiled at him. "I couldn't save Jarrod. But I could save Damu."

Don let out a breath through puffed out cheeks. "Wow." He shook his head. "Sounds like he saved you too."

I smiled at him. "He sure did." By this, Damu was close enough to hear us, so I hurried him along. "Don has something for you inside."

"Is everything okay?" Damu asked quietly.

I smiled at him and nodded. "Yes, it's more than okay."

I think Don had a new appreciation for Damu's timidness, after what I'd just told him. "Special delivery," he said gently.

We walked back inside, and Damu stopped when he saw the long tube. His hand went to cover his mouth. "I had given up hope."

"Open it," I urged him.

Damu pulled the spear out first, gasping as he did. It was just as I remembered, only it seemed better somehow. The tip was still wrapped in my old shirt, and we pulled that off to reveal the blade. Damu grinned and stood tall, holding his spear proudly. "You like?"

"Looks good," I said, unable to stop smiling.

"It's incredible," Don said.

I unwrapped my old shirt and held it up. "Good lord," I mumbled. It was so threadbare, with holes, and although it had been white, it was now stained brown. "I wore this every day."

Damu put this hand over his mouth and laughed. "I not remember it look so bad."

Don stared at the scrap of material I called a shirt. He didn't say anything, but I could see it in his eyes that he was finally understanding exactly how we'd lived in the manyatta.

Then Damu pulled out his rungu, and ran his fingers over the smooth wood, like they'd forgotten the touch.

"It looks like my golfing driver," Don said. "Can I?" Damu handed it over proudly.

"You should show him how you use it," I said.

Damu shook his head, embarrassed, like the idea was foolish.

"I'd love that," Don said, looking over the wooden club.

"Really?" Damu asked.

"Yes!"

So, out in the back yard, I put an old can on a fence post, and Damu stood about forty metres from it. He tossed the rungu in his hand, getting a feel of the weight of it, then he raised his arm back, and taking a few long strides toward the post, he launched the rungu at his target. With perfect aim and strength, the rungu knocked the tin flying of the post.

"Woo!" I cheered.

"Holy shit!" Don cried, then clapped. "That was incredible!"

Damu bowed his head, but his smile told me he was proud.

We talked for a little while, and I really liked Don. He was old enough to be my father, and maybe he looked at me like the son he never had. Maybe he felt guilt over what happened to Jarrod, I wasn't sure. But I liked him, and I enjoyed his friendship. "Hey listen," Don said, as we walked him to his police car. "The primary school in town is having a Culture Week coming up, and I reckon they'd love to see a real Maasai warrior. What do you think?" he asked, but quickly added, "You could tell them about how you lived, what you ate, that kind of stuff. Then maybe show them what you can do with that wooden club." Then he smiled. "And it might be good for the folks around town to get to know you both as well."

I liked the idea. "What do you think?" I asked Damu. "You could teach the children here some things, like I did over there."

"Me?" Damu asked, stunned.

"Yes, you," Don said with a laugh. "Let me talk to the principal about it, and I'll let you know."

WE ARRIVED at Blakeford Primary School as their community assembly started. It seemed word had passed around the small town in the last three weeks since Don Walmsley had first mentioned it to us, that Damu—the new *African* man in town—would be there.

We'd been in Blakeford for just a few months. Not only were we new to town, where some people still weren't considered local after twenty years, but I had odd coloured eyes, Damu was African, and to top it off, we were gay.

We were always going to be on the outer. I never expected anything different. For the most part, people were nice and polite, and if anything, curious.

But I swear half the town had turned out at the school, including Detective Don Walmsley in full uniform. He grinned when he saw us and gave us a wave. The school's undercover area was packed, and although most, if not all, had seen us down the main street in the last few months, nothing prepared them for the sight of Damu walking in wearing his red shuka and carrying his spear.

The crowd went silent, the kids all went "ooooooh," and the principal, standing at the microphone on stage, announced Damu's arrival. "As an exciting start to our Cultural Awareness Week, we have a very special guest..."

Damu and I walked onstage to a warm round of

applause. Damu was nervous, and no one in the crowd had the slightest clue what it took for him to get up in front of a few hundred strangers. He had more courage than any of them could imagine.

He waved his hand to the crowd. "Hello," he said. "My name is Damu, and I am Maasai."

He glanced at me, and I grinned at him.

"My name is Heath," I told them. "I spent a year living in Tanzania with the Maasai. We lived on the Serengeti. And where we're from, there are kangaroos and wombats and koalas, yes?" The kids all said yes. "Well, where Damu is from, there are elephants and giraffes and lions."

Damu told them how he'd been injured in a stampede and how I'd taught the Maasai kids how to write. I told them I was the first white man a lot of them had ever seen, and how I was given a Maasai name that meant milk. This made them laugh. Then I told them how Damu's name meant blood, and how we actually drank blood and milk. A collective "ewwwwwwww" went around the audience.

Damu told them what food they ate and how they built their houses. We showed them a map and pictures from the Internet, but all they were interested in was Damu's spear and rungu.

Damu held up the wooden club. "This is called a rungu," he told them. "We use it like weapon." He had their full attention. "Would you like me show you?"

A very loud and excited "yes!" went through the school. Damu handed me his spear to hold, and Don took an empty Coke can out into the middle of the cricket pitch. The audience gathered around and Damu waited for them to quieten. He'd been practicing a little, nervous he would miss the target in front of the audience, but he needn't have worried.

He stood alone out in the oval, a striking figure in his red traditional shuka; he took my breath away. He sized up the small target, fifty metres away, secured his grip on the handle, took four long strides and threw the rungu. The wooden club spun through the air, the crowd held their breath, and when the rungu hit the tin can, it spun a good ten metres in the air.

The crowd erupted in applause, and Damu, in his true humble way, simply gave a small wave in acknowledgment.

A morning tea was put on, a typical small town affair of cups of tea in styrofoam cups and home baked goods. I had a feeling Don had invited us to help us be accepted, so the small community could meet us on a more personal level. We talked with kids and adults alike. The kids wanted to look at the spear, the adults asked all sorts of curious questions. But Don was right. They met Damu, and taking in his soft-spoken voice, his gentle manner, they could see he was nothing to be afraid of. In fact, the kids swarmed to him. He laughed with them, and my suspicions of Don were confirmed when he stood beside me, watching Damu laughing, and he nudged me with his elbow. His smile was hidden as he sipped his tea.

"Thank you," I said to him. "It means a lot."

"No problem," he said. "Just glad to help. You know, my wife asked if you and Damu wanted to come around for dinner one night. I'd love to hear that story sometime."

"Sounds real good. I'd like that."

The children were all called back into class, the parents disappeared, and the principal asked to speak to Damu. "We'd love you to come back and talk more to the children," she said. "Being Cultural Awareness Week, you have so much to teach them."

Damu's smile was slow spreading. "I would like this. Very much."

We exchanged numbers, and Damu was positively beaming. Don said he'd be in touch about dinner plans and left.

I nodded to where our old ute was parked up the street but looked up at Damu. "Remember that day when we were walking back to the manyatta and you said you dreamed of the day you could walk in the sunshine, free to hold my hand?"

Damu eyed me cautiously. "Yes."

I held out my hand. "Damu, my handsome Maasai, you are free to hold my hand."

He slipped his rungu into the waistband of his shuka, took his spear into his left hand. "I am free because of you, Heath Crowley." He slid his right hand into mine, and together we walked, free of dreams and demons, in the warmth of the Australian sun.

~The End

ABOUT THE AUTHOR

N.R. Walker is an Australian author, who loves her genre of gay romance.
She loves writing and spends far too much time doing it, but wouldn't have it any other way.

She is many things: a mother, a wife, a sister, a writer. She has pretty, pretty boys who live in her head, who don't let her sleep at night unless she gives them life with words.

She likes it when they do dirty, dirty things... but likes it even more when they fall in love.

She used to think having people in her head talking to her was weird, until one day she happened across other writers who told her it was normal.

She's been writing ever since...

Email:
nrwalker@nrwalker.net

CONTACT N.R. WALKER

Website
Facebook
Facebook Author Page
Twitter
Instagram
Google +
Amazon
Audible
Bookbub
Email:
nrwalker@nrwalker.net

ALSO BY N.R. WALKER

Blind Faith (Blind Faith #1)

Through These Eyes (Blind Faith #2)

Blindside: Mark's Story (Blind Faith #3)

Ten in the Bin

Point of No Return – Turning Point #1

Breaking Point – Turning Point #2

Starting Point – Turning Point #3

Element of Retrofit – Thomas Elkin Series #1

Clarity of Lines – Thomas Elkin Series #2

Sense of Place – Thomas Elkin Series #3

Taxes and TARDIS

Three's Company

Red Dirt Heart

Red Dirt Heart 2

Red Dirt Heart 3

Red Dirt Heart 4

Red Dirt Christmas

Cronin's Key

Cronin's Key II

Cronin's Key III

Exchange of Hearts

The Spencer Cohen Series, Book One

The Spencer Cohen Series, Book Two

The Spencer Cohen Series, Book Three

The Spencer Cohen Series, Yanni's Story

Blood & Milk

The Weight Of It All

A Very Henry Christmas (The Weight of It All 1.5)

Perfect Catch

Switched

Imago

Imagines

Red Dirt Heart Imago

On Davis Row

Finders Keepers

Evolved

TITLES IN AUDIO:

Cronin's Key

Cronin's Key II

Cronin's Key III

Red Dirt Heart

Red Dirt Heart 2

Red Dirt Heart 3

Red Dirt Heart 4

The Weight Of It All

Switched

Point of No Return

Breaking Point

Spencer Cohen Book One

Spencer Cohen Book Two

FREE READS:

Sixty Five Hours

Learning to Feel

His Grandfather's Watch (And The Story of Billy and Hale)

The Twelfth of Never (Blind Faith 3.5)

Twelve Days of Christmas (Sixty Five Hours Christmas)

Best of Both Worlds

TRANSLATED TITLES:

Fiducia Cieca (Italian translation of Blind Faith)

Attraverso Questi Occhi (Italian translation of Through These Eyes)

Preso alla Sprovvista (Italian translation of Blindside)

Il giorno del Mai (Italian translation of Blind Faith 3.5)

Cuore di Terra Rossa (Italian translation of Red Dirt Heart)

Cuore di Terra Rossa 2 (Italian translation of Red Dirt Heart 2)

Cuore di Terra Rossa 3 (Italian translation of Red Dirt Heart 3)

Cuore di Terra Rossa 4 (Italian translation of Red Dirt Heart 4)

Confiance Aveugle (French translation of Blind Faith)

A travers ces yeux: Confiance Aveugle 2 (French translation of Through These Eyes)

Aveugle: Confiance Aveugle 3 (French translation of Blindside)

À Jamais (French translation of Blind Faith 3.5)

Cronin's Key (French translation)

Cronin's Key II (French translation)

Au Coeur de Sutton Station (French translation of Red Dirt Heart)

Partir ou rester (French translation of Red Dirt Heart 2)

Faire Face (French translation of Red Dirt Heart 3)

Trouver sa Place (French translation of Red Dirt Heart 4)

Rote Erde (German translation of Red Dirt Heart)

Rote Erde 2 (German translation of Red Dirt Heart 2)

www.ingramcontent.com/pod-product-compliance
Lightning Source LLC
Chambersburg PA
CBHW032101180726
48284CB00002B/391